Mr. Darcy
and
Elizabeth's
Secret

Ginger Schlegel

iUniverse

MR. DARCY AND ELIZABETH'S SECRET

iUniverse books may be ordered through booksellers or by contacting:

iUniverse
1663 Liberty Drive
Bloomington, IN 47403
www.iuniverse.com
1-800-Authors (1-800-288-4677)

ISBN: 978-1-5320-4844-9 (sc)
ISBN: 978-1-5320-4845-6 (e)

Library of Congress Control Number: 2018904900

Print information available on the last page.

iUniverse rev. date: 05/14/2018

To my daughter, Pauline,
for reintroducing me to *Pride and Prejudice* and for starting all of this

Please note: Any changes in spelling from the original Jane Austen version of *Pride and Prejudice* (1813) with either the characters names or any locations mentioned, are authorial choice.

Acknowledgement

I would like to thank Jane Austin for creating such time honored and enduring characters. Where would such wonderful historical fiction be without them. I would also like to thank my children and grandchildren for being with me always. Without family, we are only a shell of a person. I would like to acknowledge my publishing coordinator, Jacky Alba for her time and assistance. Finally, I would like to thank my husband David, for his patience with me while creating this story and his help in its publication.

"Happiness comes when your work and words are of benefit to yourself and others."
-The Buddha (c.563-c.483BC)

Contents

Introduction

The marriage to Mr. George Wickham was a mistake from the start. Elizabeth had married him with encouragement from her parents but without any significant thought regarding what her future would be with him. She had the false impression that the union with her new and handsome spouse would be wonderful and carefree, but regrettably, she was wrong. Lieutenant Wickham had married her with the misconception that she had a sizable dowry and would, upon her father's death, inherit a large and wealthy estate. They were both wrong.

When they first met, she found him handsome and charming, but unfortunately she had listened to his empty promises and lies; then she had married him under his false pretenses of love and security. He saw her as an easy way to obtain money and assets for his numerous gambling debts. They met at the annual Meryton ball, at the home of Lady Lucas, a prominent local socialite, just six weeks before their marriage. The ladies attending the ball were very beautiful, and the gowns they wore were of silk, with yards of skirt, full and all quite colorfully decorated. There were dozens of military officers in attendance but none more handsome than Lieutenant George Wickham. He was tall and quite well favored in appearance with his red military coat and properly cut trousers. He wore many medals on his jacket; it was to be assumed he had earned them honestly for bravery and service to country. His blond hair was cut long and pulled tight to his neck. His eyes were a dark blue. His nose was long and sharp, and his face was deeply colored from many hours out of doors. His appearance was almost feminine, but he had a definite male physique. His shoulders were broad, and he had a narrow waist. His leg muscles were strong and obviously evident in his tightly fitted uniform.

Elizabeth, in contrast, was fairly attractive and slim but was not considered beautiful by either her family or by the local townspeople. She wore a borrowed green-colored silk dress, high waisted and cut low at the neck, showing just enough bust to make men look twice. Pearls worn at the neck accented the white lace worn about the sleeves and bodice of her dress. The ensemble perfectly matched her dark hazel eyes, along with upswept and styled red hair that was decorated with the same white pearls.

The two noticed each other from across the large ballroom, and their eyes immediately connected. Lieutenant Wickham crossed the room slowly while staring at the attractive Miss Elizabeth Bennet. He had had his recent acquaintance and host, also Elizabeth's uncle, Mr. Gardnier, introduce them. Elizabeth was immediately infatuated with the handsome Lieutenant Wickham, hardly believing her luck that he would be attracted to her. Lieutenant Wickham was the first man who had ever showed her any interest, and she was overcome by his attention to her. After their introduction, he offered to get her a glass of punch, which she readily accepted. By evening's end, they had talked for hours on the veranda of the Lady Lucas's large home. In between dances, she fell under the spell of his smooth, deep voice and stories of victory in combat. He had shown no interest in the other ladies at the ball, and she succumbed to his lone admiration for her. After their initial contact, he wasted no time in inquiring as to who she was. When he heard falsely that she was the wealthy daughter of a prominent landowner and would inherit the estate upon her elderly father's passing, his interest in her grew.

Within days of their initial meeting, George Wickham had thoughts of speaking to Elizabeth's father to indicate his intentions of matrimony. Elizabeth's father, Mr. Thomas Bennet, readily gave his consent to the marriage after interviewing Lieutenant Wickham only once. Mr. Bennet was taken in by his smooth talk of love and security for his daughter. Mrs. Francis Bennet, Elizabeth's mother, who was also in agreement with the union, smiled to Lieutenant Wickham with grace and pleasure, knowing that one of her daughters would soon be married. Miss Elizabeth Bennet, age twenty, would be the first of their five daughters to be married. The wedding day was planned with excitement and anticipation for the happy couple. Unfortunately, the union would be short-lived and shameful for both Elizabeth and her family.

1

During the first days of Elizabeth Bennet and George Wickham's courting, George had been kind and considerate. He had wanted Elizabeth's family to get to know him quickly, so he was invited to tea by Mrs. Bennet the afternoon following the dance. Mrs. Bennet felt him a charming, handsome young man, and he made quite an impression with her upon his first visit. On his second visit, he took Elizabeth on a chaperoned picnic. They rode in a fine carriage to a scenic overlook that she found to be breathtaking. They rode slowly down a well-ridden road but turned off on a quiet narrow path to the destination he had previously planned out. The weather was warm, and the springtime had brought about acres of colorful tulips and yellow daffodils and bushes of lavender lilacs. After securing the horse and carriage to a shaded tree, he spread a quilt on the ground and began to remove the china dishes, silver, and crystal glassware from the picnic basket. He had brought foods Elizabeth had never tasted before, obviously trying to impress upon her naïveté. Their chaperones, well known to the Bennet family, were never far away and kept a close watch on the happy young couple. They too were impressed with the charming Lieutenant Wickham.

"What are these foods?" asked Elizabeth. "I have never seen or smelled anything quite like these before."

"This is an imported cheese from France, and this is caviar, from Russia, both considered by many to be true and rare delicacies. I had them brought in from London just this morning, especially for you." Lieutenant Wickham smiled at her. "Please enjoy the food. You will find it most delightful—something you will get quite used to eating when you are with me." He winked.

After several minutes of silence and eating, he said to her, "You are so sweet. I cannot bear to take my eyes away from your beautiful face. I must tell you—your beauty, grace, and intelligence have changed me forever, Elizabeth." He placed his gloved hand over hers, causing her to feel uncomfortable but pleasant. She had never experienced these words spoken to her before. She found herself smothered with his smooth talk and proper manners, turning her head away with a blush arising to her cheeks. She was quite taken with him and felt herself immediately and forever falling in love with him.

"I am not sure what to say, sir, but you honor me." She smiled shyly. Convinced he was making a favorable impression on her, he continued with his flirtation.

They rode back to Longbourne, her family's home, in silence, with the intense feelings of attraction growing between them. His intentions were obvious and unmistakable. She felt confident that he would ask for her hand in marriage in the near future. When they returned to Longbourne, it was late afternoon and the shadows were beginning to lengthen. The air had begun to cool, but Elizabeth felt warm. Mr. Bennet was staring out the window, watching for the carriage to pull up to the front entrance. Lieutenant Wickham helped her down and escorted her to her door, kissing her hand gently as he bade her goodbye. He noticed Mr. Bennet at the window and smiled at him. The chaperones also dismounted the carriage and nodded to Mr. Bennet with an unspoken agreement of approval.

"Did you enjoy our day?" Lieutenant Wickham said as he bowed to Elizabeth.

"Oh, yes, indeed I did. And you?" she teased.

"Yes, of course. I see your father watching us," he commented. "It is important that he approves of me."

Elizabeth smiled. "I'm sure he will when he gets to know you better—when *I* get to know you better."

"Until tomorrow?" he asked.

"Yes, until tomorrow," she answered.

Feeling comfortable that he was gaining her and her family's confidence, he smiled as he left her at her father's door.

Elizabeth expected George Wickham to call the next day but was still surprised by the midmorning knock at the door. The butler showed Lieutenant Wickham to the front parlor and announced his arrival to Mr. and Mrs. Bennet. Wickham had requested to meet with Elizabeth's parents alone. Mrs. Bennet was quite excited, anticipating the marriage proposal for her daughter. Mr. Bennet, though, was more reserved in his judgment. After receiving notice of his arrival, Elizabeth's parents entered the parlor both with anticipation and concern, not knowing what George Wickham's prospects were for their daughter.

"Welcome, Lieutenant Wickham. Please sit down. May I offer you some refreshment? Tea, perhaps?" Mrs. Bennet asked.

"Yes, thank you very much. I would like tea, but only if you join me," he answered with a smile and wink.

"Yes, we will join you—won't we, Mr. Bennet?" she said with excitement.

"Yes, a cup would be good. Mrs. Bennet, would you be so kind and pour for us?"

"Nonsense," interrupted Lieutenant Wickham. "Please allow me to pour for you." He walked with confidence to the fire, where a cast iron teakettle was always full of hot water. He tilted the pot and poured the hot liquid into two tea presses that were also ever ready. "May I add milk or sugar to your cup, Mrs. Bennet?" he asked with a false smile.

"Yes, please do," she replied. He poured a small quantity of both milk and sugar into the china cups. Thankfully, neither the cup nor the saucer was chipped. Mrs. Bennet was pleased that Elizabeth had remembered to place out, for his expected arrival, the only cups that did not have flaws in them. Lieutenant Wickham handed the freshly pressed tea to her, bowing to her slightly.

"Mr. Bennet, how would you like yours?"

"I take mine black, sir."

"We men like our tea strong and substantial, do we not, sir?" Lieutenant Wickham said with a grin.

"Thank you, sir," was all Mr. Bennet said in reply. He suddenly eyed Lieutenant Wickham with suspicion and mistrust but dismissed his concerns as unfounded, thinking his comment was only a result of his military background.

After Lieutenant Wickham settled into his chair, he expressed proper greeting to his hosts. "Good morning to both of you," he said with a nod. "What a beautiful morning. The sun is shining, the birds are singing, and the air is fresh." He paused before continuing, while reading the expressions on both of Elizabeth's parents' faces. He had become a master at reading people's thoughts—especially when they were possibly to his advantage. His ability to shift conversations and the atmosphere of the room allowed him the benefit of deception. He desperately needed Elizabeth's parents to approve of him so he could gain Elizabeth's trust and confidence in order to ultimately acquire the inheritance of Longbourne and Elizabeth's presumed wealth. His smile when talking to Mr. and Mrs. Bennet was genuine, but its sincerity was false. If he played his cards correctly, he knew he would be a wealthy man.

"Lieutenant Wickham, how nice it is to see you again. We did not expect you to call so soon," said Mrs. Bennet.

"I agree," said Mr. Bennet. "So, sir, what may we do for you this morning?"

"It is wonderful to see both of you again. Why, it seems like years since we were last together."

"Lieutenant Wickham," said Mr. Bennet. "It was just yesterday afternoon when you and our daughter Elizabeth were on a picnic together."

"Only a day? How could that possibly be? It seems like years."

"Really?" said Mr. Bennet with now growing skepticism.

"Yes." Wickham hesitated. "Well, I would like to talk with you both, if I may. You see, I must tell you how much I admire and respect your daughter. I realize we have known each other for only a few weeks, but Miss Elizabeth Bennet has assaulted my heart and soul. I would consider her advancement on me as a military operation, and I must surrender to it. Surrender I must to Miss Bennet!" He turned away from Mr. and Mrs. Bennet, but when he turned back, his smile was gone and a serious facial expression replaced his previous and pleasant conduct. "Mr. and

Mrs. Bennet," he said. "I am here to request your permission to call on Miss Elizabeth as my prospective bride. Her grace, beauty, and wit are overwhelming, and I find myself lost in her presence and lost when I am not in her presence. I find myself speechless in your presence now, just thinking of her."

"Lieutenant Wickham," Mr. Bennet answered, "you are hardly speechless. In fact, you have made yourself quite clear with your expression of admiration and ministrations for our daughter. Mrs. Bennet and I had not considered a military man for our daughter. That is a rather nomadic life, don't you think?" Leaving his tea untouched, Mr. Bennet rose from his chair and walked slowly to the window, where he looked out over the growing fields. "I would expect you to travel quite a bit, Lieutenant. That could leave our daughter alone, possibly raising a family by herself."

"Sir," Wickham replied, "if Miss Bennet would have me and I gain your confidence and approval, I would resign my naval commission to remain with her and our prospective family."

Lieutenant Wickham retained his serious demeanor. Gaining the Bennets' trust was essential if he was going to obtain the expansive estate. He hoped that once he gained Elizabeth Bennet's inheritance, he would rejoin the military and then be able to come and go as he wished. If she had any children from their union, that would be her problem, not his. He had no patience for children and had no desire to include them in his future plans with her or anyone else.

"Tell me about yourself, Lieutenant Wickham. How did you come to join the military?" Mr. Bennet asked.

"Well, it is a long story. I lived with the Darcy family of Pemberley in Derbyshire, as you may already know. I attended Cambridge with Mr. Fitzwilliam Darcy, son of Mr. James Darcy, owner of Pemberley. Unfortunately for me, I embarrassed young Darcy with my scholarly academics and champion sportsmanship. The elder Mr. Darcy had provided my passage to Cambridge, so when I excelled above his son, Fitzwilliam Darcy; I was forced to leave so the younger Mr. Darcy would not be humiliated. At first it was difficult to leave Cambridge. You see, I enjoyed the university very much. I developed deep and lasting relationships with both my professors and my fellow classmates, but after I left, I realized that leaving Cambridge provided me the opportunity to use the skills and knowledge I had acquired for advancement in military strategy. My natural skills in leadership have been noted by my superiors and are currently used to guide and instruct new recruits."

Little did the Bennets know that George Wickham had actually been relieved of his duties in the military as a result of his drunken and disorderly conduct. His behavior had been found to be both ungentlemanly and uncivil. He recently had been stripped of rank and ordered to leave the military compound immediately and without pay. It was fortunate for him that no one knew of this at the recent ball he had attended when he met Miss Elizabeth.

"Well, Lieutenant Wickham," said Mr. Bennet after hearing the Lieutenant's account of himself, "I am impressed. You should be proud, and so should your parents." Meanwhile, Mrs. Bennet continued to smile and nod her head enthusiastically throughout their guest's speech.

"Sir, I am humbled to say my parents have both passed—murdered by highwaymen when I was just a boy. I attempted to stop the robbers and save my parents, but unfortunately I was unable. I was honored for heroism for the attempt, though I was without success."

"Oh, Lieutenant Wickham," said Mrs. Bennet, "how awful that must have been for you."

"Yes, it was," he answered with his head hanging sadly. "But I have prevailed and made the most of that dreadful event."

"Tell me, sir," said Mr. Bennet. "What are your duties now in the military? Where will you be stationed next?"

"Fortunately, Mr. Bennet," he answered, "I currently have a more permanent post. I am a senior drill instructor for the military academy, teaching survival and combat skills. I am an expert marksman in both rifle and pistol. I am proficient in fencing, wrestling, and survival swimming, so unless there is active warfare here or in London, I should remain at this location for quite some time."

"Oh, Mr. Bennet," exclaimed Mrs. Bennet. "That means you will be near our daughter and will be able to see her frequently."

"Yes ma'am, I hope so."

"So it is settled then; you may have our permission to court our daughter. We hope to see you regularly, sir," said Mrs. Bennet, clapping her hands with excitement. "How wonderful it would be to have you as our son-in-law. We certainly want the best for our daughter, and you fit the bill for our Elizabeth. Don't you think so, Mr. Bennet?"

"You certainly are quite charming, and you seem sincere in your remarks. So, if Elizabeth will have you, you may have my permission to court her."

"Thank you, sir," he replied. "I promise you, you will not be discontent with your decision."

2

"What is all the excitement about?" asked Elizabeth as she walked into the parlor. Mr. and Mrs. Bennet and Lieutenant Wickham all stood at once when Elizabeth entered the room. Elizabeth smiled. "Oh, excuse me; I did not realize we had a guest."

Mrs. Bennet rushed to Elizabeth's side and said, "Oh, daughter, what exciting news. Lieutenant Wickham has come here today to ask you father's permission to call on you." She lowered her head to Elizabeth and whispered, "It seems Lieutenant Wickham is quite smitten with you."

"Oh, Mama, please do not say such things," she whispered back with a confident smile. Mrs. Bennet smiled back and continued to nod to both her daughter and Lieutenant Wickham.

"Elizabeth," Mr. Bennet announced to all, eyeing the young couple closely, "Lieutenant Wickham has come to speak with your mother and me regarding you two seeing each other formally. He has indeed asked our permission to court you. We cannot make any final decisions, of course; that would be entirely up to you. We have, though, consented to allow you to see each other."

"Thank you, Mr. Bennet," Wickham said with a bow. When he stood up, he eyed Elizabeth with a wide smile. Elizabeth returned his greeting with a shy smile and nod. "Miss Bennet, may I have the pleasure of a walk with you in your family's garden? I hear it is the most beautiful in the county. I would greatly enjoy a lesson in your gardening skills."

"Lieutenant Wickham, I certainly am no expert in gardens."

"Your modesty is a pleasant attribute," he answered. "Please allow me to escort you about the yards."

"My pleasure, sir." Elizabeth smiled and again nodded. She turned back to her parents and saw their approving facial expressions.

Elizabeth and Lieutenant Wickham slowly walked about the yard, she with her hands clasped in front of her and he with his hands clasped behind his back. They talked with their heads down, staring at the ground, but with an occasional glance and smile toward each other. Always did they stay in sight of the main house, where they knew they could be seen. How inappropriate and scandalous it would be if they were out of sight of her parents or if they were unchaperoned, even with the permission of formal courting.

"Miss Bennet, what a beautiful day. The sun is shining, the birds are singing, and the smell of flowers is so sweet. Your family's gardens are breathtaking. The balance of ornamentals mixed with perennials and herbs is masterful indeed."

"Lieutenant Wickham, you said you needed a lesson in gardening. It seems you are well versed in horticultural knowledge."

"Miss Bennet, my gardening skills are quite elementary. It is the wonderful mixture of colors and smells that I am taking advantage of at this moment." After a short distance of walking, Lieutenant Wickham stopped abruptly and turned to Elizabeth. "Miss Bennet, you have captured my heart and soul. I must confess, Miss Bennet, I have never met anyone as lively, gracious, and kind as you. Your beauty leaves me breathless. Ever since we met at the Meryton ball, I have thought of no one but you. You have made an impression on me, Miss Bennet, with your graceful movements, speech, and competent language. I have grown to love you, Elizabeth, and would be proud and honored if you would be my wife."

"Lieutenant Wickham, we have only just met. We hardly know each other. I do not know what to say."

"Say yes to me, Elizabeth, and I will make you a very happy and proud woman. I promise to care for you and our children always."

"I have come to love you also, Lieutenant Wickham, and I will consent to be your wife," she answered shyly.

"Thank you, dear, now and always." He took her hand into his, kissed her palm gently, and then reached to touch her cheek. She felt a comfort she had never felt before, and she knew she had made the correct decision with Lieutenant Wickham.

"Elizabeth, I would like to marry as soon as possible—next week, I hope, if that is agreeable to you," he said while still in the gardens and holding her hands.

"Why, Lieutenant Wickham, why so soon?" she asked. "It takes some time to plan a wedding. I thought we should wait for a few months. You said you will be stationed nearby, so traveling will not be a problem."

"Yes, of course, but the sooner we are wed, the better. My love for you only grows stronger every day, and every day without you only adds to my discourse. Besides, I know our union will be blissful and glorious." He smiled at her while she blushed deeply. They walked back to the main house hand in hand. He smiled to himself not for his marriage to Elizabeth, which he did not care about, but for the Longbourne estate he planned to inherit in the near future. Once he had ownership of the vast farmlands and their financial possibilities for himself, he would control all her money and enjoy its profits. How wonderful a plan he had made for himself.

The marriage took place one week later at the small church in Meryton, located several miles from the Longbourne farm. Two open carriages carrying the wedding party had been decorated with flowers and ribbons by Elizabeth's sisters. One of the carriages was drawn by matching white horses, borrowed by one of Mr. Bennet's clients, and carried Mr. and Mrs. Bennet, Elizabeth, and their long employed and loyal butler, Mr. Lawton. The other carriage was drawn by two of Longbourne's farm horses and carried Elizabeth's sisters. The mood was happy and lively, with hope and laughter for a prosperous and long life for the soon-to-be wedded couple. Mrs. Bennet was giddy with delight, while Mr. Bennet remained calm, though with an underlying comfort in knowing his daughter would be safe and secure. Regrettably, this was not to be.

The carriages pulled up to the church, which was filled with awaiting guests and well-wishers for the bride and groom. Mr. Bennet exited the carriage first and assisted Mrs. Bennet and then his daughter.

"Now, Elizabeth, dear," said Mrs. Bennet, "remember what I told you. Smile, nod to everyone as you walk down the aisle, and don't look nervous. Don't step on your dress, and don't let your father step on your hem either. This is your special day."

"Yes, Mother, I remember. You told me all this already," replied Elizabeth to her mother.

"Now, straighten your dress," she said again while smoothing out the back of Elizabeth's dress, which had been slightly wrinkled from the carriage ride. The dress, a light blue gown of silk with a high waist and accented with white beads, had been borrowed from Mrs. Bennet's sister.

She hoped no one would notice that the dress was not new—especially Lieutenant Wickham. Mrs. Bennet did not want the groom to know that his bride's dress was on loan and had been repaired from previous use. Elizabeth herself did not mind this, but her mother certainly did. Her red hair was worn long and decorated with white and pink roses just picked from the family's gardens. She carried a matching bouquet of roses, tied with long blue ribbons that matched her dress.

Mr. Bennet looked smart in a dark morning coat with matching trousers and shining black boots. He wore a beaver hat; it had been borrowed from his sister's late husband. Mrs. Bennet also wore a blue dress, but it was of a darker hue. It had long sleeves covered with lace and a few stains, unable to be removed, from a previous wearing. Mrs. Bennet had a tendency to spill food and drink on her clothes—especially when indulging in too much wine.

Mr. Lawton was the last to depart from the first carriage. He quickly walked to the second carriage so that he might attend to the four remaining daughters. The two younger sisters had been arguing during their ride to the church. The girls quarreled over many topics, including clothes, bonnets, and members of the opposite sex. Mr. Lawton raised his eyes to the girls as soon as he approached them, hoping to curb their inappropriate conversation. He had known the girls since infancy, and they usually followed his lead. This time, though, they did not heed his cue and continued their chattering. It was not until Mr. Bennet approached the carriage that they became silent.

"Girls," he said patiently but sternly, "today is your sister's wedding day. Please behave yourselves and respect our guests."

"Yes, Papa," replied the youngest. "But she started it." She pointed to the older sister.

"Girls," he said, now loudly.

"Yes, Papa," the youngest said again. Unable to resist, she turned to the sister next to her and proceeded to display her tongue to her in an unladylike fashion.

The sisters were dressed in their best dresses, which had been recently cleaned and were without any obvious tears. They wore matching bonnets decorated by themselves with flowers and new ribbons. There had been bitter arguing about the style of the bonnets until Mrs. Bennet chose the colors. They carried freshly picked wildflowers from the hedgerows adjacent to the cultivated fields, all tied with the same matching ribbons as the bonnets. For the time being, the entire Bennet family was happy.

The ceremony was short, with all guests smiling, happy, and relieved that the first of the five Bennet daughters was now married. Marriage had always been a concern for Mr. Bennet. He worried over the security his daughters would have after his death. Despite his occupation as a lawyer and gentleman, he never planned for the future of his family. His dedication to his books and library was always a priority for him, not their monetary future. He realized far too late the importance his family's security had to him. Elizabeth's marriage brought that to light for him now. How little he understood what a tragic mistake had been made for his daughters, but now with Elizabeth married, he felt comfortable, at least, with her future. No one realized how the upcoming months would be fateful for the entire Bennet family.

After the vows were made, guests returned to the home of Elizabeth's aunt and uncle, Lady and Sir Lucas—the same site as the Meryton ball. They had a modest home, larger than the Bennets', with a large open garden. Flowers were abundant, and the air smelled sweet and fresh. Tables were set with a simple array of eggs, sausage, breads, fruits, and vegetables for a traditional celebratory breakfast. Many of the food items and the china pieces had been donated by friends and family. Wine was distributed for tasting and drinking for all.

"Please," Mr. Bennet called out to the guests. "Allow me to be the first to congratulate my daughter's marriage to Lt. George Wickham. May their lives be joyful, successful, and fruitful." With the word "fruitful," cheers and laughs broke out among the guests. Elizabeth was a typical blushing bride, and Lieutenant Wickham smiled with delightful anticipation of their bridal night together. He was well acquainted with the female sex, but Elizabeth was innocent of her role as a wife.

Wickham had quickly grown bored of the wedding breakfast and the Bennet family. He eagerly consumed the wine, hoping it would relieve his indifference he had toward Elizabeth. The sooner he acquired the large and wealthy Longbourne estate, the happier he would be. Life would soon be profitable for him, once he had money that he could he could gamble with and spend on the women of his choice. He knew he needed money to enter large high-stakes poker games, and then he would win even larger sums of money. He knew where and when these games would be; it was just a matter of getting the money to start with. After winning at these large, profitable games, his name would be known throughout London, and those who doubted him—especially the Darcy family and his military commanders—would realize how wrong they were in their ill judgment of him. The more he drank, the grander he felt about himself and Elizabeth Bennet's inheritable estate. Her money, estate, and connections would be his ticket to security.

All during the wedding breakfast, Elizabeth spoke with their guests with kindness and grace. She walked among the tables and spoke with everyone in attendance. How happy all were to see Elizabeth marry a man of military competence and rank. Her rosy cheeks and smile gave everyone the impression of happiness and high spirit. No one seemed to notice that there were no other military personnel or any members of the groom's family in attendance. When guests started to leave, Elizabeth resumed her usual role and started to clean up the tables and distribute food to the guests as they left the wedding celebration.

"My dear daughter, today is not the day to act like a kitchen maid. It is your wedding day, and you and your new husband must be anxious to be on your way. Now please, say goodbye to your aunt, uncle, sisters, and father. Hurry now; please go."

Elizabeth nodded and smiled to her mother. "Thank you, Mama, for everything," she said, sounding slightly embarrassed. "Today has been wonderful."

"Nothing is too much for my dear Elizabeth—I mean Mrs. Wickham. Now say goodbye and go with your new husband." Again Elizabeth nodded, but she did not reply to her mother's last statement.

Elizabeth had missed her husband for much of the wedding breakfast but eventually found George talking to her uncle and father. She walked to him slowly. Her smile grew as she approached but waned when she got closer to him. She could sense that his demeanor had been affected by the large amount of alcohol he had consumed during the day.

"Elizabeth, my dear, there you are. I was wondering where you wandered off to. We really must get going, dear. It is a long way into London."

"Yes, I agree; we must start our travel." She could immediately see that the wine was affecting his speech and manner. She was quite surprised by this. She had frequently seen her mother consume too much wine, and rarely her father, but she had never seen George in this condition. She assumed it was a result of his nervousness and excitement about the marriage and possibly the anticipation of their first evening together. He had told her that he was "inexperienced," so she understood how his present condition could have occurred.

"Elizabeth, Lieutenant Wickham, again, congratulations and God protect your long journey through life," said Sir Lucas.

"Thank you, Uncle," said Elizabeth. Sir Lucas shook Lieutenant Wickham's hand and again expressed his salutations.

"Thank you, sir; thank you for everything," replied Wickham. His thanks were not for his marriage to Elizabeth but for the estate and fortune he was expecting to inherit. *How easy it is to fool these people,* he thought. He knew that as soon as he obtained her money and land, he could live easily, come and go as he pleased, and be free to have as many women as he wanted. Elizabeth was tolerable enough and maybe even enjoyable, but she was certainly not enough to satisfy an appetite for women like his.

The sound of Mrs. Bennet's voice brought him back to the present. "Lieutenant Wickham, Elizabeth—my love and best wishes go with you both. Please write often, and take care of yourselves," said Mrs. Bennet.

"Thank you again, Papa. I love you," answered Elizabeth while hugging her father. A tear slipped down her cheek, and she quickly brushed it away.

"You know you are always welcome to come home," Mr. Bennet

carefully whispered to her when he knew he would not be overheard by anyone, "for any reason."

"I know, and I appreciate that," she whispered back.

"Well, now," Mr. Bennet announced. "These newlyweds need to start their journey. Everyone, come and say goodbye." The carriage taking the couple was pulled up to the main driveway, where the guests who were still in attendance met for their final farewell. There were cheers, waving, and clapping as the happy couple entered the closed carriage. As the two gave a final wave out the window, the carriage pulled by the matching white horses left the Gardniers' home, heading toward London. The couple was expected to stop at a local tavern in the nearby town of Marion and exchange the horses and carriage for another rig rented by Lieutenant Wickham. The bridal carriage and horses would then be returned to Mr. Bennet's client.

The ride to Marion was quiet, with little verbal exchange between the couple. They sat opposite each other in the carriage with little or no touching.

"I think the ceremony and breakfast went very well. The weather was perfect, and everyone seemed to be in good spirits," Elizabeth said.

"I suppose so," he replied coolly. She was confused with his indifference and blamed it on the wine and fatigue.

"You must be tired. I know you have been traveling recently with your company."

"I am tired," he replied. *I am tired of you already*, he thought.

"We should be in Marion soon," she said. "I hope there will no delay with the carriage. We should reach London by nightfall.

"Maybe," was all he said. They remained quiet for the rest of the journey.

5

The carriage carrying the couple reached the tavern within two hours' time. The inside of the carriage had grown warm and thick with the heat of summer and the tension that had grown between Elizabeth and Wickham. She could not understand his distance with her. Afraid she had annoyed him somehow, she reached for his hand when they approached the tavern, but he pulled away immediately. Looking out the window, she could see the next carriage they would take, waiting for them. As soon as the carriage came to a stop, Wickham immediately opened the door and stepped out. He did not assist her from the carriage and did not seem to acknowledge her when he entered the tavern, suddenly walking briskly ahead of her. She stepped out of the carriage and reluctantly followed him, entering the dark tavern room alone. Once her eyes adjusted to the light, Elizabeth found the room not unpleasant, but smoke-filled and smelling of charred meat. It was clean and quiet, and few people were present. Wickham had approached the barkeeper and was speaking quietly to him. Elizabeth stood a respectable distance away, concerned she would anger her new husband more than he appeared to be already. She could not hear the conversation but understood the verbal exchange was serious between them. Their voices were becoming loud and tense. She was concerned that the exchange of the horses and rig had been compromised. When Wickham stepped away, she reluctantly approached him, asking him if there was difficulty with their plans. He brushed by her without answering her question.

Now very upset, she pleaded, "Lieutenant Wickham, what is wrong with the horses and carriage? Please tell me, I beg you."

"Oh, shut up, my dear; nothing is wrong. We are only taking a slight detour; that is all." He had a stein of beer in his hand and an impatient expression on his face. "Go find us a room for tonight. We are staying here."

"But I thought we were going to London tonight?"

"Well guess what? We are not. Now make yourself useful and get us a room!" he shouted.

His shouting and hurtful expression caused her to withdraw in confusion and fright. She had never been spoken to in this tone or manner by anyone. She did not know immediately what to do.

"Yes, of course," she timidly answered. Was it anxiety, the alcohol, or the carriage ride that made him so different? How could the man she had grown to love become so unlike the man standing before her now? She stepped back at the same time Wickham turned away from her and walked away. Not knowing what to do now, she glanced about the room. The few people in the tavern were now staring at her with indifference. A woman who appeared to be middle aged approached Elizabeth and said, "C'mon, sweetie, looks like you need to get outta here. I'll take you to a room where you can wait for Mr. Wonderful over there." She nodded toward George Wickham, who was now talking to several men. A young woman stood in the distance, snickering at Elizabeth as she was escorted to the stairway and her bridal bed.

The woman taking Elizabeth upstairs opened the door to a guest room. Elizabeth stared at the inside of the room she expected to lose her virginity in. The room was dark and colorless. A heavy wooden bed was positioned in the middle of the room with what appeared to be a worn, stained quilt covering the top. Two pillows with matching tattered shams completed the set. A small dresser with a cracked mirror hung by the window. The mirror was smoke-stained and obviously needed washing. The look on Elizabeth's face needed no further explanation. She was confused, stultified, and tired all at the same time.

"Yeah, I know, it's not the king's palace; but you know, none of us knows what's gonna happen to us. We just take life as it comes and try to survive it. Remember that, honey; we women survive, despite the men in our lives." With that said, she turned and walked out of the room and shut the door.

After the woman left, Elizabeth walked slowly to the edge of the bed, where she sat quietly. Her thoughts were scrambled and confused. The bed groaned loudly even with slight movement. She shifted her weight with no improvement in the squeaking of the mattress, only adding to her confusion. How long was Lieutenant Wickham going to be? She did not understand his change in plans. If he wanted to change their plans, that would be fine, but she also wanted to be informed about the change.

As she sat on the bed, a loud knock sounded at the door. Before she could answer, George Wickham burst into the room. The smell of alcohol reeked on his breath and clothes.

"There you are; I've been looking all over for you," he said, slurring his words. "What are you doing here? You should be downstairs having a drink with me. After all, it's our wedding day and we should be celebrating. It's not every day a man finds a woman like you to marry." He laughed.

She smiled shyly and said, "Are you pleased with this room?"

"What the hell do I care about the room? Anywhere you are, sweetheart, is fine with me," he said loudly while swinging his arms about him.

"Lieutenant Wickham," she asked. "Why have our plans changed?"

"I told you," he said sternly. "They have. Now, what difference does it make where we stay? We are here now, so let's have a drink."

"Yes, if you wish," she answered quietly. He stepped back and gestured for her to proceed in front of him. She walked slowly out the door, gathered up her skirts, and proceeded down the stairs to the taproom. The room was now filled with people laughing, drinking, and conversing loudly. The smoke from cigars was thickening, making her cough and choke. Her eyes were starting to sting from the tobacco fumes and fireplace smoke.

"Pull up a chair and sit down; it may be a long night," he said to her.

"Please, sir, I would prefer to stay upstairs until you have finished your business."

"Have it your way," he said, casually casting off her request. He turned and walked away from her as if she were not present. Reluctantly, she retreated to the stairway and returned to their room, not knowing when she would see her bridegroom again.

It was well past midnight when George Wickham staggered up the stairs and into their room. He was drunk and was ataxic in his walk. It was dark, with only a single candle lit to guide him into bed. He had difficulty stripping off his uniform, leaving it on the floor in a heap. Elizabeth had undressed early and put on a bridal gown in anticipation of her husband's early arrival. She was disappointed and relieved that he had not returned upstairs for hours after she left him downstairs. The stench of alcohol and an unfamiliar perfume was overwhelming and disappointing, but Elizabeth was actually relieved that her new husband did not demand her wifely duties that night. Within minutes of his arrival in bed, he was snoring loudly.

6

The next morning proved to be difficult. Elizabeth had awoken early, gotten out of bed, and dressed, still leaving her husband sleeping in bed. She performed her morning toilet and ordered breakfast to be delivered to their room. Wickham awoke to the sound of the door opening and a tray of food being set loudly onto the table.

"What the hell is going on?" he yelled out.

"It is just the maid bringing us breakfast. I thought you would like to eat here this morning instead of the main dining room downstairs." He made no further comment but sat up in bed, swinging his legs over the side. His lack of clothes startled the maid, who turned her head away. She was not surprised to see men behave in such a manner. Years of working in the inn had numbed her to such sights. It upset and shocked Elizabeth, though, that her husband would be so bold as to expose himself to strangers. Never having seen a naked man before caused Elizabeth to also turn her head away in embarrassment. The maid left quickly, recognizing the symptoms of the gentleman's illness due to an evening of heavy drinking.

"Would you like some breakfast, dear?" Elizabeth asked.

"No, I would not, and I don't appreciate you spending my money like this." He spread his arms about the room. "You can eat downstairs like everyone else."

"I am sorry, sir; I thought this would be a pleasant surprise for you," she answered.

"Well, it's not." He walked unsteadily to the washbasin and rinsed his face. He dried it with a towel and turned to look at Elizabeth. "What are you staring at? What's the matter; haven't you seen a naked man before? Of course, you're a virgin princess." Speechless, Elizabeth immediately cast down her eyes to avoid the argument she felt brewing. "Well, get over here and give me a kiss; we are married, you know," Wickham said with a slight slur and agitation to his words.

"Yes, of course," she whispered. She walked slowly to him, her hands clenched in front of her. When she was closer to him, he stepped forward and grabbed both of her arms, pulling her closer. She still could smell alcohol on his breath. His morning whiskers were rough on her face as she brushed against him. She tried to pull away, but he was strong and forceful. He kissed her hard, now moving his right hand from her arm and holding the back of her head, preventing her from pulling away. His physical strength forced her backward until her legs hit the bed. She then fell onto the bed, lying on her back. She tried to get up and get away from him, but the magnitude of his strength proved too much.

"You won't get away from me, Elizabeth, and you will never deny me. Understand?" He paused. "Did you hear me? Answer me!"

"Yes, I understand," she whispered back. He reached under her skirts, eventually pulling them up to her waist. He tore her underclothes while pulling them down. His eventual attack on her was brutal, aggressive, and uncaring, leaving her bloodied and whimpering in pain.

"Oh, shut up, Elizabeth. Get up and get my breakfast. At least you know now what it means to be my wife." She got up slowly, feeling slightly dizzy. She adjusted her skirts and walked to the breakfast tray still sitting on the table. She poured a cup of tea, but her hands were shaking. Thankfully, she did not spill any of the tea.

"Hurry up, Elizabeth, we haven't got all day," he said while sitting on the edge of the bed, still completely naked. She placed the food next to him on a small table close to the bed. Wickham drank the tea, taking large bites of the food placed before him. "Get our bags packed. We will be leaving within the hour," he said out loud, though his speech was not directed at Elizabeth. She made no verbal comment but slowly walked to the bedside stand and packed their bags for travel.

7

They traveled in silence for the remaining trip to London. The rocking and movement of the carriage did nothing for Wickham's disposition. Elizabeth could sense his continued morning-after hangover and foul mood—surely the effect of the prior evening's alcohol consumption. Her thoughts kept returning to this morning and his sudden personal attack upon her. She did not understand what provoked his behavior. This was not the man she had fallen in love with just weeks before: the man who courted her, saying he loved her and would care for her—the man her parents had approved of for her. *Is this what marriage is about?* She could not believe her father behaved this way. She could not ask her mother about such things. If she had the opportunity while in London, she would attempt to talk to her aunt Gardnier, sister to her father. She trusted her and knew she would be honest with her. She would explain to her what marriage was.

The couple finally arrived at the small house Wickham had procured for them. It was located on the outskirts of the city, near the waterfront, in one of the poorest and roughest neighborhoods of the city. The neighborhood was known for crime, brawling, and taverns. The carriage pulled up, and again Wickham stepped down from the carriage without any thought to assisting Elizabeth. She needed to pull up her skirts to exit the carriage and nearly slipped in the mud that covered the street. She could smell the strong odor of oil from the shipping boats and rotting fish left to spoil in the sun and heat. She did not eat breakfast after she was assaulted by her husband, and she could feel bile creeping up her throat. Taking deep breaths, she would not allow herself to be sick or cry. There was no drive leading to the house, which sat close to the street. There were no gardens, grass, or pathways—nowhere for her to walk, which was something she had always enjoyed. Looking around, she knew she would not be walking for her leisure again soon. Little did she know that she would to be walking alone for a very long distance in the near future.

The house was indeed small, with chipped and peeling gray paint on the outside. The front door was not latched, the doorknob was missing, and the hinges did not appear to allow the loosely hanging door to close. The windows on either side of the front door were dirty and cracked. The slate doorstep sat unevenly, with overgrowth covering much of its surface. Her face paled at the sight of the house, and she felt a mistake must have been made by the driver, thinking he might have brought them to the wrong address.

"George, where are we? What is this place?" she asked.

"This, my dear, is your new home. This is where you will stay while I am away. It is close to the waterfront, and most importantly, it is cheap. You will save money living here, so I don't want to hear any of your negative comments about this place. As long as you don't spend any money, you can do what you want with the place. The rent is paid for six months."

"George, you will be staying here also. You told my parents that you would resign your commission and stay with me."

"Well, I changed my mind," he answered sternly. He thought, *As soon as I inherit the Longbourne estate, I will have enough money to spend and do as I please.* "So get your baggage and let us see what you have here."

Again Elizabeth had a sinking feeling that something was terribly wrong. This was not what she had wished for in a marriage. She could not understand how she had gone so wrong with her initial impression of Lt. George Wickham.

8

Upon opening the door to the house, Elizabeth was shocked by what she saw inside. Her eyes widened, and her mouth dropped open. Before her was a small room, filthy, with broken, overturned furniture. The few curtains at the windows were stained and torn. She walked slowly through the rooms, finding the same scene throughout. The kitchen housed a rusty, broken water pump. Startled rats hurried away as she attempted to open a cupboard. She jumped back and screamed as they disappeared down a broken floorboard. The stove was also rusty, had a broken leg, and was missing the oven door. There was no sign of wood, and the smell was indicative of rot.

"What's all the noise about?"

"Rats in the kitchen. George, look at this place. It is filthy; the furniture is broken, and the pump is rusted solid. What are we going to do?"

"You're going to clean this up, that's what. I'm going into the city. I'll be back around suppertime. Have something ready for me to eat."

"But, George, we have no food. I need some money to get some supplies. I do not even know where to go to get food. We will need everything to get started," she pleaded.

"All right, here is some money, but that's all you get. You hear me?"

"Yes," she whispered back, now close to tears.

"Good, now get busy. I'll be back."

Her disbelief was almost overwhelming when she heard the slam of the broken door as he left. Tears streamed down her face as she once more looked around the room in shock and rejection. Within one day, the only life she had ever known and loved was lost forever, but she had to stop feeling sorry for herself. She had to think of what she was going to do. Who could help her? Where could she go for food? How was she going to clean and repair this house? The only people she knew here in London were her aunt and uncle Gardnier, and she did not know how to find them. Slowly, she walked to the front room, took off her gloves, straightened an overturned table and set her bag on it. Looking about the room, she found a rusty bucket that thankfully did not have holes in it. Walking outside, she saw a water pump not far from the house. She walked briskly to the pump, lifted the handle, and gave it several strokes. A small trickle of brown water came out of the spout, and after several more strokes, clear water started to flow. She filled the bucket to three-quarters full, turned, and started to walk down the path back toward the house. Almost back to the front door, she met an older woman. She was thin and bent over at the shoulders, wearing a worn, dirty dress that was torn at the hem. Both of her shoes were worn; one had a thin rope tied around it to secure the sole to the top of the shoe. Her hair was sparse, gray, and tied at the back of her neck. Despite her haggard appearance, she had a sparkle in her eyes. When she smiled to greet Elizabeth, her toothless grin lifted Elizabeth's spirits. She was carrying an empty bucket and appeared to be heading toward the communal water pump.

"Good morning, honey. I can see from your looks you ain't from around here."

"Good morning to you also, ma'am. No, I am not from here. My husband and I just arrived today. We will be living in the house just ahead," she said as she nodded in the direction of the impoverished, run-down shanty she was now going to call home.

The old woman looked at Elizabeth with doubt. "You gonna live in that shack? What kinda husband you got, let a proper lady like you live there?"

"He is in the military," she said with embarrassment.

"Doesn't matter; no lady should live in a place like that," she mumbled to herself as she started to walk away.

"Please wait," Elizabeth called after her. "Where can I buy some food? We have nothing to eat."

"Down the road a bit is a bakery. You could try there," she answered.

"Thank you!" Elizabeth shouted back to the old woman, who was now well down the path and nearly out of earshot.

9

Elizabeth carried the water bucket back to the house. When she opened the door, she was grateful that her bag was still sitting on the table. At least someone had not stolen it while she was away. She carried the water to the kitchen and set the bucket down, making sure she made a loud noise in hopes of scaring any remaining rats away. She did not know where to start cleaning the filthy room. She had no rags or brush to scrub the tables or floor with, but she knew she had to figure out something soon. George was due to be home in several hours, and she still had to get food for supper. Going to her bag, she looked through her belongings, finding a hairbrush that she could use on the floors and a petticoat she could use for a cleaning rag. Rolling up her sleeves, and removing her underskirts so they would not be soiled or torn, she tucked the front of her skirt into her waistband and started first with the tables. She scrubbed them with the brush and then rinsed with her petticoat. It did not take long before the water was dark brown from the filthy tabletop. She emptied the water into the sink and was thankful the water disappeared down the drain and did not leak onto the floor. She walked back to the well and retrieved another bucket of water. After an hour, the floor was clean, but not as clean as she would have preferred. Realizing she could do no more, she again emptied the last of the dirty water down the drain. She put her underskirts back on, straightened her clothes, and proceeded to the bakery the old woman had told her about earlier in the day.

The walk was not far, and Elizabeth, used to walking longer distances, reached the bakery in a short time. She selected a small loaf of bread, several ham hocks, a small sack of flour, vegetables that looked to be overripe and turning soft, and a tin of tea. She hurried home to make a soup for tonight's dinner. The only pot she had to make the soup was the same bucket she had washed the floor with. After getting another bucket of water, she cleaned the vegetables, broke them into the smallest pieces she could without a knife, and set the water to boil on the unlevel stove. The wood left outside, next to the back door, was rotting but dry. She was able to light a fire in the stove with a flint starter she found next to the stove. She was thankful she did not have to use the oven, as she was sure the stovepipe was obstructed, which would possibly cause the smoke to back up into the room. While the water was heating, she did her best to straighten up the front parlor. She had made no attempt to attend to the bedroom. She hoped that George would help her with that after he returned.

She returned to the kitchen and put the ham bone and vegetables into the hot water to simmer. As soon as it boiled, she would make a flour paste to add to the mixture, thickening the broth.

# *10*

George Wickham returned about an hour after the soup was done. He threw open the door, nearly taking it completely off its hinges.

"Elizabeth, where in the hell are you?" he shouted. She could smell alcohol on his person and clothes soon after he opened the door and immediately felt a combination of desperation and fear within her.

"I am in the kitchen; supper is almost ready," she timidly answered.

"It better be," he mumbled to himself. He took his coat was off and tossed it onto a chair. His hair was uncombed and loose. His eyes were bloodshot, and he sported a day's growth of whiskers. His trousers were stained with beer, and his boots were muddied.

"Elizabeth, where is this dinner you were supposed to make?" he asked with a slight slur of his words.

"Here, sit down. I have some soup made, and I bought some bread." She had found two chipped china cups and one cracked plate in the cupboard. Within minutes, she washed them with the last of the water she had in the bucket and had them set on the cleaned table. "Please, sit down. I will pour you some soup, and here is some bread to go with it."

"What is it?" he growled.

"It is vegetable soup with a ham broth."

"It smells awful."

"It is the best I could do with the few supplies we have," she answered more sternly. She sat across the table from him, ready to spoon the soup into his cup. After she did, she set the cup in front of him and reached to break the bread. He took a sip of the soup and, to her sudden surprise, stood up from his chair and threw the soup cup and bread across the room.

"That tastes awful, and this place looks awful," he shouted. Before she could react, he grasped the table edge and effortlessly flipped the table onto its side, spilling the food onto the floor. She gasped in horror at what he had done. She stood up and backed away from him. Her lack of comprehension angered him further as he now glared at her.

"What's the matter with you? Can't you cook and clean? What good are you, anyway? I told you I wanted this place cleaned up. What have you been doing all day? Sitting around?"

"George, what is the matter? Are you ill? What has happened to you?" she pleaded, now with tears in her eyes.

"You are worthless; that's the matter with you," he shouted to her. As soon as he finished shouting, he grasped her arm, and before she could react, he slapped her as hard as he could, knocking her to the floor. He reached out, grabbed her hair, and slapped her again. She lay on the floor, dazed and weak from the pain he had suddenly inflicted upon her.

"You're worthless," he repeated at her as she lay on the floor. "Now clean this up!" He left the kitchen, grabbed his coat, and left the house. It took several minutes before she could regain her senses and have the courage and strength to stand. She felt dizzy, but the symptoms passed quickly. Her face felt burning hot, and she could taste blood in her mouth. She felt something sharp on her tongue and was concerned that a tooth was broken. *What has happened to him? Did I misjudge him entirely?* She could not believe she had made such a terrible mistake in her choice of marriage partners. Looking about the room, she slowly picked up the table and found the cups and plate. One of the cups had smashed into many pieces, and the other had cracked in half. The plate now had a large shard missing. The soup had spilled all over the floor and splashed against the wall. With the rag of a petticoat she had used for cleaning, she slowly began wiping up the spilled food. Her face continued to be burning hot, and her eye was beginning to swell shut, but she continued to clean the floor. Nausea with a bile taste rose to her throat, but she ignored the discomfort and continued with her work until it was done. She did not want her husband to see that she had not done what he demanded.

Already she was beginning to feel constant fear because of her husband, George Wickham.

After she finished cleaning the room, she found her small hand mirror in her bag. Afraid to look at herself, she took a deep breath and held the mirror up to her face. The damage was more than she expected. The swelling and bruising of her face extended from her chin and lips to above her eye. Her left eye was now completely swollen shut, with a deep purple bruise extending across her nose. Her lip was cut, but the blood she had tasted had clotted already, allowing no further blood to seep from its edges. With nothing more she could do tonight, she stumbled into the makeshift bedroom. She placed her underskirt on the bed and then lay down, falling asleep immediately.

11

Elizabeth awoke the next morning to the sound of hammering. She estimated it was midmorning by the angle of sun coming through the small, dirty windows. Her face was very sore, and unfortunately the swelling had not abated. Her eye was still swollen, but she could now open it very slightly. Her lips felt tight, but she could now open and close her jaw. The slop jar she had used the day before had yet to be emptied, but she used it again, knowing she would need to take care of that at her soonest opportunity.

She exited the bedroom to find a small older man repairing the hinges of the front door.

"Morning, ma'am." He smiled at her, seemingly not surprised by her appearance. "My wife says you and your husband are going to be living here. She thought you might need a hand around here, and by the look of things, I guess she was right."

"Thank you," she answered, turning her head away from the welcome stranger.

"That's okay, ma'am; glad I could help. The wife says you are a real lady. Husband's gone a might, so she sent me over here to see what needs to be done," he said as a matter of fact.

"Again, thank you, sir. I tried to fix a broken cabinet in the kitchen yesterday, but I fell off a chair I was using to reach the cabinet," she lied, touching her face.

"Yeah, that happens sometimes. Well, the door is fixed. When I come back, I'll look at that cabinet for you," he said calmly. He picked up his tools and walked out the door quietly, shutting it as he left.

Elizabeth was now alone again. Without money, and having no family connections, she did not know where to go or what to do. Feeling totally alone, she felt overwhelmed and at a complete loss. She felt worthless and abandoned. What a fool she had been. As she sat in a chair, contemplating her next decision, she heard the door open slowly. Recognizing the red uniform, she rose to Lieutenant Wickham's arrival. He was carrying a satchel and a small bouquet of flowers recently picked from the roadside.

"Elizabeth, dear," Wickham said sheepishly, "are you all right? I just wanted to say I am sorry for my actions last night. I must tell you I have never done anything like that before. I do not know what came over me."

She looked at him in disbelief. "No, I am not all right, sir," she answered curtly.

"I brought you these," he said as he handed her the flowers. "I also brought some food." Elizabeth looked at the satchel without emotion; nor did she reach out to take it when he offered it to her. "Elizabeth, I beg your utmost forgiveness. I must tell you how very sorry I am. We are passionate people, Elizabeth, and we belong together. Being together just demonstrates the excitement and love I have for you. As I said, I do not know what came over me last night. I just lost all sense of proper behavior and reason. I have nothing to say in my defense. You must believe I love and cherish you now and always will."

"You were drunk," she said with anger.

"Yes, and that is also inexcusable," he answered.

"Yes, it is," she said slowly.

"What can I do to make amends?"

"I do not know, sir." She sat back slowly in the chair, turning her face away from him. She detected a faint smell of unfamiliar perfume in the air and on his clothes that was not hers.

"Please let me help you. I have brought food. We will have something to eat, and together we will clean our house and make it a home." She thought for a long moment and then slowly nodded in agreement.

12

They spent the rest of the day together, cleaning the small house, though little conversation was exchanged between them. Wickham made several trips to the well, bringing in water. He had brought several cooking pots and a kettle to heat water for tea. She made them tea and served this with bread and hard sausage from Wickham's satchel. She did not ask where he obtained the food or how he paid for it, but he obviously had some money. Slowly they worked together cleaning the house, but he made no attempt to repair the furniture, windows, or cupboards. He watched her struggle to turn the dirty mattress but made no attempt to help her. Once the mattress had been turned, its contents spilled onto the floor. Elizabeth could see rat droppings mixed within the straw stuffing, and she fought hard to ignore them. She just hoped the rats themselves had abandoned their mattress home. Elizabeth and Wickham still had no bedcovers, so she placed her underskirt on the bed as a makeshift bed sheet. As soon as most of the cleaning was done, Wickham started to pace the floor, kick at the chair legs, and brush invisible dirt from the table. By late afternoon, Elizabeth could detect a restlessness and irritability in her husband that she was starting to recognize and associate with recent his alcohol use. She knew he would be leaving again soon.

Within the hour of completing their cleaning, he said to her, "Elizabeth dear, I need to go out and get a few things. I won't be long." She did not verbally respond but simply nodded. She was tired, and she continued to have pain in her face. She thought she would lie down for a while but wanted to wait until after George left. She did not want him to think she was "lazy and avoiding her chores." He put on his red military coat, checked to make sure his uniform was in proper order, and left without looking back or saying goodbye to her.

After he left, her confusion returned, and tears of exhaustion and betrayal overcame her. The light from outside the window was beginning to fade, so she walked to the well to get water for the morning. She was afraid to walk in the darkness for fear of tripping or losing her way. Darkness had always frightened her, ever since she was a little girl, but she never knew why. Being unable to find her way in the dark caused an anxiety she was never able to control. On her way back from the well, she met the old woman on the path. The woman had picked various plants from along the path that she would use to season her soups and stews. Elizabeth had seen these used by the cook her father had employed, but she did not know the names of the plants and herbs; nor did she know how to use them.

"Good evening," Elizabeth said to the woman. "I wish to thank you and your husband for helping me today." She was suddenly aware of her appearance and the obvious trauma to her face. "Please pardon my looks. I have been working diligently in our home, and I fell while reaching up into the upper shelves of the kitchen cabinets."

"Yes, my dear, we all seem to fall once in a while," the old woman said with obvious acknowledgment and understanding of Elizabeth's injuries. Elizabeth smiled slowly and quietly walked toward the house with her own head down in mutual unsaid agreement.

Wickham had not returned yet when she returned to the house. She lit a candle and put water in the kettle for tea. There was enough food left for one light supper, but no more. She chose to leave the food for him and hope he would not be too hungry or intoxicated when he returned. Hours passed, and George did not come back. Exhausted and hungry, Elizabeth walked into the bedroom and lay on the bed, immediately falling asleep.

13

Elizabeth awoke as light was just beginning to come through the window—the same broken window that had not yet been replaced. Yesterday's washing helped to allow more light to enter the room, but that had not improved the dark atmosphere inside. George had not come home during the night, and she again awoke alone and saddened by her unexpected and unexplained plight. The swelling of her face had begun to subside, but the bruising had worsened. Her jaw was still sore, but she could now open and close her mouth. She had not yet changed her dress since leaving the tavern two days ago. Never before had she gone days without changing her clothes. She felt dirty and unwashed. Using the water she had pumped the previous night, she washed her face gently, though she had no soap. Her hands were dirty, and her nails were split and broken, but she cleaned them as best as she could. Not only had she used her hairbrush to clean the floor, but she had also used her nailbrush to clean the few dishes she had.

After washing, she ate a small biscuit and drank some cold leftover tea. Not feeling hungry and not having eaten since the evening before, she was surprised she could eat at all. Today she was determined to venture out into the local streets and city to find what little food she had money for. She missed her family terribly, and she hoped to someday soon find her aunt and uncle's house. She needed to speak with her aunt about the past day's events. Her aunt would tell her the truth about marriage and what she needed to do to improve her current situation. She had to find a way out of her present dilemma. She remembered the advice given to her by the woman in the tavern. She was determined to survive this hell she was now in.

Judging by the sun's height in the sky, she ascertained it to be midmorning. Running her fingers through her hair and pulling it back without a ribbon to tie it, she started to leave the house, but she stopped short on hearing the front door open.

"Elizabeth, where in the hell are you?" She did not answer back immediately, and he called out again. "Elizabeth, can't you hear me, woman? Answer me when I call you!"

Gathering her courage, she simply answered, "I am here, George."

"Good. Get me something to eat," he demanded. He walked into the kitchen, and she was shocked by his appearance. His military coat was stained with mud and torn at the sleeve. His trousers were also torn and stained from not only mud but also from food and beer. His face was bruised, and he had a cut above his right eye. He reeked of alcohol and cigar smoke.

"Are you all right? Have you been hurt?" she asked.

"No, I fell down; now get me some food," he said while sitting down hard in a chair. She made what little food they had and put the two remaining biscuits on a plate in front of him.

"I said I want some food, not this garbage!"

"That is all we have, sir," she said without empathy.

"You bitch, you have eaten all the food and spent all the money, haven't you? You spoiled brat. By God, I'll show you how to be my wife." He stood quickly, kicking the chair out from under him, grabbed Elizabeth by the wrist, and dragged her into the bedroom.

"No, George, don't do this. I promise you there is no money. I did not spend it. We have no food."

"Shut up, slut. I know about women like you. You are all alike." He pushed her down onto the bed and slapped hard on her already bruised and partially healed face. The pain was excruciating, and she nearly fainted from the impact. He tore at her clothes with a strength she did not realize he was capable of.

"Please stop; do not hurt me," she begged, but he ignored her pleas. "Why are you doing this? Please stop!" she called out, now crying and trying to push him away.

"Go ahead and fight, woman; it won't help you," he laughed. "You whore," he snarled at her. Within minutes, her clothes were ripped off her and shredded. She lay on the bed completely naked, openly exposed to his demands. She tried to cover herself with her hands, but he was too strong. He grabbed her wrists and dragged her to the front door. After kicking it open with his foot, he dragged her outside and then turned and went back in. He then slammed the door shut, leaving her outside. She crawled to the back door, opened it as quietly as she could, and entered the kitchen. She was hoping to avoid him, but he was waiting for her. He now pulled her up off the floor and dragged her into the bedroom. She was too traumatized, weak, and scared to scream.

After he finished with her, he said, "Now clean yourself up and get me some food." She sat up on the bed but felt dizzy. The room was spinning, and it took several moments before she could adjust her eyes. She put on the few remaining underclothes that were not torn or stained, along with the one remaining dress from her bag. Uncomfortable from her assault, she walked slowly into the kitchen. Wickham was sitting at the table, now upright, eating the biscuits and drinking the tea. He looked up at her and quietly said, "I am sorry; I didn't mean to hurt you. I don't know what comes over me sometimes. But Elizabeth, we need each other, and we will always love each other. We need to be strong for each other." What he really needed was her inheritance and her money, and he needed it soon. His gambling debts were starting to accumulate again. He was talking more to himself than to her, and she ignored him.

14

After he finished his breakfast, Wickham walked into the bedroom, lay on the bed, and soon fell asleep, snoring loudly. She cleaned up what few dishes they had with what little water was left. Her thoughts were scattered as she worked, but she knew she had to make some serious decisions, as her life could not continue on its current destructive path. She did not believe he was sorry for his actions, and she knew he would continue to hurt her. She knew he would kill her one of these times. She again fixed her hair and washed her face gently as she could without causing more trauma and pain. She quietly counted what little money she had left over, picked up what belongings she had, put them into her bag, and walked out the door, not bothering to close it.

Not knowing where to walk, she proceeded to the street as it followed the edge of the waterfront. She had not walked far when she met the older woman she had seen and talked to several times at the water pump.

"There you are, my dear," the old woman said. "You are going the wrong way to get back to your house, aren't you?"

"Please, could you help me?" asked Elizabeth. "I need to find the neighborhood called Cheapside. I have relatives who live there, and I need to find them."

"Looks like you might have fallen again, sweetie," the old woman observed.

"Yes, yes I did," Elizabeth answered with embarrassment.

"I see. Well, you need to keep walking on this street for several blocks, then turn at Harris Street. Keep walking and you should find it directly. It may take you a while to get there, but you will. I suggest you hurry along before your husband wakes up and finds you gone."

"How did you know he was sleeping?" Elizabeth asked.

The old woman eyed Elizabeth for a moment and then said, "I know men, dear." Elizabeth simply nodded and turned away. "Now get going, sweetie, and remember: don't look no one directly and just keep walking. Don't stop for no one, even if they talk to you, hear me? This part of the city can be dangerous to women."

"Yes, and thank you."

The old woman made no further comment but turned away and walked in the direction she had come from.

15

Elizabeth kept walking, picking up her pace, and she progressed across the city, following the old woman's directions. Despite her having few belongings, her bag was heavy across her shoulder, but she proceeded without hesitation. The discomfort she felt from the heavy bag was minimal compared to the pain she had experienced at the hand of George Wickham. Her face and jaw hurt, and her vision was limited because of the swelling of her eyes. Her arms and legs were bruised and cut from his fists. The horrid thoughts of George Wickham only encouraged her to keep walking. The farther she was from her husband and the closer to her family, the better for all.

The daylight progressed to darkness, and she grew tired. The lack of daylight caused long shadows to appear, and her fear of darkness started to grip her soul. The progressive loss of daylight caused the families of London to retreat to their homes, and the men and women of London's nightlife presented themselves on the street. Remembering the old woman's words, she made no eye contact with anyone, kept her head down, and proceeded on her course. She ignored her hunger and thirst, knowing she had to keep walking. By now George Wickham would know she was gone, but she knew that as long as she was away from him, she could make it to her aunt and uncle's home of refuge. However, by the early morning hours, she could walk no more. She found an unoccupied doorway stoop and curled herself into the opening. She wrapped her skirts around her and hugged her small bag to her chest. She put her head down and fell asleep, but rest would not be long for Elizabeth. A loud noise awoke her suddenly only one hour after she fell asleep.

"What are you doing here?" shouted the shopkeeper who owned the doorway she was sleeping in. "Get along with you. We don't need your kind around here. Now get going, and don't come back." Scared and alone, she cried softly but knew her tears would be ill spent. The short time she had slept had reenergized her enough to get up and continue her journey. By dawn, the street vendors started to appear again, and she started to feel safe again. Her hunger was minimal, but her thirst was great. She knew she would need to ask for directions and where she could obtain water soon. She noticed a well-dressed, handsome gentleman standing next to his carriage, conversing with his driver. He appeared calm and was obviously well-spoken and comfortable with his surroundings. She shyly approached him and asked for directions.

"Please, sir, could you give me directions to a part of the city called Cheapside? I think it is close by. I have lost my direction and need to find my family. They live there, and I need to get to their home rather quickly."

"Are you hurt, ma'am? May I help you?" he asked with obvious concern. She kept her head down, but he could see by her battered and bruised face, cut lip, and swollen eyes that she had been beaten—beaten by someone very strong and angry.

"No, sir, but thank you. Once I reach my destination, I will be all right. My family will help me," she said slowly. With relief, she found she was only several blocks from her destination. The thoughts of seeing her aunt's and uncle's faces and experiencing the security of their home again gave her the confidence to continue.

"Thank you again, sir, for your kindness."

"You are welcome, ma'am. Are you sure you are all right?"

"Yes, sir. I will be fine once I reach my family," she slowly replied.

"Safe journey to you, then," the man answered, bowing slightly to her.

By midday, she found the house. Walking eagerly to the door, she knocked as loudly as her weakened condition would allow. Her aunt's maid answered the door and looked upon Elizabeth with disbelief.

"My God, child, what are you doing here? What happened? Hurry, come in before you faint!" the maid said. She reached out and held on to Elizabeth's arm as she guided her into the front room. As soon as she sat,

Mrs. Gardnier entered the room. Looking at Elizabeth in disbelief, she immediately sent the maid to locate Mr. Gardnier, demanding he come at once.

"Elizabeth, let me help you with your bag. Cook!" she yelled, not taking her eyes from Elizabeth. "Cook, where are you? Come at once."

Cook entered the room wheezing and moving as fast as she could, still holding a dishrag.

"Yes ma'am, what can I do for you?" She stopped, stared at Elizabeth, and whispered, "What has happened?"

"Where is Mr. Gardnier? Quickly, get Mrs. Wickham some hot soup. Hurry now!"

"Yes ma'am, right away." She turned and hurried out, while at the same time Mr. Gardnier entered the parlor.

"By God, what has happened here? Elizabeth, what has happened?"

"Mr. Gardnier, we can ask her questions later; now she needs some food, drink, and much-needed rest. Her injuries need attending to immediately. Come, help me, Mr. Gardnier; help me take Elizabeth upstairs." Together they lifted Elizabeth from the chair and carried her upstairs and into a small guest room. They laid her down on the bed, and then Mrs. Gardnier started to remove Elizabeth's shawl. Mr. Gardnier started to turn away, but he quickly turned back at the sound of Mrs. Gardnier's gasp upon seeing the extent of Elizabeth's bruised and swollen face. Dried blood remained in her hair and on her clothes. Cook quietly entered the room and set the bowl of hot soup on the bedside table.

"Thank you, Cook," whispered Mrs. Gardnier. She then turned back toward Elizabeth and said, "My dear, let me clean and dress these wounds; then I want you to eat some of this soup." Elizabeth, now weakened from lack of food and exhausted from her long journey, was only able to nod in agreement. "Mr. Gardnier, please fetch me a basin of warm water, some clean clothes, the jar of that special cream I got from the apothecary last week, and some bandages."

"I'll be right back, dear," he answered reluctantly. Within minutes, Mr. Gardnier and the maid returned with the items requested. Quickly, Mrs. Gardnier and the maid cleaned and dressed Elizabeth's wounds while Mr. Gardnier stood back watching with utmost concern for his niece. "Mrs. Gardnier, please excuse me; I will return within the half hour," Mr. Gardnier said softly. His wife did not answer him but only nodded without turning to face him.

As soon as Elizabeth's wounds were dressed, Mrs. Gardnier began to spoon feed the soup to Elizabeth.

"Easy now, dear; take your time. You will be all right now. You are safe here with us." From Mrs. Gardnier's earlier years of nursing, she recognized the wounds of abuse and knew from the moment she saw Elizabeth's face and general appearance that she had been beaten. She also suspected who gave her the beating. When the soup was nearly gone, Elizabeth waved away any further soup and attempted to close her eyes.

"Yes, dear, you close your eyes and get some rest. You certainly need it. You are safe now."

"Please, Aunt, stay with me; do not leave me alone," Elizabeth whispered.

"You will not be alone. I need to speak with your uncle, but the maid is here, and she will stay until I return. I will just be gone for a few minutes." Elizabeth nodded in understanding, laid her head back onto the pillow, and fell asleep immediately.

16

Mrs. Gardnier entered the study to find her husband writing frantically. He looked up briefly but returned to his writing without speaking to his wife.

"What are you doing, sir?"

"I am writing to her father to let him know we are going to provide Elizabeth sanctuary here. Then I will write my solicitor, asking him to look into the background of Lieutenant Wickham—something I should have done before they were married. Maybe I could have prevented this."

"My dear husband, Lieutenant Wickham fooled all of us with his smooth talk and gallant stories of accomplishment and glory. No one is to blame for what has happened. He fooled all of us. I just wish I knew why."

"Yes, he sure was polished," Mr. Gardnier responded quietly.

"I will stay with her; please join us when you are ready," she said. He looked up briefly with a look of anger and disgust but returned to his writing without any further conversation.

Elizabeth slept much of the day, sometimes peacefully and other times fitfully. Mr. and Mrs. Gardnier, along with the maid, took turns sitting with her all through the first day. She awoke by early evening. Cook prepared her another bowl of soup, which she managed to eat herself, though she did so slowly. Her face was swollen and painful, with both eyes nearly swollen shut, but she could now move her jaw, indicating that there was no fracture.

"Elizabeth, dear, please let me help you up. It is important you do not lie in bed too long. Some people have been known to experience sudden death from being in bed too long. It is not clear why this happens, but I did see this happen during my days of nursing at the hospital. The maid will change your sheets while you are up."

"Thank you, aunt," Elizabeth said quietly. She sat in the chair while the maid quickly removed the bedclothes, replaced them with fresh linens, and then left the room, leaving Elizabeth and her aunt alone.

"Elizabeth, your uncle and I will not ask you any questions now, while you are so weak, but as soon as you feel well enough, we would like to hear what has happened to you."

"Yes, of course. It has been very difficult few days, but I need to speak with both of you." She was silent for a moment and then said, "Oh, Aunt, I did not know what marriage meant. While we are alone, I need to hear from you what is expected from me and what is permitted between husband and wife."

"Elizabeth, I can tell by your appearance that you did not experience what love and marriage are all about. Marriage is love, gentle and kind, without hitting, slapping, or verbal abuse. The marriage act is something mutually agreed upon by husband and wife. You and all of us were misled by Lieutenant Wickham. We suspect everything he told us was lies—lies given to us for some unknown reason."

Elizabeth did not respond but turned her head away while silent tears streamed down her face.

Her sleep that night was savaged with dreams of broken furniture, rats, and George Wickham's hateful words. The old woman's wise advice was interrupting her but was of no help in keeping her calm. She awoke by early dawn, shaking and cold.

Her uncle, who had sat with her all night, immediately responded to her distress by holding her hand and whispering comforting words. "Elizabeth, dear, you are here with us now. You are safe. Please rest and get well." He was extremely distressed to see his beloved niece in such physical and emotional turmoil.

By midday, Elizabeth felt rested enough to bathe, dress, and join the family downstairs. She noticed a clean dress lying out on a chair, inviting her to come downstairs for a midday meal. Sitting at the table with the family, Cook presented her with a thicker soup. She consumed this with fruit and soft bread with fresh butter, but meat would be difficult for her to chew. Embarrassed, she was unable to finish her meal and requested to leave the dining table early.

"Please, Aunt, may I be excused? I am feeling more tired than I thought."

"Yes, of course dear, but first, please come to the front parlor with your uncle and me. We are still very concerned about you."

"Yes, of course. You have been so kind to take me in. You both must be very curious about what brought me here so soon after my marriage." She stood up slowly from the table and left the room. She walked to the front parlor, where she was soon joined by her aunt and uncle.

Once seated, Mr. Gardnier asked, "Elizabeth, may I get you anything? A glass of wine, perhaps?"

"No thank you, Uncle," she replied.

The three remained quiet for a brief moment, gathering their thoughts. Then Mrs. Gardnier said, "Elizabeth, your uncle has written your father, letting him know that we are providing you with sanctuary and that you will be staying with us for the time being. You must know you are always welcome and are safe here with us here."

"Yes, Aunt, and I am most thankful for that. Actually, you cannot know how truly grateful I am that you are both here and have accepted me into your home."

"We do know," replied Mr. Gardnier. "Now, Elizabeth, if you are able, please tell us what has happened to you—and, I assume, what Lieutenant Wickham has done also."

"Take your time, dear," said Mrs. Gardnier while eyeing her husband. "If you are not ready yet, please wait until you are,"

"No, Aunt, I am ready." Elizabeth took a deep breath and slowly told her story, starting with leaving Longbourne and continuing to how she came to be at her family's home. She included the details of Lieutenant Wickham's verbal and physical assaults starting on their wedding night, but she also spoke of how a kind, well-dressed gentleman gave her directions to reach her uncle's home when she was lost and walking alone in the city. She was embarrassed to talk about her ordeal with her uncle present, but she felt it necessary to do. They deserved to hear the truth from her after taking her into their home, feeding her, providing fresh clothing, and caring for her wounds. As she continued to tell her story, she could feel the tension she carried start to leave her body. Mrs. Gardnier watched Elizabeth without emotion, but Mr. Gardnier exhibited restlessness and increasing anger. Eventually he stood from his chair and started to pace the room.

"Do we know where Lieutenant Wickham is now?" asked Mr. Gardnier.

"He had gone to bed just before I left. That was three days ago, Uncle," answered Elizabeth quietly.

"Do we expect him to show his face here?" he asked.

"I do not know, but I would not be surprised. After all, I am still married to him," she again answered, now bowing her head.

"Yes, well, I suppose we will just have to deal with him and his disgusting behavior. We will deal with this when it happens. I must tell both of you that Lieutenant Wickham is not welcome here and I do not want him in my home or near my family. That includes all of my family. If he does come here looking for you, Elizabeth, and if you wish to see him, you must receive him outside of our home."

"Yes, Uncle, I understand. Please," she said sadly, "I am so sorry for all of this. I apologize for your inconvenience and for the concern you have for your family regarding my husband. I never imagined any of this could happen."

"Elizabeth, dear," Mrs. Gardnier said, "we were all fooled by Lieutenant Wickham. What I do not understand is why? What did he think he would accomplish with his lies and clever speeches to us?"

"All I can think of, dear," Mr. Gardnier said to his wife, "is that Lieutenant Wickham must feel Elizabeth and her family are wealthy landowners and he hopes to one day to obtain large amounts of money upon our brother's death."

"Why would he possibly think that? Who would tell him the Bennets are wealthy?" asked Mrs. Gardnier. "They certainly do not have a large, expansive estate, servants, or connections to London's elite."

"I do not understand. I never gave George any inclination that I had any wealth or that I would inherit any land or estate," Elizabeth interjected.

"Of course you did not, dear," said Mrs. Gardnier. "I am sure Lieutenant Wickham is looking for any quick path to money."

"Well," said Mr. Gardnier, "I am going to inquire after Lieutenant Wickham. I will see what my solicitor has discovered." He stood slowly and walked out of the parlor in deep thought.

"It is going to be all right, Elizabeth," said Mrs. Gardnier. "Remember: you are safe here. He cannot hurt you anymore." Elizabeth sighed and slowly bent her head forward and stared at the floor. "Elizabeth, let me get you another cup of tea."

"Thank you, Aunt. That would be nice."

18

Shortly after Mrs. Gardnier left the parlor, Elizabeth heard the front door open and close, followed by loud voices that permeated the entire downstairs.

"I told you, sir; Elizabeth will not see you!" shouted Mr. Gardnier. "You are to leave this house immediately or I will summon a constable. You will not be recognized by our family!"

"Sir, I beg your pardon, but I must speak to my wife. I can only imagine what Elizabeth's appearance may appear to be, but this has been a terrible misunderstanding. I need to apologize for my abhorrent behavior. Too much drink overpowers my thoughts, causing me to behave in an ungentlemanly way. I beg you, sir; allow me to see my wife."

"Absolutely not. Elizabeth has suffered enough. She has been severely injured at your hand and now needs rest and the nursing care of her family."

"I understand," said Wickham humbly. "Please allow me to return when she is feeling better. I will need to talk with her before I leave for my next duty call."

"You told Elizabeth's father that you resigned your commission and that you have a permanent assignment here. It was believed you would not be traveling."

"Oh yes, of course," said Wickham reluctantly. "I have just been notified that my commander is in desperate need of my services and unable to release me at this time."

"Sir," said Mr. Gardnier, "pardon my thoughts, but I do not believe you and I strongly suspect you are lying." Both men stared at each other for several moments before Lieutenant Wickham stepped back and bowed slightly before turning away and leaving quickly out of the door.

Mrs. Gardnier, having listened to the conversation from an adjacent hallway, stepped forward, exposing her presence to her husband. "Oh, sir, what a despicable man. I am proud of you for calling him the liar that he is. I suspect you are correct in your accusation of him not being truthful, but now what will you do?"

"I will write Elizabeth's father immediately about this current event. He must know what has happened. He may want to come here himself to see Elizabeth."

As soon as he finished, Elizabeth appeared. "Please, Uncle, do not let my father come here and see me like this. He will be so upset. I have disappointed him so by marrying George Wickham."

"Elizabeth, he must know, but I will ask him to stay away for now, if that is what you wish."

"It is, sir." With that, Elizabeth sadly left her aunt and uncle's company and returned to her room, where she would remain for the rest of the day.

Meanwhile, George Wickham left the Gardniers' home quickly, with his temper in check, but could feel his pique near the point of explosion. He again needed to gain Elizabeth's trust so he might commandeer her inheritance and the Longbourne estate, which he was convinced she had. She was his wife, and through his marital rights, he could demand her return; but he also realized his utmost charm and acceptable manners would gain more than his threats and fists. He would return in the morning to see Elizabeth and start courting her again if necessary. For now, he needed a drink, so he proceeded to the nearest tavern and into the arms of a more-than-willing barmaid.

Elizabeth sat in a straight-backed chair next to the window, lost in thought. She stared out of the upstairs window, watching both the traffic in the street and the pedestrians shopping, laughing, and gossiping among themselves. She just could not understand how her life had taken such a drastic and unpleasant turn. By now her father already knew her plight and would be coming for her. Would he still love her? Of course he would, but she also realized their relationship would be forever changed.

A thunderstorm had rolled into the city during the afternoon. The flashes of light and loud crashes of thunder seemed to shake the roof and house shingles. What would a thunderstorm be like at the small dirty house by the river's edge she had shared with Wickham? Would the roof leak? Would the doors hold back the rain and wind? A strong storm might bring the building down. She shuddered to think what her life would be like had she stayed there with George Wickham.

20

By morning the storm had passed and the day appeared bright and clear. The rain had washed much of the smoke-filled air away, causing a freshness that was much appreciated. Elizabeth was feeling stronger every day, and she was starting to miss her daily walks. The bruising and swelling of her face was nearly healed, so she decided to go for a walk outside. It was still early morning, so the temperature was comfortable. She would not go far—only to the nearby park. At this time of day, she would not require an escort, and besides, walking alone was not unfamiliar to her. She had recently walked across the entire city of London alone. Realizing she would probably be alone for the rest of her life, she dressed in the one dress she still owned, put on her aunt's cloak with matching hood, and stepped out into the cool sunshine.

Elizabeth stood on the front doorstep for several minutes, breathing in the fresh air and enjoying the conversation exchanged among the local birds and park squirrels. She did not realize how much she had missed the familiarity of the outdoors along with the comfort of her family and her home. What had she been thinking marrying George Wickham? How could she have been such a fool? As she stood there, more thoughts started to invade her. What if she was now pregnant? Where would she go, alone and with a child? Even if she was not pregnant, her mere association with George Wickham would cause her to be shackled emotionally to him forever. She hoped she would never see him again, but unfortunately knew that would never happen. Despite these consuming thoughts, she was determined to enjoy the bright sunshine and beautiful day.

She stepped down the stairs and walked toward the nearby park.

She knew the area well from her childhood and felt comfortable with her surroundings. The more she walked, the better she felt. Her spirits lifted, and her mood quickly elevated. At this point, nothing could ruin her day. But then she saw that familiar red coat coming toward her with the determination she dreaded. Had he been outside her aunt and uncle's home, watching and waiting for her? She looked around, hoping to escape, but there was nowhere she could go. She realized that he had now seen her and was deliberately and quickly approaching her.

"Well, Elizabeth my dear, how pleased I am to see you up and around on this lovely morning. You simply glow in the out of doors. You know, you must do this more often. I noticed you were starting to look somewhat sickly lately." He took her elbow and gently steered her toward a nearby park bench to sit and continue their impending conversation. She stiffened when he touched her, but she allowed him to guide her off the worn path to the public bench. Because the bench was narrow, they sat close to each other but fortunately did not touch.

"Elizabeth," he said quietly, looking out among the other people now strolling about the park, "we seem to have encountered a misunderstanding and started our marriage out wrongly, but I am here today or correct any misgivings. You know I love you and wish you to be happy." He reached for her hand, but she quietly pulled back, not wanting to make a public scene. He also did not want to draw undue attention and allowed her to hold her hands in her lap while he continued his speech.

"I wish you had not left our home and gone to the presumed protection of your family. You rightly belong to me, you know, but I want you to come to me of your own free will and into my love and trusting heart. I know we can recover from this current misunderstanding." They both remained silent for a short while without making any eye contact. Despite the fresh and comfortable air, Elizabeth was starting to feel warm. She could feel her pulse quicken and face flush. Wickham could sense her discomfort and again attempted to reach for her hand. She did not respond to his advance and turned her face away from him, struggling to hold back tears. She was determined not to be defeated by him anymore. The words given to her in the tavern returned: "We women survive."

"Elizabeth," Wickham said, "I wish you will return with me. I will look into more comfortable living arrangements and possibly find a maid to help with cooking and cleaning. I realize a proper lady like yourself should not have to toil as you recently did. We should be able to find acceptable lodgings in the city and start over."

Gathering her courage and taking a deep breath, Elizabeth turned toward her husband and said, "Lieutenant Wickham, you have demonstrated to me that you are an unfaithful, abusive, and angry man. You have treated me most uncivilly and rudely. You have abused and hurt me. I do not trust you, and I do not think I ever will, so I am telling you now that I refuse to accompany you back to our current home or any other home. In fact, we should separate legally and eventually dissolve our marriage. As a gentleman in the king's military, I would expect you to respect my wishes." George Wickham sat quietly and listened, but she could see his jaw tighten and his fists open and close. His anger was building, and her concern for her safety heightened. She was somewhat comforted by their being in a public arena. She had noticed a constable standing just within the park—certainly within shouting distance if she needed his assistance.

"Elizabeth," Wickham said sternly, "I am within my marital rights to demand you come with me. In fact, I can physically take you against your will. You are my legal wife, and you are obligated to obey me. I had hoped we could resolve our differences with civility, but, as you have stated, I am a gentleman. With that said, I am willing to negotiate with you."

"Negotiate?" she answered.

"Yes, negotiate. I am willing to separate and dissolve our marriage, as you phrase it," he said sarcastically. "But you must turn over your inheritance to me now."

"What inheritance?" she said.

"The Longbourne estate. Your father's estate—the one you are to inherit upon his death," he answered unexpectedly.

"You thought I was to inherit an estate? You married me because you thought I was a wealthy heiress?" she asked. She stared at him and then started to laugh. "You, sir, are a bigger fool than I was for marrying you."

"What are you saying?" he asked loudly. "Answer me now!" His shouting brought about the attention of several visitors of the park, but they quickly turned away, trying to ignore the increasing eruption between the couple sitting on the bench.

Elizabeth sat quietly, looking out onto the park. She then turned toward him and calmly answered, "Longbourne is a one-hundred-acre farm that has been losing money every year for the past ten years. Only one half of the land is tillable; the other acreage is a combination of wetlands and pastureland. The whole farm is not worth much except for the grassland used to feed the animals. So you see, sir, you have been fooled into thinking Longbourne was a wealthy estate and I was worth marrying only to gain the value of the estate. Even when my father passes, the house and farm are entailed to my distant male cousin—a cousin I have never even met."

"What are you saying?" he shouted.

"You heard me. I have no inheritance—no money."

"You bitch!" he yelled. "You are worthless. You are less than worthless. You slut! To think I thought you were actually worth marrying!"

"Well, the joke was on you," she smiled.

He stood slowly, turned, and stared down at her. "You and your family are finished. Well, the last laugh will be on you, my dear. I will never release you from your vows. You will be married to me forever. You will never be able to court or marry again. You will live out the rest of your days alone and in my shadow. If you ever try to be with any other man, your reputation as a married woman separated from her husband because of infidelity will be announced all over England. You will be known as the biggest adulteress in the whole country."

"I have never been unfaithful to you," she exclaimed.

"That will never be proven, my dear. The local gossip will be widespread and unstoppable. Now, with my creditors calling in loans under your family's name, it will be difficult to prove."

"How dare you make such accusations," she said.

"Elizabeth, I will be the last one standing in this war. I will accuse you of compiling my debts. Your name will appear on all of the bills, loans, and the credit I will acquire from now on. I will see to it that you will be responsible to my creditors from now until long after I die. I will name you as the responsible party in our marital separation. I will spread the word of your infidelity, drunkenness, and mental instability. You and your family will be ruined. Your crazy mother will not be able to show her face in the village, and your wild sisters will have no chance for suitors or husbands. My image will haunt you now and forever. If you are ever seen with another man, the scandal will finish you." He turned to walk away but stopped and resumed his angry glare. "One more thing: if you are with child from our few marital encounters, I will denounce the child as mine, and you and your bastard will be penniless and forced into menial labor for the rest of your miserable lives. Think all this over, my dear. Now enjoy your day. It will be the last one you will enjoy. Remember one more thing, my dear: I always win." With that he turned and walked away.

Elizabeth hoped he was bluffing, but deep inside, she knew he was not. Deceit and anger were powerful enemies, and she definitely had acquired an enemy today. He walked away, carrying his head high and his shoulders as straight as any military man would. He was angry, and his threats were not empty. He left her with no hope and no future. She needed to accept his threats and live the rest of her life in hopeless despair. She knew her father would come for her, but even his support was no match for George Wickham's reach regarding her future.

21

After Wickham left, Elizabeth sat at the bench for almost one hour, contemplating what he had said and what he had threatened to do to both her and family. She knew his declaration was valid and would forever follow her. What if she was with child? Where would she go, and how would she make a living alone? With nothing more for her to consider, she stood and slowly walked back to her aunt and uncle's house.

When she entered the house, Mrs. Gardnier said, "There you are. Did you have a nice walk? It is so nice to see you up and around again. The fresh air and sunshine have always brightened both your skin and mood." She stared at Elizabeth's sad face. "What's wrong, dear? I can tell by your face and expression that something has happened."

"Yes, something has happened," said Elizabeth sadly.

"Is that Elizabeth? Has she returned from her walk?" called out Mr. Gardnier. He entered the front hallway to find the two women standing quietly, and he noted the nonverbal exchange between the two of them. "Something has happened. What has happened?" he demanded.

"George Wickham was waiting for me outside. We had quite an enlightening conversation," said Elizabeth matter-of-factly.

"Please, dear, come into the parlor, sit down, and tell us what happened," said Mrs. Gardnier.

"I cannot wait to hear what Lieutenant Wickham has to say now," said Mr. Gardnier sarcastically. Elizabeth removed her bonnet and coat, and hung then up on the hall tree. The three walked into the parlor and sat down. Elizabeth took a deep breath and then proceeded to tell her aunt and uncle about George Wickham's assumption and threats.

After Elizabeth finished, it took several minutes before anyone could speak. Then Mrs. Gardnier said, "My God, how could he say such things? How could he do this to you? Is he mad? He will never get away with these threats."

"My dear," said Mr. Gardnier calmly. "I am certain Lieutenant Wickham can do this. Elizabeth is, after all, his legal wife. She belongs to him, and according to the vows, she must honor and obey him. She is indeed responsible for his debts and will be until they are paid. She may not court or even be seen with another man as long as they are legally married, as he will cause disgrace to her, the family, and any children born of their union."

"Oh, how Papa will be so upset. I have disappointed him so," said Elizabeth.

"Nonsense, child; none of this was your fault. We were all taken in by Lieutenant Wickham's stories," answered Mrs. Gardnier.

"Yes, we were—especially me," replied Elizabeth sadly.

"Elizabeth, dear, your father will be here this afternoon to take you home. He must not see you this way. He is so worried about you. Please pick your spirits up and show him how strong you are."

"Yes, Aunt, I will," was all she could say.

22

By midafternoon, Elizabeth was indeed anxious to see her father. Wickham's threats had been forgotten for a short time until Mr. Bennet's carriage approached the Gardniers' front steps. Mr. Bennet stepped out of the coach and into the anxious arms of his daughter.

"Elizabeth, I am so glad to see you," he said as he held her at arm's length. "Are you all right? Your uncle has written me and informed me of the terrible events that occurred to you over the past several days. You must know that scoundrel will never hurt you again—not as long as I am alive. He will never hurt you again. Oh, daughter, what a fool I have been to allow this to happen to you."

"Papa, it is all right. We are together again, and we are both safe. Please come in; Aunt and Uncle are very anxious to see you again." Together they walked into the house and were greeted warmly by Mr. Bennet's sister and brother-in-law.

"Brother," called Mrs. Gardnier. "How good to see you; please come in. You must be tired from your long journey. May Cook fix you something to eat or drink?"

"Something from my brother-in-law's cabinet may be more appropriate," said Mr. Bennet. "Then the three of you will need to inform me of the most current events." He then disappeared into Mr. Gardnier's study and quietly shut the door.

Both Elizabeth and Mrs. Gardnier stared at the closed door with the acceptance that a decision would be made regarding Elizabeth's future. It would be made with confidence and trust and without the instability of Mrs. Bennet's impulsive comments. Approximately two hours after the men retreated into Mr. Gardnier's study, they reappeared, neither happy nor sad. Both slightly influenced by alcohol, they requested the presence of both ladies in the front parlor.

"Well, ladies," said Mr. Gardnier. "It certainly has been an eventful day." He put his feet up on a table in order to make himself more comfortable.

"Please take your feet off the table, sir. We have guests present," requested his wife.

Shyly he did as he was told and sat himself more upright.

"Ladies," Mr. Bennet said, clearing his throat. "My brother has informed me of what has happened over the past few weeks and what has transpired just today. All of this saddens me terribly, but I am so grateful that Elizabeth is now safe and with us again. I realize that you have had a very difficult time, but that is now over." He looked directly at his daughter.

"Papa," Elizabeth interrupted. "George spoke to me only this morning. He made threats not only to me but also to our family. We cannot ignore this!"

"Yes, daughter," he replied calmly. "Your uncle has told me what he said. I would, though, like to hear what he said, directly from you. Please start from the beginning and tell me the whole story." Elizabeth took a deep breath and proceeded to recall her earlier conversation with George Wickham.

After she was finished, Mr. Bennet said, "Well, Elizabeth, part of what Lieutenant Wickham says is true. You are still married to him, and he does have rights regarding that bond." Elizabeth knew her father well and had seen him study the law and review cases previously tried. He had now exited the role of her father and entered the role of her attorney. This both comforted and cautioned her regarding his actions and decisions. She never knew which personality would succeed, but whatever the result, she knew it would be the best for her. Whenever her father and uncle, both practicing attorneys and gentlemen, put their heads together, only positive outcomes occurred.

"Papa, have you made any decisions regarding our plight?"

"Yes, I have. We will return to Longbourne as if nothing has happened. According to Lieutenant Wickham's own account, he was recalled into active duty and has left for his port of call. We may not know if this is true, but for now, through a mutual decision, you will wait for him to return from this newly assigned post."

"Is that not acting only on the defense as opposed to the offense?"

"Not at all, daughter. I will call this a responsible decision based on Lieutenant Wickham's military responsibility. We can refer to his absence as the reason you have returned to Longbourne. So let us use this as a reason for your return, until we need to make another decision; then, if we need to, we can certainly address this again."

"Papa, I love you. How lucky I am to have you as a father and always with me. I was very concerned you would never acknowledge me again," Elizabeth said.

"Elizabeth, that will never happen. Now, let us have supper. We have a long journey home tomorrow," Mr. Bennet answered.

The ride to Longbourne the next day was long, made longer by the relative silence between father and daughter. Despite the lack of communication made, Elizabeth and her father understood each other's thoughts perfectly well. Their nonverbal exchange left no doubt about the positive feelings they had for each other. Their bond was unbreakable. This latest difficulty caused by Lieutenant Wickham only made their relationship stronger.

When they were within one mile from Longbourne, it was Mr. Bennet who spoke first. "Elizabeth, your mother and sisters are aware of the difficulties with Lieutenant Wickham, but not to the extent that I am. I think it best that we leave it at that. You know your mother and her 'nerves,' so let us not make a difficult situation impossible."

"Yes, Papa," was all she said in answer.

They approached Longbourne, and Elizabeth sat higher in her seat, her anxiety rising significantly with the sound of each hoofbeat. She could envision her mother and sisters ready to greet them happily. Despite her anxiety, she smiled with the comfort of seeing the rest of her family again.

"Elizabeth, my beautiful married daughter," her mother said when they arrived, holding her daughter close, "you are back home with us. I am so happy you will be waiting here for your husband to return from his military duty. What a surprise to hear he was called to active duty again. I am sure you would rather be with him, but we are so happy to have you with us again. Don't you agree, Mr. Bennet?"

"Yes, of course, dear wife," was all he replied.

23

The weeks passed living at Longbourne while George Wickham's debts continued to grow. Elizabeth worked day and night in whatever menial jobs she could find, trying to keep up with his creditors. It grew to be too much, and she sold most of her personal possessions to earn money. She was reduced to doing washing and repairing the clothes of many of the local women. Gossip spread throughout the village, and her spirits started to drop.

"Oh, Papa, what am I to do?" Elizabeth asked. "I have no money and no home. George's gambling debts have exceeded any money I would ever dream to have. He has left me in shame and disgrace. I am in more debt than anyone could possibly imagine. When I walk to Meryton, the townspeople stare and turn their heads, whispering. I'm sure my husband owes money to just about everyone in Meryton. I appreciate the money that you have given me to help with his debts, but you cannot give me any more; nor will I accept any more." Her voice grew quieter. "You, mother, and my sisters need your money if you wish to continue to live at Longbourne. I cannot allow you to lose Longbourne because of me."

"Yes, I have seen the townspeople staring and whispering myself. I have sent an inquiry to your uncle to ask his opinion on our future decisions regarding both you and Lieutenant Wickham," said Mr. Bennet. The look on his face showed saddened sorrow for the unfortunate situation of his daughter. Mr. Gardnier continued to be aware of Elizabeth's current and growing financial situation and would help any way he could. George Wickham's threats were proving to be true. Perhaps leaving Longbourne and going back to London would help stop the local gossip. It also could provide more opportunities for Elizabeth to earn money, but the more she earned, the faster the debts occurred. She was sure Lieutenant Wickham was aware of her every move and of her financial situation.

Within days of writing to Mr. Gardnier, a letter arrived at Longbourne from Elizabeth's uncle. Mr. Bennet opened the letter slowly and with concern regarding its uncertain contents. He was hoping his brother-in-law would have good news for him, but he was also sure the letter's arrival would mean Elizabeth would need to leave Longbourne. Mr. Bennet read the letter quickly and then reread it again more slowly, his expression turning grim.

My dear brother,

I have received your letter dated one week prior, requesting my opinion regarding my niece's current financial and marital situation. This is indeed an unfortunate situation for Elizabeth and your family. I was hoping the situation had not become this serious. I have recently heard of Lieutenant Wickham's debts and exploits but did not realize how desperate my niece's situation had become. Apparently Lieutenant Wickham owes money to just about anyone in London who was unfortunately taken in by his smooth manner and was willing to lend him money. His creditors are now anxious for repayment, most with high interest added.

To my understanding, he has not been seen in or about the city for many months. I fear that many of his creditors here will soon start to look to you and my niece for their payment. Because of this, I have acquired another means for Elizabeth to obtain money to meet some of these debts. I have heard Mr. Fitzwilliam Darcy, the master of Pemberley, in Derbyshire, needs additional kitchen staff for the upcoming holiday season and possibly beyond that. I took the liberty of inquiring about this position. The master cook, Mrs. Enders, a German immigrant, is willing to accept Elizabeth as a kitchen assistant. I realize that this may be unbecoming to you and your family, but it will be solid, steady employment for the next year. I know of Mr. Darcy, and he is an honorable man known to be honest, truthful, and very good to his employees. Please let me know your thoughts and concerns regarding this possibility. I look forward to your response.

Sincerely, your brother-in-law,
Mr. Gardnier

After reading the letter for the second time, Mr. Bennet stood from his desk and walked toward the large bay window in his study. He gazed upon the vast farmland of Longbourne without expression. He was unable to feel any emotion, knowing that his daughter, Elizabeth, would be leaving their home to become a humble kitchen servant for the honorable Mr. Fitzwilliam Darcy of Pemberley. He had heard of the expansive manor, with its huge, impressive home, a hundred tenant's homes, thousands of acres of farmland, and thoroughbred horses. How he despised George Wickham for doing this to his daughter and family. He despised himself for having allowed this to happen to her.

Elizabeth was taking a stroll among the gardens of Longbourne, but she was unable to see anything or smell the wonderful fragrances that surrounded her. The reds and oranges of early autumn were breathtaking, but Elizabeth was unable to appreciate their color as a result of her melancholy mood. She continued to speculate on her immediate and distant future, but she knew her life would soon be changing. The uncertainty was disturbing. At least she had not shown the symptoms of pregnancy, and for now she would not have to take on that responsibility.

"Elizabeth," Mr. Bennet called to her, "please come into the library; I have news from my brother for you."

"Yes, Papa," Elizabeth said. "I will be there directly."

"Well, my dear," Mr. Bennet said to Elizabeth after she settled into one of his overstuffed chairs, "I have received a response from your uncle, Mr. Gardnier. Here is his letter; I would like you to read it." He handed the letter to her. "Elizabeth, I know this is not something either you, your mother, or I would have wanted for you, but we need to look at this situation realistically. Our financial status is precarious." As he was speaking, Mr. Bennet paced about the room with a now serious concern upon his face. The love for his daughter was unquestionable, and his conversation with her was difficult and inevitable.

"Yes, Papa, I understand," said Elizabeth quietly. "When will I be leaving?" she asked without emotion.

"Tomorrow, my dear," replied Mr. Bennet. "You will be leaving on the coach from Meryton and then take a private carriage to the manor. Mr. Darcy provides transportation for his people when starting and leaving his employ."

"That is generous of him," stated Elizabeth.

"Yes," he replied. "He is a very generous man." She stared at the carpet so her father could not see her tear-streaked face.

24

Elizabeth first entered the back kitchen door of Pemberley carrying only a small tapestry bag. Her clothing, jewelry, and personal belongings had been sold long since to help pay her husband's mounting debts. She was sad but remained proud of who she was. She would not let her financial situation and current marital conflict interfere with her pride. She met Mrs. Enders, the master cook, almost immediately upon entering the kitchen. She was a stern-appearing overweight woman in her midfifties. She was quite short, with gray-colored hair pulled back from her face in a tight bun. She wore a gray dress covered with a white apron and spoke with a heavy German accent. She was the daughter of a local brewer and was rumored never to have been married, despite her being called "Mrs." The elder Mr. Darcy had met her in while visiting in a local pub and fancied her cooking. After several visits there to sample her expansive cooking skills, he finally asked her to come to Pemberley to be the master cook for him, his family, and the entire estate of Pemberley. She agreed on the condition that she be given complete control of the kitchen. The elder Mr. Darcy accepted her terms.

She approached Elizabeth. "Who are you? Are you the new kitchen maid? Answer me, girl; who are you?" asked Mrs. Enders impatiently. Elizabeth walked slowly to her new place of employment, knowing she was being observed by the many servants and members of the kitchen staff. She knew her manner and mode of dress did not match her surroundings, for her present appearance did not match that of a typical kitchen servant. Her borrowed dress was a dark orange muslin with a matching bonnet and shawl. She smelled sweetly of lily of the valley, but soon that would change to wood smoke and baked bread.

"Yes ma'am, my name is Elizabeth Bennet." She deliberately did not include her recent new last name of Wickham or include the fact she was married. Excluding the title of "Mrs." made her feel guilty, but she was also concerned someone would recognize her husband's name. She needed to keep this a secret. "I was sent here by my uncle, Mr. Gardnier, from London," she said quietly. "I was told I would be working for you in the kitchen as your assistant. My uncle told me you were kind, efficient, and a very excellent cook. I hope I can live up to the standards you have established here at Pemberley."

"I know Mr. Gardnier and his wife. Both are pleasant and polite. They are good to their cook, and outside of myself, their staff are also excellent cooks," said Mrs. Enders.

"Thank you, Mrs. Enders. As I said, I hope I can live up to your standards," said Elizabeth.

"I hope so; otherwise, I do not have the time or patience to teach someone who knows nothing of a kitchen. You do know how to cook, don't you?"

"Oh yes, ma'am, I do," said Elizabeth. Elizabeth's cooking skills were poor, but she hoped she could learn quickly, before Mrs. Enders realized how limited her abilities were.

"Good. Mr. Hickey here will show you to your room. You can put your things away. Change into the uniform that has been left for you, then come back here so I can show you what your duties will be," said Mrs. Enders impatiently.

"Thank you ma'am," said Elizabeth shyly, but Mrs. Enders had already turned away from her and gone back to her business.

She followed Mr. Hickey out of a side door from the kitchen and up a short flight of stairs to the maid's quarters. The servant quarters were well away from the main house, so she saw nothing of the manor house. They walked past several rooms before finally coming to hers at the end of the narrow hallway. The hallway was well lighted, from the outside windows that were facing the south side of the house, toward the main drive. There she could see the open fields, some newly harvested. Rare sunlight for this time of year was peering through the windows. She entered her room with a pleasant surprise. The room was small, clean, and freshly swept. It had been freshly painted, and she could not detect any unpleasant odors. The room contained a single bed, already made up with a quilt and feather pillow; a dresser; a nightstand; and small dressing table. A bowl and water pitcher stood on the dressing table, ready for washing. A mirror atop the dresser also reflected light from the outside. Thankfully, it was not cracked.

"Thank you very much, sir; the room is very nice, and I'm sure I will be comfortable here," Elizabeth said to Mr. Hickey.

"I'm sure you will. Mr. Darcy has a reputation of taking care of his servants. As long as you do your work, stay out of the main house unless told otherwise, and don't gossip too much, you should be all right here," said Mr. Hickey. "Well, I'll leave you to get settled. Don't linger too long or Mrs. Enders will get angry with you. Believe me; you do not want her to be angry with you." Mr. Hickey's slight Irish accent made Elizabeth smile in comfort.

"Thank you again, Mr. Hickey, I'll remember that."

He turned to leave and closed the door gently behind him. She placed her bag on the dresser and sat on the bed, facing the window. She opened it and stared out at the field. It was dark yellow from recent mowing but lush with mature trees on the hillside. A pond circled with wildflowers was breathtaking but somehow made her feel sad. *Well*, she thought, *my situation could be much worse. I could be in a dirty town outside the slums of London, working over a hot oven and listening to the unpleasant sounds made by traveling men and the women employed by a tavern keeper. I myself could be in the position of entertaining men, but thankfully I am not—at least not yet.*

She returned to the kitchen after unpacking her few belongings and saw Mrs. Enders scolding one of the kitchen maids. From what Elizabeth could hear, the maid had covered a simmering pot on the stove, allowing its contents to boil over onto the cast iron stovetop. She could smell and see the burned food smoking on the stove. Elizabeth felt sorry for the young girl receiving the scolding from the angered Mrs. Enders. Elizabeth kept her distance from the altercation but then approached cautiously when the conversation finished.

"I wish to thank you, Mrs. Enders, for allowing me to come to

Pemberley and be part of your kitchen staff. I appreciate the opportunity you are giving me."

"Never mind that; get this apron on, and let's see what you know about the kitchen," said Mrs. Enders impatiently. "We cook not only for Mr. Darcy and his sister, Miss Georgiana Darcy, but also for many of the unmarried working tenants, stable hands, and groundskeepers. Mr. Darcy employs over one hundred people, and he takes a personal interest in all of them. That includes what they eat, so let's get moving here."

Elizabeth noted that Mrs. Enders was as efficient as her uncle had said she would be. She moved about the kitchen quickly and made no unnecessary movements. "Hurry now; come over here. Start with cutting up these vegetables," she ordered. Elizabeth started her work immediately that first day, and the day did not stop until well after nightfall. For the first several days, she walked back to her room at nightfall exhausted, barely having time to remove her apron before falling asleep on top of the quilt.

The work days were much of the same, with the days starting just before dawn. She cut up meat and vegetables, and stirred large pots of stews and soups. She kneaded dough and lifted the hot trays of freshly baked bread and rolls from the ovens. She discovered that much of the food made was also distributed to the needy families of Pemberley. The work was hard and hot, and she was more tired than she had ever been in her entire life. When she wasn't preparing food for the cooks, she was hauling water from the outside well. Mr. Darcy had installed an inside water pump directly into the kitchen, but Mrs. Enders had ordered her to haul water in from the outside well. She felt the physical labor would strengthen her back and shoulders, allowing her to stand and work longer hours. On the days of hauling water, she felt exhaustion and pain over her entire body. She missed her family—especially her father. She missed his stimulating conversation and hearty laugh. She had not heard anyone laugh in the past few months. The days were long, and the nights were short and lonely. She did not miss her husband, George Wickham; in fact, she hoped she would never see him again, even if it meant she would have to stay in the kitchen of Pemberley forever.

Weeks passed with the same routine every day. Elizabeth awoke early and worked late. She was tired but fell into her daily chores without complaint. After she had been at Pemberley for eight weeks, Mrs. Enders called her aside just as she was entering the kitchen after her morning routine of water distribution.

"Elizabeth, come over here; I have a job for you," said Mrs. Enders.

"Yes ma'am, what do you request of me?" asked Elizabeth.

"Elizabeth, the master, Mr. Darcy, is expecting guests this afternoon. I want you to change into the dress you were wearing when you came here, and take this tray of breads and meat into the front sitting room. Mr. Darcy will entertain his guests there. Go on now, hurry up and be sure you are out of the room before the guests arrive" said Mrs. Enders loudly.

"Yes ma'am, as you request," replied Elizabeth. She hurried to her room and changed from her apron into the same simple orange dress she had worn when she came to Pemberley. It was still clean, but the hem was worn and the lace on the sleeve was torn. She glanced in the mirror and was saddened by her appearance. She looked and felt years older than she had just eight weeks prior. Unfortunately, she was becoming settled with her new station in life.

She went back to the kitchen, picked up the tray of prepared food, and proceeded to the front parlor, which was used exclusively for Mr. Darcy when he entertained business guests from London. She found her way easily despite her being allowed to enter only a few of the one hundred rooms of Pemberley. She entered the parlor, thankful that no one had arrived yet. She set the cumbersome tray down on a large table in the center of the room. Next to the tray was a decanter of brandy with several matching crystal tumblers. The room had a very masculine look and feel. The walls were paneled with a dark wood but accented with gold and yellow drapes. The accenting chairs and divan had matching gold and yellow designs. The colors of the room were properly matched and very pleasant to the eye. She looked around the room, thinking it was the most beautiful room she had ever seen. A large fireplace was located on a far wall, with a small fire ablaze in it already. The room was not overheated and was very comfortable. A few mounted deer and elk heads, as well as a large moose head, were displayed on one of the walls. She found these quite fascinating, as she had never seen animals that had been hunted, with their heads and skins mounted on the walls. Several pictures were on the marble mantelpiece. She presumed these were of the Darcy family. A rosewood pianoforte was also in the room. How comfortable everything looked. Despite being tired, she dared not sit down to rest. She knew Mr. Darcy would be along soon, and she did not want to be present when he entered to greet his guests. She also knew Mrs. Enders would scold her for lingering at her duties.

She left the room and started back toward the kitchen. She walked down the long hallway, and her eye caught the open door of the library. She looked in and could not believe the sight of the tall bookcases holding thousands of volumes. Elizabeth could not resist the allure of the books and quietly entered the room. Looking around the room to be sure no one else was there, she walked farther into the library and approached the bookcases. The room smelled of leather from the bound books with a slight musty odor from a recently smoked cigar. She did not detect a hint of the dust that normally accompanied her father's library. Not unfamiliar with the smell, she found that the room made her homesick for her father's own library. She reached for a book, slowly opened it, and started to read. She heard a noise behind her and turned quickly, only to see the master of Pemberley, Mr. Darcy, staring at her.

"You there—what are you doing in here?" a surprised and somewhat angered Darcy said. "Who do you think you are, opening and reading the books from the Pemberley library? Servants do not usually linger in here. What do you have in your hands?"

He was an attractive man, but she had seen men more handsome. He was well dressed with a dark coat and matching trousers. His shirt and matching cravat were cream colored. A small pearl held his cravat in place. He wore tall, shiny black boots and had an impressive and arrogant air about him.

"Excuse me, sir; I did not mean to trespass," exclaimed Elizabeth. "I was walking down the hall from the parlor to the kitchen and saw all these wonderful books. I could not help myself from entering this beautiful room. I could not resist opening and reading just one from this wonderful collection. You have all the works from Shakespeare, Dante, and the stories of Faust."

"You, a servant girl, would know of these literary artists?" asked Darcy with slight surprise.

"Yes, I attended schools in London as a child and learned to appreciate the writing of many authors. My father is an attorney who continues to read daily; in fact, he is most unhappy without a book in his hands. Before I came here, I also read daily. I believe books hold the power of knowledge for all of mankind."

"You said you have read these books and know these authors?" said Darcy as he swept his arm across the room.

"Oh yes, I have read many of these and all of Mr. Shakespeare's plays and sonnets. I found them quite thought provoking and at times sensual." Immediately she knew she had spoken inappropriately and turned her head away from his downcast smile. "Your library has so much more than my father's library. It is all so wonderful," said Elizabeth as she continued to look around.

"Well, my family have been collectors of books. Many of these date back generations," answered Darcy.

"I'm sure they do. I have taken up too much of your time, so please, sir, if you will excuse me, I need to return to my duties in the kitchen before Mrs. Enders wonders when I am. I do not want her to think I am neglecting my duties," said Elizabeth.

"Of course, ma'am," he replied. He stepped away from the door to let her pass but followed her with his eyes down the corridor until he could no longer see her. Meeting her made him think of a line from Shakespeare's *Henry V*, act 5, scene 2: "You have witchcraft in your lips." He had never seen such a fine-looking woman in all his life. She looked vaguely familiar; he thought he had seen her before but could not recall the time or place. It would be quite unusual for a person of his station to meet someone of her social class. Perhaps he would remember in time.

25

The day after their first encounter in the library, Darcy and Elizabeth met again when he saw her pumping water from the outside well. She was dressed in a grease-stained white apron and dirty black shoes. Her hair was pulled back away from her face with a black scarf. It covered most of her long red hair, but he could see her thick tresses hanging below the scarf. When he saw her, he stopped his course and watched her from across the open lawn. He noticed her movements were graceful despite the heavy water buckets she was carrying. He continued to watch her until she was about to enter the back kitchen door she was so used to using. When she stopped to shift her weight, she looked up to see him staring at her. She was embarrassed and wanted to look away but could not take her eyes off him. He certainly was an attractive man, but she could not think of him as anyone but her employer. After a few prolonged minutes, they both looked away and resumed their chores. He was on his way to the stables for his morning ride, and she was to start the noontime meal for the farm workers. Once she entered the kitchen, she dropped the full buckets of water down next to the large cast iron stove. Her shoulders were sore and tired, but she knew her continued employment was contingent upon her working hard. She was ready to start cutting up vegetables when Mrs. Enders called over to her.

"Elizabeth, what took you so long? Hurry up, girl, and get busy with those vegetables," she called out.

"Yes, Mrs. Enders," replied Elizabeth. "Right away." She did not think anymore of Mr. Darcy that day.

After Elizabeth was out of sight, Darcy proceeded to the stables. His daily ride on his favorite horse was one of the few pleasures he looked forward to. Managing the large, busy manor and farmlands took most of his time, leaving little opportunity for pleasure. He did not mind the busy schedule he had, as long as he could exercise his horse. Just before reaching the stable, he turned his head back to the kitchen door, but she was gone. He was not sure why he did this, but since he did not see Elizabeth, he turned back to the stable, ready for his ride.

Later that evening, as Darcy sat with his sister Georgiana, his thoughts began to wander to Elizabeth and whether she had prepared his evening meal. He was quiet, consumed with his image of her. "Are you well, brother?" asked Georgiana. "You are quiet tonight, not at all like yourself."

"Yes, my apologies, Georgiana. I am well—just thinking about the day."

Georgiana answered him, "All is well with the manor is it not? Is there anything I should be concerned about?"

"No, of course not, sister; all is well. You need not worry about anything," he replied.

She smiled, but her concern for him continued. "I went riding today," she finally said to him. "Mr. Hickey accompanied me on one of the horses. He said this horse was one of the gentler horses we own. We went to the meadow, at the river's edge. You know the place—we went riding there as children. It was really quite nice. The fall colors and the trees were rich and bright, and the air was not too cold. I really had a wonderful time." Darcy continued his silence, not hearing her words. "Brother, are you sure you are all right? Have you heard what I said?" asked Georgiana.

"I'm sorry, sweetheart, what did you say? My apologies for my distant thoughts tonight. I am just caught up in my own thoughts this evening. Please go on with your conversation."

"I said I went riding with Mr. Hickey as my chaperone today down by the river. It was very nice," repeated Georgiana.

"Sister, I would rather you allow me to chaperone you when you ride. You are not that skilled as a rider yet. I do not approve; nor do I think it is appropriate for you to be out alone with only one of the stable hands," said Darcy firmly.

"Brother, it was totally innocent, and Mr. Hickey is a perfect gentleman."

"Georgiana, you heard me; you will only go out with me as your chaperone from now on," said Darcy with a stern paternal expression. "We will go out tomorrow after breakfast if you would like."

"Very well, brother; as you wish," said Georgiana obediently.

26

Following the first few days after their initial meeting in the library, Elizabeth and Darcy saw each other occasionally but only from a distance. Weeks passed, and Darcy and Elizabeth would nod to each other informally from a distance but did not speak. The only exchanges between them were indifferent glances in each other's direction, their thoughts confined to their own duties. Gradually Mr. Darcy started to find himself thinking about Elizabeth at least daily and at different times of the day. These thoughts would occur while writing at his desk, riding his horse, inspecting the farmlands, or riding in his carriage while in London on business. He would think about her toiling at her chores, hoping they were not too difficult, and that her clothes looked worn and stained. It bothered him that such a beautiful, graceful, and intelligent woman had to labor as she did. Was it wrong to think of a servant woman the way he did? He knew of other gentlemen who had used their servant women for their own personal pleasures, but he had never considered doing these things. He talked frequently to Mr. Hickey regarding matters of the manor, but otherwise he kept to himself regarding his staff. So why did this woman invade his thoughts? What was so different about her? He just could not understand what was happening to him. He had all these thoughts about a woman whose name he did not even know. She looked vaguely familiar; maybe he knew her from some other time or occasion. He continued to ponder where he had seen this woman before, confused as to why he couldn't remember.

Darcy remained busy as usual until a morning in early December, when he was again walking to the stables for his daily ride. He heard a call of alarm and pain from the direction of the well and saw that Elizabeth had fallen near the outside water pump. The recently filled water buckets had spilled onto the gravel path as she lay on the ground. She was bleeding from a cut on her forehead, the blood streaking her face and dripping onto her collar and apron. Her legs were bent behind her, and her skirts were wrapped around her waist, exposing her stocking legs to the cold. One of her stockings was torn, and he could see an abrasion on her knee. She started to get up but slipped again on the ice that was quickly forming from the spilled water. Darcy sprinted to her side, nearly falling himself.

"Miss, are you all right? No, of course you are not. Forgive me. You are hurt and bleeding. Please, let me help you," said Darcy.

"Thank you, sir; I'm not hurt," said Elizabeth slowly. As she started to get up, she sat back down hard, now holding her head where the cut was beginning to swell. Dirt and small bits of gravel adhered to the blood on her face and knee.

"Please, let me help you," said Darcy again.

"I need to get this water into the kitchen or Mrs. Enders will be angry at me again," said Elizabeth. She looked at his face, seeing his handsome face and dark, caring eyes looking back at her with obvious concern.

"Do not worry about Mrs. Enders; I will talk to her. Now please come with me into the house so you may be attended to," said Darcy calmly.

She stood slowly, allowing Mr. Darcy to help her. His strong arms felt comfortable around her. She had forgotten how wonderful it felt to have a man care for her. He continued to hold on to her and guide her into the manor house, deliberately avoiding the kitchen and Mrs. Enders's eventual scorn.

"Please, sit down here," said Darcy once they had entered a small front foyer room of the manor house. He steered her to a small dark green settee. Matching end tables and a coffee table also matched the wood from the settee. A bright copper coffee-and-tea set sat on the center of the coffee table. The wallpaper was an older floral pattern but attractive, and pictures on the walls accented the color of the furniture. The room definitely had a feminine feel.

"You are so kind to attend to me," said Elizabeth as she looked up at him. His dark eyes showed warmth and compassion—things she had not experienced before from a man. She stared at him for what seemed like a very long time. She briefly remembered Lieutenant Wickham's same kind words and attendance when they first started courting.

"Are you sure you are all right?" asked Darcy. "You looked as if you were lost for a moment." It was at that time that Elizabeth recognized Mr. Darcy as the gentleman who gave her directions when she was lost in London and trying to find her way to her aunt and uncle's house many months ago. She hoped he did not recognize her.

"Excuse me, sir," replied Elizabeth, "I am all right. I just forgot where I was for a moment." Darcy looked back at her with continued concern.

"What is your name? I have seen you in my library, out at the kitchen water pump, and from a distance from other areas of the manor, but yet I do not know your name."

"My name is Elizabeth Bennet, sir," said Elizabeth slowly.

"Please let me get the housekeeper; she will attend to your injuries," said Darcy.

"No, sir, please do not do that. I can get care for myself," she answered.

"I absolutely insist," said Darcy sternly. He walked quickly to the pull cord, close to the settee, to summon his housekeeper, Mrs. Bergman. Elizabeth watched him walk with determination in his step. She felt frightened, and a slight chill fell over her. Looking back, Darcy noticed her distress and reached for a light blanket lying across on the settee, to cover her shoulders. He sat beside her with his arm about her exposed shoulder until the housekeeper entered the room. He did not release his hold on Elizabeth or stand when the housekeeper arrived.

"Mrs. Bergman, Miss Bennet fell outside near the water pump. She has been injured. Please attend to her injuries. I will return momentarily," said Darcy.

"Yes, sir, of course," answered Mrs. Bergman. "I'll take care of her immediately."

Darcy slowly released his hold upon Elizabeth and rose, his eyes never leaving her. He bent close to her. She could detect a faint smell of leather and horseflesh on his clothes. "I will let the kitchen staff know what happened and where you are," Darcy whispered into Elizabeth's ear. Darcy stood again, looked directly at Mrs. Bergman, and said, "Please stay with her until I return. I shall not be long."

Mrs. Bergman had been the housekeeper at Pemberley for almost forty years. She was a young immigrant bride from Sweden, who had been traveling through England on her way to America when her husband became ill with smallpox. He died within days of falling ill with the disease. Mrs. Bergman, young and alone in a strange country, and barely able to speak English, was taken in by the Darcy family to care for the children of their servants. She decided to stay on with the family rather than continue on to America alone. She became the housekeeper shortly after the current Mr. Darcy was born, and the Darcy family had been grateful for her service ever since.

Mr. Darcy walked to the hallway entrance and briefly turned to look again at Elizabeth. He kept his hand on the doorframe as he watched his housekeeper attending to the cut on Elizabeth's forehead. He then left the room and walked toward the kitchen. Mr. Darcy entered the kitchen and found it very active, as it was midday. He saw approximately a dozen workers busy with their chores for the majority of Pemberley's main meal. The air was hot and close, and it held a mix of smells, all of them quite pleasant. Several ovens were in use for the making of breads and roasting of meats. Cast iron pots were full with fresh stews and soups nearly ready to be fed to the people of Pemberley. Darcy felt humbled in the company of these efficient workers, yet he was proud knowing how much was being accomplished for his people. He could hear Mrs. Enders giving orders to one of the stable boys, who was carrying the buckets of water that Elizabeth had dropped when she fell.

"Where is that woman who was supposed to bring in the water over an hour ago?" barked Mrs. Enders, waving a large cooking ladle. "When she shows up, let me know. Now take that water over to that far oven." She pointed to a large black stove at the far end of the kitchen, where a cook was waiting.

"Yes ma'am, I will," replied the boy. He hurried over to where he was told, anxious to leave Mrs. Enders's angry mood.

Mr. Darcy worked his way over to where Mrs. Enders was standing, careful to avoid bumping into anyone or disrupt their work.

"Mrs. Enders," Darcy called out above the loud noise level. "Please, if I may, a word with you." Many of the staff had now recognized the master, stopped what they were doing and curtseyed or bowed as he walked passed. The noise level dropped immediately, as most of the kitchen staff had never seen the master in the kitchen before. Miss Georgiana had come to the kitchen many times to discuss menus with the cooks, but never the master himself. By the time Mr. Darcy reached Mrs. Enders, the room was nearly quiet.

"Mr. Darcy, what a pleasure for you to come to my kitchen. What can I do for you, sir?" Mrs. Enders curtseyed. "How pleased we are to see you here. Is everything all right? Is there a problem?"

"No, no problem, Mrs. Enders. I wanted to let you know that Miss Elizabeth Bennet fell this morning on the ice outside while pumping water at the well. She was hurt, and Mrs. Bergman is attending to her in the front sitting room."

"Well, I hope she is all right," said Mrs. Enders with surprise. She found it quite curious that the master himself would let her know about a member of her staff. Of course other kitchen staff had injured themselves, but Mr. Darcy himself had never come to discuss such things to her. "Yes, I'm sure she will be fine, Mrs. Enders. May I speak with you in private?"

"Yes, sir, as you wish," was her reply.

"Please let us talk out in the hallway, where we will not disturb the others," said Darcy. He stepped back and allowed her to pass in front of him, as a gentleman would, and out into the cooler hallway.

After they were out of earshot, Mr. Darcy said, "Mrs. Enders, when I was walking to the stables this morning, I found Miss Bennet had fallen on the gravel pathway after she apparently slipped on the ice. She was carrying two heavy buckets of water into the kitchen. May I ask why water is being carried into the manor house when we recently had a pump installed directly in the kitchen? It was my impression that carrying water would be unnecessary after the installation of the inside water pump."

"Yes, that is true, sir," stammered Mrs. Enders, "but I have found that carrying water buckets helps the new staff become stronger and helps with morale and discipline. I run a very efficient kitchen, and I need everyone to follow orders, sir."

"I am well aware of your efficiency and excellent cooking skills, and I compliment you on that. I am requesting you not have the girls and women haul water from the outside well. We have plenty of stable hands, so I would prefer they do this for you," said Darcy.

"Yes, sir, if that is what you wish, and thank you, sir," said Mrs. Enders with a curtsey.

Darcy bowed slightly and turned to proceed down the hallway and back toward the front room, where Elizabeth was waiting. Mrs. Enders watched him leave, thinking their conversation had been very curious. After all, he had never interfered with her kitchen management in the past. She wondered if Elizabeth had something to do with the master's new interest in the food preparation.

When he returned to the front room, he was pleased that Elizabeth looked better. The color of her face had returned to normal, and a bandage had been applied to the cut on her forehead. Her disheveled clothing had been straightened, and she was sipping what appeared to be a cup of hot tea. While looking at her, he saw a beauty he had not seen before and noted a graceful and intelligent pose despite her recent trauma. Mrs. Bergman had remained in attendance as he had instructed her. She had moved a chair directly in front of Elizabeth, and they were talking quietly. As soon as Mrs. Bergman noticed that Mr. Darcy had entered the room, she stood to greet him. Elizabeth also started to stand, but Darcy immediately requested she stay seated.

"Please, Miss Bennet, stay where you are. There is no need for you to stress yourself further," said Darcy. He then turned his attention to his housekeeper. "Mrs. Bergman, thank you for taking such good care of our patient. We both appreciate your help."

"You are welcome, sir; is there anything else I may assist you with?"

"No, Mrs. Bergman. Thank you again; you may return to your duties." Mrs. Bergman curtseyed slightly to Mr. Darcy, briefly looked at Elizabeth, and left the room, quietly shutting the door behind her.

Both Elizabeth and Darcy were quiet for a few moments until Elizabeth said, "Thank you again, sir, for your kindness. I had heard from my uncle that you were a generous man."

"You are very welcome," said Darcy shyly. He sat down next to her on the settee and turned toward her. Their eyes met. They again were quiet, and then both started to speak at once. Both stopped abruptly and looked at each other, starting to laugh.

"Please, ladies first. What were you going to say?" asked Darcy.

"What did Mrs. Enders say? Is she angry at me? Sometimes she gets so angry with me. I just cannot seem to do anything right for her. I try the best I can, but sometimes it just isn't good enough," said Elizabeth solemnly. "My cooking skills have improved, but Mrs. Enders tells me my culinary skills are lacking." Darcy laughed at her proclamation but knew she was probably leaving herself short.

"Miss Bennet, please tell me, how did you come to Pemberley?" asked Darcy. "I remember I caught you in my library several weeks ago. I have seen you several times since, but only from a distance."

"I am most humbled, sir," said Elizabeth. "I was sent here by my father at the request of my uncle, Mr. Gardnier of London. He had heard that Pemberley needed additional kitchen help with the upcoming holidays, so he sent an inquiry to your master cook, Mrs. Enders. She reluctantly agreed to take me into your employ over the winter season. Your increased number of holiday parties and balls required more kitchen staff. So here I am." She looked directly at him while explaining her abbreviated story of how she came to be at Pemberley. For the first time, she noticed his heart-stopping good looks and his immaculate riding clothes that took her breath away. He certainly cut a fine masculine figure of a man. He listened intently and without any look of mistrust or dislike.

"Excuse me, Miss Bennet, but I consider myself a fairly good judge of people, and you are not a kitchen maid or a servant. Your hands have seen hard work, but the rest of you suggests education and intelligence. You also have a wedding ring on your left hand, so please tell me again how you came to Pemberley." She looked away from him and searched for words that would not bring tears of shame or embarrassment. "Please tell me. I suspect you are holding a secret, but I can assure you it will be safe with me," he said.

"Sir," she finally said, "my story is difficult but probably not unbelievable or untold by other women. I was married nine months ago to a man who deceived me into the marriage vows. He married me in hopes of acquiring my family home and its acreage. He had considerable debt from gambling and once he acquired my family home, he intended to sell my family homestead to satisfy his creditors. He did not realize that upon my father's death, our family home would be entailed to my distant male cousin. Once he found out the terms of the will, he left. I have not received any word from him, and I do not know where he is.

My estranged husband's debts are considerable, and to my understanding they continue to grow. I am here to earn money and repay my father for his generosity in paying off some of his creditors. The entire situation was scandalous for my parents and for my remaining unmarried sisters. So it was determined by both my father and uncle that I should leave Longbourne and come here."

"I see," said Mr. Darcy. "Longbourne—is that your home?"

"Yes, it is. It is my family's farm. It is a modest farm—only own one hundred acres or so. We have some cash crops and a few livestock. It is enough to make our living, but no more. My parents and sisters still live and work there. I hope they are well. I do miss them very much. I have received only two letters from my father since I arrived here almost three months ago. The last letter I received from my father came several weeks ago. The gossip that was being spread within the town regarding my trouble was difficult for my family, so I hope all is well there."

"I can understand how difficult gossip can be. My family has been a victim of gossip also, so I know and can understand how you feel," he replied. "How awful all this must be for you."

"It's really not that bad. Everyone here has been very nice—even Mrs. Enders, except when she is mad at me," chuckled Elizabeth.

Darcy grinned at her remark concerning her supervisor. "You must be very close to your father and miss him very much."

"Yes, I do, but last I heard from him, he was well, and so were my mother and sisters."

"How many sisters do you have?" asked Darcy.

"I have four: one older than myself and three younger," replied Elizabeth happily. Darcy smiled and looked away from her, gazing about the room.

His eyes settled again on her and he said, "I have a younger sister, whom I would miss very much if she did not live here with me, so I understand how you could miss your family."

"I have never seen your sister, but I have heard her playing the pianoforte. She is very good," said Elizabeth.

"Yes, she is; I am very proud of her," answered Darcy.

They were both quiet for some time. Then Elizabeth said, "This room is very nice. It is so open and bright. The sun shining in makes a beautiful pattern of colors on the wall." The burgundy-colored drapes had been pulled back to expose large windows with rose-tinted panes near the ceiling. A crystal vase cut the incoming light, causing the multicolored shapes she saw. The room itself was not large, but it was comfortable and appropriate for intimate conversation. The small divan they were sitting on and one matching mahogany chair with the tables were the only furniture needed in the room. The mauve tapestry upholstery complemented the burgundy swag at the windows. Whoever had coordinated the furniture and colors had impeccable taste. Was she having an intimate conversation with the master of Pemberley in this room? She could not believe she was exposing herself to him and telling this incredibly handsome man her story of false love and deceit. She felt safe and contented in this room and was glad Mr. Darcy had brought her here.

"How are you now, Miss Bennet?" asked Darcy.

"I am well, sir. Again, how can I thank you for your kindness?" said Elizabeth. She looked directly into his eyes and again realized what an incredibly handsome man he was. His eyes were dark and clear, his hair black with a slight curl. For the first time, she noticed he was not dressed in a formal coat, silk shirt, or cravat, which she had always seen him dressed in before. He had on light-colored riding breeches and boots. Looking at her own dirty apron and shoes, she felt embarrassed.

"Miss Bennet, if you feel well enough, would you like a tour of the mansion? I would like to show you my home."

"I-I guess that would be nice," stammered Elizabeth, "but my clothes are not proper enough to be walking about this beautiful home."

"Nonsense," he replied. "Please walk with me." As they stood, he looked at her to be sure she was steady. Once he felt she was secure, he took her hand and entwined it with his lower arm. He then placed his own hand on top of hers. Together they walked into the hallway and proceeded with the house tour.

Room by room, they walked through the entire first floor. He spoke of his family's heritage dating back generations. He described his lineage and pedigree. He talked for what to Elizabeth seemed like forever about his parents and sister. His mother had a title, though he chose not to use one himself. He was entitled to use the name "Lord Darcy" but felt better without it. She learned he had an extended family of aunts, uncles, and cousins. He spoke fondly of his cousin Richard, who was in the military like George Wickham. The mere mention of the military and the fact that his cousin might know of her estranged husband frightened her. She hoped they did not know each other. If anyone ever knew of her life here, despite the hard work she did, her life here would end. George Wickham needed to be her secret. Her thoughts were wandering, but when she listened to his calming words, she listened to him proudly repeat the story of his family and home.

"The main mansion was built in 1490, during the Renaissance Era. It was originally built as a military defense post, but when no longer needed, it was eventually acquired and taken over by my mother's great-grandfather and transformed into the home it is today. At one time, the mansion was host to lavish parties and soirées for many of the country's royalty. Those extravagant parties and the unworked land have gradually been replaced by working farmers and tenants supplying food, livestock, and fowl to many families in England. The estate has approximately fifty thousand acres and one hundred farmhouses for those who work the land and harvest the fruit and vegetables.

"Was the mansion always this large?" she asked.

"Several additions have been made over the years. The last addition was built in 1750, and the mansion is what you see now."

"It is overwhelming to me and so beautiful."

"My grandparents and mother worked very hard to make the mansion as you see it. Georgiana and I have done very little in regard to redecorating since our parents' deaths. Sometime soon, though, someone will need to take a serious look at this massive home and appraise both its appearance and function."

"It is not uncommon for any home or building to need an update for both its construction and function; I am sure Pemberley is not unusual in that regard," she simply stated.

"No, I suppose not," he answered.

As they walked about the mansion, discussing the architecture, paintings, furniture, etc., he grew more comfortable with her. He did detect, though, a sense of withholding in her speech and manner. He felt perhaps it was due to her recent fall.

"That must be a huge responsibility for you as master of this vast estate" she heard herself say.

"My father managed the estate. He taught me its workings, and now I manage it. That is the way it is."

The afternoon passed, and neither realized the length of time spent. When they finished their walk through the lower floor of the mansion, it was near nightfall and time for the evening meal.

"Miss Bennet, please forgive my manners," said Darcy. He suddenly realized he had been talking all afternoon and had ignored her probable need for food, drink, and toilet. "I have been very selfish with my behavior this afternoon. You must be hungry and thirsty. Please come with me to the dining room tonight and have your evening meal with me."

"Oh, Mr. Darcy, I cannot. My dress is inappropriate for dining in your company. Look; I still have on my kitchen apron, and my hair is not brushed properly. My shoes are both dirty and worn. I beg you, sir; I cannot dine with you. I am not suitable enough."

"Very well, then; come with me. My housekeeper, Mrs. Bergman, will take you where you can freshen yourself and change into more appropriate clothing if that will help you feel more comfortable. Please accept my invitation and be my guest for dinner."

Elizabeth was surprised and taken aback by his forward manner. She hesitated with her answer but finally agreed to his invitation. She hoped she wasn't making a mistake.

27

Elizabeth followed Mrs. Bergman to an upstairs dressing room. There she was surprised to see a bath ready for her. The water was hot and felt very pleasant. She had not had a real tub bath since she arrived at Pemberley. She had missed what she had always taken for granted. She could have sat in the tub for hours but knew she could not. A dress and underclothes were laid out for her. She knew she had lost weight since coming to Pemberley, and thus she did not feel comfortable asking anyone to help her dress. After all, she was still one of the kitchen staff members. The dress prepared for her was made of a dark burgundy silk and had a modest collar and lace sleeves. It was slightly large for her, but she was grateful it was clean and not torn. She wondered who the dress belonged to and hoped she would not be upset that she was wearing it. She did not think it unusual that this unmarried man had spare women's clothing available.

After dressing, she brushed her hair and pinned it in place. After she applied a dab of cologne, also available to her, at her neck, she followed Mrs. Bergman back to the dining room.

Mr. Darcy was waiting for her in the dining room. He also had bathed and dressed for dinner. He was handsome in a dark green frock, a starched white silk shirt, a matching cravat, and dark trousers. The boots he had worn during the day had been replaced with white stockings and black slippers. He had a glass of wine in his hand and was facing the lit fireplace. When she entered, he turned and smiled at her. "Good evening," he said, bowing slightly. "How lovely you look."

"Thank you, sir, and good evening to you also," she answered. She hoped he did not notice she was not properly laced and the dress was ill fitting. "I hope the owner of this dress does not mind me wearing it," she said.

"I am sure she will not. It belonged to my mother."

They looked at each other for a brief moment before Mr. Darcy spoke. "May I offer you a glass of wine? I have a variety of blends for you to choose from." Again she felt uncomfortable with her present surroundings and had never drunk much alcohol before, but she agreed to a small glass of sweet white wine. He poured the wine into a small stemmed crystal glass, their hands touching briefly. A feeling of warmth spread through her. She thanked him for the glass and then stepped back from him. His eyes lingered upon hers and then looked away while he set the wine decanter back on the sideboard. He too felt warm and slightly uncomfortable being alone in a woman's presence for the first time in his life. Miss Bennet stirred something in him that no woman ever had. What was happening to him?

The evening meal of roasted venison, sweet potatoes, and vegetables was delicious. She did not realize how hungry she was until she sat down to the meal. The wine seemed to increase her appetite, and she had not eaten since early morning. The bread that she had been used to making since coming to Pemberley was warm and freshly made. The melting butter added to the tasteful aromas in the room. Once again she felt homesick for her family and Longbourne.

The evening progressed without incident. Elizabeth and Darcy carried on with simple conversation, carefully avoiding any personal or private topics, including Elizabeth's marriage. The meal was served by members of the kitchen staff. The staff went about their usual duties of serving the master of the home without taking any usual notice that Elizabeth was dining with the master of Pemberley. Throughout the weeks that followed, no mention was made by the staff to Elizabeth regarding that first evening meal. She was sure that gossip was exchanged out of her earshot. Little did Elizabeth know that there would be many further meals with Mr. Darcy.

After the meal ended and the plates and crystal had been cleared from the table, both Darcy and Elizabeth felt awkward, not knowing what to say to each other.

It was Elizabeth who first spoke. "Mr. Darcy, this has been a wonderful day and evening. Never could I have imagined what this day would entail when I awoke this morning. But like any other day, it must end. Sir, the meal was delicious and the company excellent, but I must say good night. My day starts early, so I need to retire for the night." She lowered her head during the last sentence, and her words were close to a whisper.

"Yes, of course," said Darcy. "I too will say good night." He stood from the chair he had sat in during the meal, bowed slightly to Elizabeth, and abruptly left the room. She remained in her chair for several minutes and then got up and left the dining room, walking briskly to her own room, which was located in the servants' wing of the manor.

Mr. Darcy had retreated to his sitting room adjacent to his bedchamber. A fire was already set and ablaze, making the room warm and comfortable. Winter had arrived, and a chill had started to settle through the mansion. The change of seasons never bothered him, but for some reason, this season was different. He was not sure why. He poured himself a full snifter of brandy, slowly swirling the amber contents and inhaling its aroma. He sat in his favorite large chair next to the fire and started at the flames. He had removed his coat and cravat, and loosened his shirt collar. He felt distressed, though he was still not sure why. He remained restless throughout the night, unable to sleep and pacing about his sitting room until almost dawn. Thoughts of Elizabeth Bennet kept returning, leaving him tired, chilled, and unable to rest. She had stirred something deep within him that he was unable to recognize or appreciate. He knew he had to see her again. He had to understand what was happening to him. She had said she was married but her husband had deserted her, leaving her saddled with much of his debt and feeling ashamed. Who would do this to someone as lovely and gracious as she? Was there something he did not know about her? What was her secret?

The evening had ended quite abruptly with her returning to her room in the servants' quarters. He had to remind himself that she was one of the many kitchen staff hired to help with the holidays that were quickly approaching. How would he get through these upcoming days feeling the way he did? She had said she did not know where her husband was or whether he was still alive. She did not say what her husband's occupation was. *Is it possible that children are involved and that is her secret?* He had not thought of that during the day. He knew he was being foolish to fall in love with a married woman—possibly one with a child. His involvement with such a woman would cause scandal for him and his own family. He had to think of Georgiana and her future. This type of gossip would ruin her chance of a marriage and proper standing in their social circle. The servants would start talking, if they had not already, adding fuel to the spreading rumors. Her wearing a wedding ring would be a constant reminder to him of her marital vows.

The night passed slowly for Darcy, without sleep. By dawn, he knew he had to speak with Elizabeth regarding his feelings toward her. If her feelings were mutual, and he suspected they were, then they would have their own secret to keep.

Meanwhile, Elizabeth had returned to her own room. It seemed so small and cramped compared to the large rooms she had seen during the day. She sat on the bed and stared at the single lit candle that supplied the room's only light. Its flame danced against the wall, illuminating a pattern that seemed to call out to her, but she could not understand its meaning. It was not the beautiful pattern of light she had seen in the front parlor early this afternoon, but almost an angry light. She was tired but was unsure if this was from the unusual events of the day or the effects of the wine she had consumed. Her head hurt, but again she was not sure why. She continued to have some swelling and bruising around the laceration on her forehead. She touched the bandage, but there was no seepage from the wound. Her thoughts were confused, and she had trouble sorting out the day. *How did all of this happen, and what will tomorrow bring? What a wonderful man Mr. Darcy is, and how different he is from George Wickham.* The more she knew Mr. Darcy, the more anger she felt toward her husband. She eventually fell asleep, but she too had restless thoughts.

She awoke before dawn, as she usually did. She washed quickly using the cold water in the basin on the dressing table. She had left the clothes she had been wearing when she fell in the upstairs dressing room that Mrs. Bergman had taken her to in order to change her clothing the evening before. Thankfully she had a spare gray dress, but she did not have an apron to put on over it. She knew Mrs. Enders would be upset that she would not have the proper attire for work, but there was nothing she could do about it. She would just have to face the wrath from the master cook.

She left her room and walked down the narrow hallway of the servants' quarters and approached the kitchen door. To her surprise, Mrs. Bergman was waiting for her.

"Good morning, Mrs. Bergman," said Elizabeth with a shock in both her voice and her expression. "I do not think I have ever seen you here this early in the morning. I am glad, though, to see you. I left my soiled clothing in the upstairs dressing room yesterday, and I need to retrieve it. I am sorry if this has been inconvenient for you, but I will come and get it as soon as possible."

"Elizabeth," whispered Mrs. Bergman, "I am here at the request of Mr. Darcy. He asked me to come and inquire if you would meet him this morning for breakfast. He left word for me last night to attend to your head wound and have you meet with him this morning."

"Oh, Mrs. Bergman, I must report to work this morning," said Elizabeth. "I did not complete my chores yesterday, so I am sure Mrs. Enders will be quite upset with me." Both women stared at each other for a short time before Elizabeth spoke. "Mrs. Bergman, please tell me," asked Elizabeth shyly. "I feel very uncomfortable about this. I am just a servant here and have no place dining with the master. Gossip will spread here, and I will be dismissed. I need this job to repay my father's debt toward me. I feel I can trust you. Please tell me what to do."

Mrs. Bergman smiled at Elizabeth and said, "My dear, I have to tell you I have never seen the master in such a state. I have known him since he was a boy, but his behavior and manner are something I have seen before. I can see a change in you also. Please join him this morning; it will be fine. And yes, you can trust me."

"What shall I say to Mrs. Enders?" asked Elizabeth.

"Rest assured, child, I will take care of everything," answered Mrs. Bergman.

Elizabeth felt she could trust this kind and gentle woman, so she accepted Mr. Darcy's invitation.

Cautiously, Elizabeth returned to the manor house and went to the main dining room, where she had eaten dinner the night before. Again she felt uncomfortable with her attire. Not wearing the clothes she felt would be proper for this occasion was upsetting for her. Her upbringing had required her to dress for a meal, but here she was wearing a worn servant's dress to a breakfast with a man known for his affluence and proper manners. She entered the room, but no one was there. The room felt cold with no fire lit. The dining table was bare, without dishes, glassware, or food. She felt embarrassed and assumed she must have misunderstood the housekeeper. She hoped she would be able to return to the kitchen before anyone knew she was missing. She turned to leave, only to walk directly into Mr. Darcy.

Instinctively she stepped back, saying, "Oh, excuse me; I did not realize you were present." Too embarrassed to say anything further, she kept silent, lowering her eyes to the floor. She noticed he was wearing riding clothes similar to the ones he had been wearing yesterday. This made her feel more comfortable with her own attire.

"There you are; I was looking for you," he said, smiling while bending his head to look at her face. She looked up to him, now smiling herself. "Good morning; I hope you slept well."

"Yes, yes I did," she lied. "And you? Did you sleep well?"

"Yes, very well," he replied. "Are you well this morning? How is your head?" He pointed toward the previous day's injury. "I see a fresh bandage has been applied. I hope Mrs. Bergman is taking care of that for you."

"Yes, she is. She has been very kind to me," she stammered. She looked directly into his dark, handsome face and said slowly, "Mr. Darcy, I do not understand what is happening here. Yesterday, after I fell, you came to my aid, we spent the afternoon touring your beautiful home, and then we had dinner together last night." She stopped to catch her breath and think through her words. "Then Mrs. Bergman met me at the kitchen door this morning and told me you wish to have breakfast with me. I have to tell you, sir, I am confused about all of this."

Darcy continued to look straight into her eyes, thinking she was the most beautiful woman he had ever seen. His heart was pounding, and he felt the most anxious he had ever been in his life. Finally he said, "Miss Bennet, I too am confused, but please let us walk to the breakfast room and talk. If we do not eat, Mrs. Bergman and Mrs. Enders will be quite upset with both of us." His smile sent a warm feeling throughout her. He took her elbow, and together they walked down the hallway and turned a corner to another wing of the house she had not yet seen.

The room they found themselves in was much smaller than the large dining room used the evening before. It was painted a light yellow with large windows. The drapes were turned back, allowing the morning sun to spill into the room. The furniture consisted of a round table with six high-backed chairs. The pattern on the chair seats was yellow with large embroidered flowers. The china matched the chair seats, giving the room a feminine look, much unlike many of the other rooms she had seen the previous day. Paintings on the walls complemented the color scheme. The sideboard held dishes of eggs, meats, fruits, and fresh pastries ready to be served. Two servants were present, standing by the sideboard, ready to serve their master and his guest.

"What a beautiful room this is," Elizabeth said while looking about. "It is so unlike many of the other rooms. Why is this so different?"

"This room was used by my mother when she entertained guests for breakfast and luncheons. She decorated it. It was her favorite room in the entire mansion. Now it is used only by my sister Georgiana. No one has wanted to change anything since my mother died."

"I see no reason to change anything; it is perfect," she replied.

"Thank you," he whispered.

She looked at him curiously, again wondering why she was here with him. "May I ask, sir—if your sister is the only person who uses this room, where do you have breakfast?"

He smiled gently and answered, "When Georgiana is not here, I usually have breakfast either at my desk or upstairs in my sitting room."

"That sounds rather lonely to me."

"Yes, it sometimes is. Now let us eat before the 'troops' come in and take our food away."

Mr. Darcy guided Elizabeth to the table and pulled a chair out for her. After she sat, he helped her push the chair up to the table. He reached out to grasp her hand in his but stopped short when one of the servants moved toward the table to pour coffee into the fine china cups for them. Elizabeth and Darcy avoided each other's eyes until the servants backed away from the table, waiting for orders from their master. Mr. Darcy took his eyes away from Elizabeth and dismissed the servants from the room. As they left, he requested they shut the door, giving them the privacy he wanted.

He put his hand over the top of hers immediately after the servants left. He looked at Elizabeth and said, "I need to confess to you that I was unable to sleep last night. I could not stop thinking of you. I paced the floor most of night. If I was not pacing, I could not stop thinking of you," he repeated. "Elizabeth, something is happening to me. I do not know what, but it is something I have never experienced before. I think you are the most beautiful woman I have ever seen. You are intelligent, graceful, and kind. Miss Bennet, I need to confess to you that I think I am falling in love with you."

Both were silent but continued to stare at each other. A small tear started to trickle down Elizabeth's cheek. She did not know what to say.

Mr. Darcy spoke again, softly. "Miss Bennet, I know this must be a surprise for you, but I cannot hold back my feelings for you. In the short time that I have known you, my heart has been taken hostage by you, and I see no means of escape. I can sense you feel the same."

Elizabeth turned her head away from him and quietly said, "Mr. Darcy, I too need to confess to you my own restlessness last night. I could not stop thinking of you either. You have stirred something in me that I also have never felt before. I have never experienced the kindness or warmth that you have given me. I also do not understand what is happening to me or how this could happen." She stopped for a moment. "At first I thought my feelings were because I was overwhelmed with my presence in this beautiful home, and by your kindness, but I think not." She took a sip of her coffee, forgetting that she had not sweetened it with sugar. She was not used to the bitter taste and immediately put the cup down and showed an expression of dislike.

"Miss Bennet," Darcy said, "Is something wrong with the coffee? Did you burn yourself?"

She smiled. "No. I just forgot the sugar; that is all."

He smiled back, reached out with his free hand, and moved the china sugar bowl to her. With her free hand, she spooned a teaspoon of sugar into her coffee and stirred, being careful not to touch the sides of the cup with the teaspoon. She knew making too much noise while stirring with her spoon was very impolite. She took another sip of coffee and was pleased with its sweet taste.

She looked at Mr. Darcy and smiled while returning the cup to its saucer. She collected her thoughts and said, "Mr. Darcy, I am at a loss for words. I too have developed strong feelings for you that I am struggling with. I do not know why or how it could have happened." She paused before continuing. "I believe I am still married. As I told you yesterday, I was married to a man who deceived me but then deserted me once he discovered I had no wealth for him to inherit. I am here to earn money to repay my father, who agreed to help me with the mounting debts my husband has accumulated. Mr. Darcy, I am your servant; how can anything more come of this?"

They were quiet for several minutes, both relieved with their confessions.

"Miss Bennet—oh, I am sorry; may I call you Elizabeth?"

"Yes, yes, please do," she answered quickly.

"And you must call me Fitzwilliam."

"Yes, I will, but is it proper?"

"Yes, I will make it proper," he said with a gleam in his eyes. His face then suddenly went grim. "Elizabeth, you must do something for me."

"What? What can I do? You look so cross; what is the matter?" Elizabeth asked with sudden concern.

"We must eat breakfast or Mrs. Bergman and Mrs. Enders will both be very angry with us, and you know we do not want Mrs. Enders angry with us." He smiled.

Elizabeth smiled back. "Yes, I know very well."

They stood and walked together to the sideboard. Mr. Darcy helped himself to large portions of food, but Elizabeth took only small portions. She had lost her appetite for breakfast with the events of the morning. They ate in silence, looking at each other only occasionally, now with their faces facing down toward their plates. When finished, Elizabeth stood and started to clear away the china, but Mr. Darcy stopped her.

"Elizabeth, you do not need to do that. That is why we have servants," he said.

"Yes, I know; I am one of them," she answered solemnly.

"Elizabeth, I do not want you to be my servant, cook, or maid. I want

you to be my companion. You once told me you have read the works of
Shakespeare. Do you remember *The Tempest*, act 3, scene 1: 'I would not
wish any companion in the world but you'?"

"Yes, I do, but I still do not understand all of this," she answered
sternly. "I do not wish to be my master's companion."

"Please forgive me for suggesting you be my mistress; I only wish
to know you better. I wish to discuss poetry, poets, authors, gardens, or
whatever comes to mind. I do not understand any of this either, but I do
know this is not some simple sonnet, but a real scenario that you and I
are living in. This is something we both feel and must face."

"Sir, Shakespeare writes of fairy tales, but love isn't a fairy tale. I do
not think I can do this," she said quietly.

"Elizabeth, come walk with me. I would like to show you something."

They left the breakfast room and walked slowly to the side door
leading toward a small portico. It faced a large meadow not far from the
servants' quarters. This was the same meadow she admired from her
room from time to time. She could see the hallway she walked daily
through the windows facing the open field. The beautiful colors of fall
had turned brown with the winter months fast approaching. A faint
frozen mist covered the lawn, trees, and shrubbery, indicating winter
had arrived overnight. The air was cool, and she shuddered from the
slight cold breeze. She wrapped her arms around herself, trying to protect
herself from the change in temperature.

"You must be chilled, Elizabeth. Let me call for a wrap for you."

"No, I am fine."

"No, you are not," he answered back sternly. He turned and called out
to one of the servants just walking past. "Excuse me; Miss Bennet needs
a wrap. Please fetch one from the nearby closet for her now."

"Yes, sir, right away," the servant said. He disappeared but returned
quickly with a rabbit coat for her and a wool coat for Mr. Darcy. Darcy
helped her with the coat and then put on his own coat. He thanked
the servant, who soon disappeared back into the house, eager to leave
Elizabeth and Mr. Darcy alone. As soon as the servant left, Elizabeth
knew the gossip mill would start. She feared her secret would soon be
discovered.

When Elizabeth felt they were alone, she said, "Thank you,

Fitzwilliam; I suppose I was colder than I thought. This feels so comfortable and warm. I have never worn anything like this before."

"It looks well on you," he complimented. She smiled back at him but did not dare hold his gaze too long.

They walked down the path, away from the mansion. They purposely did not walk close together, staying at least three feet apart, acting within the accepted rules of social diplomacy. Darcy had his hands clasped behind his back, and Elizabeth continued to hug herself. They did not want the gossip that had already been started about them being together to flare into something more. They stayed within sight of the manor house and always within sight of anyone watching.

"The gardens in the summer are really quite lovely. We have yellow day lilies, red-leafed coral bells, daisies, black-eyed Susans, and lavender-colored hostas. One of my favorites is bleeding hearts. The pink and white colors are among the first to be seen in the springtime. I am proud to say we have purple and white lilac bushes. I had them transported from the Balkan Mountains several years ago, and they are growing nicely. The spring flowers are very fragrant, and their scent will fill the air in the early morning."

"Why, Mr. Darcy, I did not realize you were such a garden enthusiast."

"Horticulture was one of the mandatory classes I took while at Cambridge. Again, I thought it was silly at the time, but the class has proved useful in my managing of the estate. We have gardeners, but knowing the flowering plants myself has proven to be helpful."

"I am sure it has," she responded. "Our gardens at Longbourne are also quite lovely. I love walking through them—especially in the early morning when the dew is still fresh and wet. The air is cool then, and I have the gardens all to myself. Living with six other people in a three-bedroom house can be overcrowding, so the solitude of walking can be invigorating. Here the mansion and the grounds are just beautiful, and the fields seem to go on forever, unlike home, where I can see our neighbor's fence and hear their livestock." After a moment of silence between them, she asked, "Is this what you wanted me to see, sir?"

"Yes, it is. I wanted to share all of this with you," he answered.

"Fitzwilliam, what are we doing?" she finally said once they knew they were out of earshot of anyone who might be within listening distance.

"We are following our hearts, Elizabeth."

"You know this is impossible. Until I know otherwise, I am a married woman," she said.

"I realize that, Elizabeth, and we need to find your husband and somehow resolve this."

"Fitzwilliam, if he is still alive and we are together, that would be scandal. It would ruin the reputation of you, me, and our families. Your sister—she will be ruined because of my marital situation."

"Elizabeth, when was the last time you saw your husband?"

"About eight months ago. We have been married two months, though I did not see him the last month or so. After the last beating I received from him, I gathered what little I had and left. I managed to walk to my aunt and uncle's home on the other side of London, and I stayed with them for a while until I could gather enough courage to face my family. Then I left to go back home to Longbourne."

"Did he contact you at all?"

Just before I returned home, he found me at my aunt and uncle's home. He wanted me to return, but I refused. That was when I told him about my lack of an inheritance. He was so angry at me; I cannot describe his mood or behavior. My uncle was ready to call a constable, but he left, and I never saw him again."

"Are you telling me you walked across the city of London all by yourself?"

"Yes, I did. It took me two days, but I did it. A very wise woman told me once that women do what they need to do to survive. I never forgot those words."

"Oh, Elizabeth, I am so sorry. You certainly did not deserve to be left stranded, alone and hurt, without money or resources." Both were silent for several minutes but continued to walk.

The cool breeze felt refreshing upon Elizabeth's face, and she inhaled deeply. She had always enjoyed walking, but since coming to Pemberley, her work had required her to stay indoors or near the kitchen. She did not realize until now how much she had missed her walks.

Finally, Darcy said to her quietly, "Elizabeth, do you have any children?"

She hesitated before saying, "No, I do not. Someday I would like to have children, but to answer your question, I do not have any children now." Again they were silent, lost in their own thoughts.

They walked in silence for most of the morning, enjoying the cool and fresh air. Eventually they came to the stables.

"Do you ride, Elizabeth?" he asked.

"Yes, I do have some riding experience, but it has been a very long time. In fact, the last time I rode was when I was a child. My family was visiting a family friend outside of Leeds. They had horses and my sisters and I took turns riding double on a horse. Of course, someone was holding on to the bridle and walking, but I remember it was quite exciting. The horse was gray, and I thought it was huge, but of course I was only five or six years of age." She chuckled.

Darcy smiled back at her. He had turned his head to watch her as she told her story, thinking, *How could this wonderful woman be abused and abandoned by anyone?* He knew in his heart he could never do such a thing to her.

"I would like to take you riding, Elizabeth, even if it is just a carriage ride."

Oh, how she would have loved a carriage ride with Mr. Darcy, but the scandal of them being together would ruin his reputation and that of his sister, Georgiana.

"Oh, Fitzwilliam, I do not see how this can continue," she whispered, more to herself than to him.

By midday they had walked back to the manor house. The air had warmed slightly, and both Elizabeth and Darcy had removed their coats. She handed the fur she had been wearing back to Darcy and thanked him. She then smiled shyly and said, "I must return to my chores in the kitchen. Have you not forgotten, sir, that I am here to earn money to repay my father for what I have borrowed from him already? The debts I still owe are significant."

"No, I have not forgotten," he said sternly.

She lowered her head and said, "Mr. Darcy, I cannot love you or anyone else. I feel nothing about love. Love is a leap that requires trust and confidence, but I am not yet ready to jump."

"Yes, yes, you will love again. You will take that leap, and when you do, I will catch you. I will show you how to laugh, trust, and love again. I will take care of you," he said.

"I do not think I can ever trust again," she answered quietly.

"Yes, you will; I promise. I will take you down that path."

She finally looked up at him and managed a faint smile, but she could not believe his words—at least not yet.

"I beg you, sir, do not call on me again; this cannot work for us," said Elizabeth. With that she turned and quickly disappeared, walking toward her room and the servants' quarters.

When she entered her room, she noticed the white apron she had left in the manor house had been washed, dried, and starched. It was lying on her bed, ready for her to put back on and wear to work. She sat down quietly, facing the window. She faced the open meadow that she had learned to love. She knew every bush, tree, and blade of grass. It had just started to snow, and she watched the large white flakes swirl around the windowpane. Within a few minutes, she stood and put on her work apron over her gray dress. She sadly looked into the mirror and left the room, walking to the kitchen, hoping to forget Mr. Fitzwilliam Darcy.

Darcy watched Elizabeth turn and walk away, feeling both sadness and anger—sadness that she was leaving him, and anger that he was letting her go. How could he do this? How could he abandon her like her husband did? Who was this man? He had to find out who he was and whether or not he was still alive. The story of her being beaten by her husband, walking through the streets of London, and looking for her family's home suddenly brought back the memory of seeing a young woman, hurt and scared, asking him for directions. Elizabeth Bennet was that woman he had seen and spoken to. He now recognized her underneath the bruises, cuts, and swollen eyes. His anger increased when he remembered how badly she was injured. He had not immediately recognized her, because of her bruised and swollen face. He knew what he needed to do. He quietly returned to his study and started to write an inquiry to his solicitor, Mr. Joseph Fellows in London. He called on Mr. Hickey to have the post delivered that day and then ordered his carriage. He would travel to London tomorrow, arriving by midafternoon. There he would find Elizabeth Bennet's husband.

He ate little of his evening meal, again preoccupied with thoughts of Elizabeth and concerns of what he might find the next day. Georgiana talked throughout the meal, but he did not hear her words. He excused himself early from the table and returned to his room. His sleep was fitful, and he arose early to depart for London. Georgiana had expected to travel with him as she usually did, but he apologized to her that he could not take her with him on this trip. He did not know what to expect or what he would discover. He was not ready to discuss Elizabeth with her or anyone else. He did not want to expose his sister to possible or unfortunate events that he might encounter with Elizabeth's abusive husband.

Thankfully, the trip into London was uneventful, and he met with Mr. Fellows at his office by late afternoon. They exchanged the usual business greetings, and Darcy was offered a gentlemen's whiskey and cigar. Darcy accepted the glass and settled into a chair opposite the large desk occupied by Mr. Fellows.

"Well, Mr. Darcy, I have news for you, but you will not like what I have to say," said Mr. Fellows.

"Well, sir, say what you need to say," replied Darcy.

"I found Miss Elizabeth Bennet's husband," Mr. Fellows said. He paused before continuing. "It is George Wickham," he said flatly. Darcy sat silently for a long moment, swirling his whiskey.

"You said George Wickham?"

"Yes, I did. I sent one of my best investigators out on this job. The results of the investigation are written in this report, but I will summarize it for you." He handed Mr. Darcy a parcel wrapped in brown paper for him to read at a future point. "George Wickham met Miss Elizabeth Bennet approximately ten months ago. He was deeply in debt at the time and was looking for an easy way to resolve his financial difficulties. He met Miss Bennet at a party given by her aunt, Lady Lucas of Meryton, and assumed she was a wealthy woman. He thought that if he married her, he could inherit her family's estate for her money and continue his habit of gambling. When he learned of his mistake and discovered she did not have inheritable money, he disappeared into the bowels of London, leaving her penniless and responsible for his debts. He has since been accumulating more gambling obligations.

"My investigator located Wickham just yesterday. He apparently has been terminated from his military post and currently is living with a whore down near the river. By the way, His Royal Majesty's guard is also looking for him for past offenses. Anyway, he is apparently deep in debt and needs money." Darcy nodded. "Well, what would you like to do?"

"Did Miss Bennet know of Wickham's situation before they married?" asked Darcy.

"No, sir, she did not; unfortunately she was a victim of his scheme to acquire her family's estate. He lied to her and misguided her to get her to marry him, in hopes that he might assume her estate. Her family and friends were also taken in by his stories and lies. I can only imagine what he must have said to them. This is all documented in my report for you."

"I see," said Darcy. He finished his whiskey in one swallow and then stood from his chair. He set the glass down on the office desk. "I thank you, sir, for your prompt investigation and findings regarding this matter. I will not take up any more of your time. Good day, sir."

Darcy left his solicitor's office and stepped into his waiting carriage. He needed to substantiate Mr. Fellows's findings and find George Wickham himself. He knew of a popular gambling house at the river's edge that was known for cheating men, marked cards, and homeless drunkards. Women were known to entertain men for whatever was offered them in payment. He had heard of stories of fighting, stabbings, and murders that occurred at all hours of the day and night. Honest men and women dared not go into this place of fear of robbery and even death. He knew this would be just the place George Wickham would go. He decided to go there and see for himself the man he had hated since his early manhood. Darcy needed to disguise his appearance, as he would not want to enter an establishment such as this dressed as a wealthy man. He also did not want George Wickham to recognize him.

He did not dare take his fine carriage into the bowery, so he had his driver leave him several miles away from the gambling house. He approached a poor homeless beggar man and paid him handsomely for his shirt, coat, boots, and hat. He smudged dirt onto his face, hair, and hands. The whiskey already on his breath completed his unfavorable appearance.

He ordered his driver to return to the hotel he would be staying at that night and informed both his driver and his aide that they would be leaving for Pemberley in the early morning. The driver reluctantly agreed and left his master alone on the dark London street.

Darcy walked several miles through busy London. A variety of men, women, and children of multiple ethnic backgrounds were all about him, going about their chores with no regard to a poor, homeless-looking man dressed in dirty and torn clothes and smelling of whiskey. The closer he walked to the river, though, the fewer people he saw. Finally, near the river's edge, he saw the gambling house he knew he would find Wickham in. He approached the door with both apprehension and determination. He opened it and walked into a darkened room filled with cigar smoke; it smelled of stale, cheap perfume and cooking grease. His eyes adjusted quickly to the poor light, and he saw several men sitting at tables, playing cards and laughing. Women of entertainment walked about flirting and serving tall steins of beer. It took him only a few minutes to spot George Wickham sitting at a corner table, drinking liquor and talking with several men. A woman wearing a low-cut off-the-shoulder dress that exposed her large breasts was seated on his lap. He had one arm around her waist; the other held a cigar. She too had her arm around his shoulder and was holding a glass of whiskey. While they laughed, he frequently kissed and nuzzled her shoulder, exposing her breasts and nipples.

Darcy sat at the far corner of the bar, watching Wickham with increasing disgust and hate. He ordered a beer and drank slowly, contemplating his plan for exposing Wickham for the man he was. Did Elizabeth know this side of Wickham? She knew of his gambling and debts, but did she know of his careless disregard for others, his disgusting behavior, or his infidelity? He hoped she would never find out the kind of man he really was.

The longer he watched Wickham, the more hatred he felt for the man. Childhood memories of the two of them playing together returned to Darcy's mind. The laughter they enjoyed back then had turned ugly after what Wickham did to Darcy's parents. Flashbacks of the final family confrontation resurfaced while Darcy watched George Wickham fondle a woman in public with no concern for anyone except himself. *Is this how he treated Elizabeth?* He finished his beer and left the gambling house, with Wickham never knowing he was there. He quietly walked back to the hotel, eager to bathe and change his clothes. He was eager to return to Pemberley and talk to Elizabeth.

28

He left London in the early morning and was thankful the journey was uneventful. His thoughts were in turmoil after seeing George Wickham again. His obnoxious behavior in the tavern made Darcy disgusted and angry. He was unable to focus on anything except the unpleasant memories of George Wickham with his beloved Elizabeth. Georgiana was waiting for him, anxious to hear of the latest news, gossip, or any upcoming social events. She was immediately shocked by his unkempt appearance. He told her hurriedly that he had no news and brushed past her, anxious to return to his study. There he shut the door, asking that no one disturb him.

Darcy immediately approached a large painting, a favorite of his father's, located on a far wall. He pulled the painting aside, revealing a locked wall safe where his father kept his most important business papers. He and Mr. Fellows were the only two people who knew the combination of the safe. He unlocked it and searched for the family documents that had been carefully stored away many years ago. He remembered well the day of the final family confrontation, when George Wickham was banned by the Darcy family from Pemberley forever.

Georgiana was not yet born when Fitzwilliam Darcy and George Wickham were boyhood friends. Wickham's father had been an associate of the elder Mr. Darcy. The two boys, close in age, had attended the same schools, church services, and social events. They learned to ride horses, they went fishing, and, occasionally, under their parents' watchful eye, they hunted pheasants together.

All was well until tragedy struck the Wickham family when the boys were in their midteens. Young George Wickham and his parents were riding home from a party when their carriage was stopped by highwaymen and robbed. The elder Mr. Wickham was shot and killed. George's mother was beaten unconscious and assaulted. She died later that night, never regaining consciousness. Young George escaped injury by hiding under the carriage. The robbers probably never knew he was at the scene; if they had known, he probably would have been killed also. He witnessed the crime and never attempted to stop the assault upon his mother. Young George was unable to identify the assailants, and they were never apprehended.

After the deaths of George's parents, the Darcy family took George into their home to be raised along with Fitzwilliam and baby Georgiana, who was named after Mrs. Darcy's aunt. George had always been mischievous, even as a young child. He drowned a family puppy and then lied about the incident, blaming one of their servants. He stole from friends and neighbors. He spied upon the servant girls while they were bathing and dressing. He frequently cheated on exams at school but somehow was never caught or expelled for his actions. Young Fitzwilliam knew of some of George Wickham's trickery but never repeated the stories to his parents, as George was his friend.

Approximately one year after the death of Wickham's parents, George began stealing from the Darcy family. First it was cigars and brandy from the elder Mr. Darcy's study; then it was Mrs. Darcy's jewelry. He started disappearing from Pemberley for sometimes days at a time. He began seeing and learning the ways of women prostitutes and learning to gamble at the local pubs. The Darcy family worried about him, assuming his behavior was due to the loss of his parents, but his delinquent pattern continued. Mr. Darcy frequently traveled to the establishments where young George had been seen, hoping to change his behavior, but never with success.

The final accusation that resulted in George being dismissed from Pemberley occurred when George was eighteen years old. He accused Mrs. Darcy of infidelity with the elder Mr. Wickham, resulting in the conception of young George himself. He claimed to be the illegitimate son of Mrs. Darcy, thus eligible for a third of the entire Pemberley estate. The gossip, scandal, and embarrassment resulted in the Darcy family being shunned from their friends and society. The rumors continued for months. Mr. Darcy hired investigators and attorneys to clear his wife's name. Finally, documentation proved the charges against Mrs. Darcy to be false, but the scandal had caused illness to Mrs. Darcy, causing her to take to her bed. She died as a result of prolonged bed rest, unfortunately before proving that the accusations made by George Wickham were false and before her name and reputation had been cleared. Mr. Darcy ordered George Wickham removed from his home, never to be acknowledged by the family again.

The death of Mrs. Darcy was difficult for Fitzwilliam's father. He also took to his bed and approximately two years later died, resulting in twenty-one-year-old Fitzwilliam becoming master of Pemberley and guardian of ten-year-old Georgiana. Fitzwilliam Darcy forever blamed George Wickham for the death of his parents.

Darcy slowly and carefully reread the sad story told by the family documents that had been stored in the safe for the past several years. Shortly before the elder Mr. Darcy's death, he requested Fitzwilliam keep the documents secure, concerned that George Wickham would return to claim a false inheritance. Fitzwilliam assured his father he would keep his mother's name and reputation unblemished. He promised his father that George Wickham would never gain the Darcy money or estate.

Evening had descended upon Pemberley when Darcy emerged from his study. He ate a quick meal and continued to avoid Georgiana. He felt guilty about leaving her alone so much over the past two weeks but was unable to discuss his situation concerning Elizabeth yet. The evening had turned cold, and snow was falling outside on the ground. The Christmas holiday was now two weeks away. The mansion was being decorated by Georgiana, with Mrs. Bergman's guidance. Georgiana loved the midwinter holidays, and Darcy would expect the decorating of the mansion to be completed within the week. He had just finished his meal and retreated to the library when Mrs. Bergman entered. Mr. Darcy held a snifter of brandy from the decanter and was staring at the flames in the fireplace, lost in thought.

"Good evening, Mr. Darcy," Mrs. Bergman said with a smile. "Is there anything else you require tonight?"

"Good evening to you also, Mrs. Bergman; I will not need your services anymore tonight. You may retire if you wish."

Mrs. Bergman did not immediately leave the library, and Darcy could sense she needed to speak to him. He was aware of Mrs. Bergman's advancing age but always knew she would continue with the family until her inability to continue and her eventual death. He would be eternally grateful for her many years of faithful service to the Darcy family. She had become much more than a servant; she was a member of their family.

"I see the house has started its transformation for the holidays," he eventually said. "It will look lovely, I'm sure. I know Georgiana is anticipating the upcoming parties."

"Yes, she is. You know, we are expecting a small gathering this coming Thursday."

"Really? My apologies, ma'am; I must have forgotten," he said with surprise.

"Yes," she said. "Your aunt, her guest, your uncle, several cousins, and a few friends are expected. I anticipate about twelve people, sir."

"That will be fine, Mrs. Bergman. I am sure you and Georgiana have everything in order."

"Thank you, sir. I will say good night, sir." She curtseyed and turned and had started to leave the room when Darcy called out to her.

"Mrs. Bergman, may I ask, Have you seen Miss Bennet? Have you attended to her injuries?"

"Yes, sir, I saw her just this morning. Her cuts and bruises are healing nicely," she replied.

"So she is well, then?" he asked.

"Yes, sir, I would say so." Mrs. Bergman paused for a moment and then said, "Miss Bennet seems like a lovely person. She is very kind to everyone here—quite smart too. Just this afternoon, she asked me if she could read one of the books here. I told her it would be all right. I hope that meets with your approval, sir."

"Yes, yes it does, Mrs. Bergman. Miss Bennet may read any of the books here," he said eagerly.

"Well, good night, sir."

"Yes, good night, Mrs. Bergman," he said slowly.

Mrs. Bergman left the room, leaving Fitzwilliam Darcy alone with his thoughts.

Darcy awoke early the next morning to meet his sister for breakfast. She was in an especially bright and cheery mood with the holidays approaching. They chatted throughout their meal concerning the upcoming holiday events. Georgiana and Mrs. Enders had planned the menus, which she eagerly discussed with her brother. They both knew he would agree to whatever they had planned. He asked Georgiana if she would like to go riding after breakfast, and she eagerly agreed. After their meal, Georgiana quickly changed her clothes into her riding attire and met her brother by the side door closest to the stables. While Darcy walked toward the door, he looked outside, hoping to see Elizabeth, but because she was no longer allowed to carry water from the outside well, she was not outside.

Brother and sister walked to the stables, holding hands and swinging their arms while laughing. "You seem very happy today, brother," Georgiana said.

"Yes, I am, little sister—very happy indeed," he answered. There was a light snowfall, but nothing that would interrupt their morning ride. The horses had already been saddled for them per Darcy's instructions. Darcy helped Georgiana up onto her sidesaddle and then mounted his own horse. He cautioned his sister not to ride too fast, as there might be a thin layer of ice under the snow. Remembering Elizabeth's recent fall, he did not want the same to happen to his sister. She agreed with his concerns, and they both trotted slowly down the gravel path until they were almost out of sight of the mansion.

After almost a half hour of riding, Darcy slowed his horse to a walking pace. Georgiana followed her brother's lead and slowed her horse also. They came to an open area where the sun had melted the snow. They stopped and dismounted from their horses. The horses were given treats and tied to nearby bushes. Darcy asked Georgiana if she would walk with him. Again he felt angry at himself for being rude to her the day before. After considerable self-reflection, he decided to talk to his sister about his relationship with Elizabeth. He did not want to discuss any details, but he felt he needed to be honest with her.

"Georgiana, I know I have been aloof lately, and I wanted to explain what has happened to me lately," he said.

"Brother, you sound serious; what is wrong? I know you have been sullen lately," she said.

"I am sorry, sister; I do not mean to be melancholy," he replied. "Georgiana"—he took her hand in his—"I have met somebody and fallen in love."

"Oh, brother, how wonderful. Who is it? Do I know her? When will I meet her?" she said excitedly.

"Georgiana," he replied quietly, "there is a complication. You see, she is married, though her husband has deserted her. She has not seen him in almost a year. We do not know where or if he will return. The situation is difficult, and I am unable to discuss any specifics with you presently."

"I see," she said quietly with her head downcast. "What will you do?"

"I do not know yet, but we will resolve this; I promise you." He looked directly into her eyes. "I do not want you to worry about this, and I do not wish you to discuss this with anyone; do you understand?"

"Yes, I understand, brother."

"Good, now let us get back to the mansion before it gets colder. I do not want you to get a chill. After all"—he smiled at her—"we have a party to get ready for." He paused. "Georgiana, I must make a request of you."

"Yes, anything, brother."

"Please keep this to yourself until the complication of her marriage has been resolved. I would not wish for any vicious rumors to start."

She smiled at him while nodding in agreement.

They returned to the mansion by midday and had a quick meal. Georgiana was anxious to resume decorating the mansion. Darcy, though, retreated again to his study. He had summoned Mrs. Bergman to his study. Within minutes, Mrs. Bergman appeared at the study door.

"Yes, Mr. Darcy, you summoned me?"

"Yes, yes, I did, Mrs. Bergman," he replied. "Please come in and close the door." She did as Mr. Darcy requested and closed the door, turning to face him quietly. He had been facing away from her, but he turned to face her when she closed the door. They both stared at each other without speaking. It was Fitzwilliam Darcy who spoke first as he gestured for her to sit in one of the large chairs.

"Mrs. Bergman, you have been with the family for a long time now."

"Yes, sir, almost forty years now. I was with your father for ten years before he married your mother. That was when I met Mrs. Darcy—when she came here as a bride. A beautiful woman she was. It was a very sad day when she passed. We all miss her very much," she said solemnly.

"Yes, it was a sad day." He paused. "Mrs. Bergman, do you remember the circumstances in which my mother died?"

"Yes, sir, I do," she said slowly. "It was that awful Wickham boy who sent her to her bed with his gossip and lies. He killed her and almost ruined the family, he did. I just don't know what happened to him." She shook her head as she spoke. "His parents were right nice folks, they were, but that Wickham boy was true evil."

Mr. Darcy stood and stared at his mother's portrait that still hung above the fireplace.

"Mrs. Bergman, while I was in London, I discovered some very upsetting news." He turned to face Mrs. Bergman as he continued. "Did you know that Miss Elizabeth Bennet is married?"

"Well, sir, I presumed she was. She is wearing a wedding ring. I just assumed she was widowed. She has never said anything, and I don't ask anything. I figure if she wants to tell me, she will, but I don't ask anything, sir."

"Yes, I know, Mrs. Bergman. Well, I was recently informed that Miss Bennet's husband is still alive. I saw him in London myself at one of those gambling houses down by the river. It is George Wickham."

"My God," she said as she clasped her chest with one hand and covered her mouth with the other. "Does she know about him? Does she know what an awful man he is? Does she know what he did to this family?"

"Yes, she knows what an awful man he is, and no, she does not know about Wickham's relationship with this family. Mr. Fellows, my solicitor, informed me they were married under false pretenses. He married her assuming she had money, and when he found out she did not, he abandoned her, leaving her penniless. That is how she came here to work for us. She came to earn money and pay his debts." As he spoke, he started to pace the room.

"The poor child, left alone by the likes of him," Mrs. Bergman said. "He should be whipped like a mean horse for what he's done to both her and to this family."

"Yes, well, Mrs. Bergman, we do not whip horses or people here at Pemberley—remember?"

"Yes, I do, sir, but if we did, he would deserve it!"

Both were quiet until Mrs. Bergman stood and approached Mr. Darcy. She spoke slowly. "Forgive me, Mr. Darcy, but I have known you since infancy. I see something different in you lately."

"What do you mean?"

"I mean, sir, since Miss Bennet has arrived, you have been distracted—not at all like your normal self. When you are with Miss Bennet, you are happy and smiling—in fact, the happiest I have ever seen you. I have watched the two of you. You know, Miss Bennet is a fine young lady. She is kind, polite, and a real lady. If you don't mind me saying, she doesn't belong in that kitchen."

"Yes, yes, I know," he whispered, more to himself than to Mrs. Bergman.

"I could go and fetch her, Mr. Darcy, and bring her here if you would like, sir," she said.

Darcy was quiet for a few moments. He then smiled at Mrs. Bergman and said, "Yes, please do, and please let Mrs. Enders know she will not be back in the kitchen."

"Yes, sir," she said, smiling broadly.

Shortly after, Mrs. Bergman returned with Elizabeth, who was dressed in the simple dress she had been wearing when she arrived at Pemberley. Her hair was brushed, but it was not pinned, as it had been when she had dinner with Mr. Darcy the week prior. She was smiling shyly and whispered, "Thank you," to Mrs. Bergman.

"You are welcome, my dear, and good luck," she whispered back. Mrs. Bergman left the study smiling and closed the door behind her.

Both Elizabeth and Darcy stared at each other, not knowing what to say.

Finally he approached her slowly and took her hands into his and said, "Elizabeth, I have missed you. While I was gone, I thought of you constantly. It is as if you have taken possession of my soul."

"Fitzwilliam, I feel the same, but it is wrong to feel this way about someone when I may still be married to someone else. I am afraid gossip is going to start if I do not return to my chores."

"Forget the gossipers," he said sternly.

"But what are we to do? I think nothing can be done now. I don't know where he is or if he is ever returning. I do not know if he is even alive." Darcy let go of her hands, but they continued to look at each other.

"Elizabeth, I found your husband," he said bluntly.

"What, he is alive?" she said with surprise and disbelief. "Where did you find him, and why did you have to find him? Dear God, why does he have to be alive? He is such an evil man; you have no idea what a monster he is. My God. George—George Wickham—is alive. He said I would never be rid of him, and he was correct." Elizabeth was near tears. She turned her head away, no longer able to look at Darcy.

"I could not believe what I was told by my solicitor yesterday."

"Your solicitor?"

"Yes. After we came back from our walk a few days ago, I sent an inquiry to my solicitor in London. He had an investigation conducted, and they found George Wickham alive and well. I still cannot believe this news, Elizabeth." Darcy started to pace the room anxiously. "Mr. Wickham—Mr. George Wickham—is your husband," he repeated, speaking more to himself than to Elizabeth. Darcy still could not believe his own words, even though he knew they were true. His look of shock and bewilderment upon his face, coupled with the final acknowledgment of her words, produced a look of misunderstanding. He had heard this news from his solicitor, Mr. Fellows, but he was still bewildered by his own words. The thought of George Wickham entering his life again after all these years was overwhelming to him. His face was reddened, and his words angry. Elizabeth could not comprehend his anger or expression.

"Yes," she stammered, "he is my husband. You know of George Wickham? Of course you would; he probably owes you money also."

Darcy started to pace the floor, looking first at her and then downward at the carpet. At first he ran a hand through his hair as he paced the floor. He then stopped, turned, and stared at her from the far end of the room. His eyes were ablaze with fury. She did not know what to think about his sudden change in mood. He did not speak for what seemed like a very long time. He started to pace the floor again with his hands clamped tightly behind his back, now staring straight ahead though seeing nothing. She had seen him do this previously—especially when he was deep in thought. He walked back to her and seemed to stare through to her soul. She could not read his face, and this frightened her.

"Please say something," she pleaded. He walked to the sideboard and poured whiskey into two glasses. He handed one to her.

Finally he spoke. "Elizabeth, please sit down with me and drink this; we need to talk."

He led her to the settee, where they sat side by side, but both turned enough to be able to see each other comfortably. He drank his whiskey in one swallow and set his glass down. She finished hers more slowly, never taking her eyes from his face. He took her glass when she finished and put it next to his on the smaller side table. He put one arm over the back of the settee and the other across her hands, which she had clasped in her lap.

"Elizabeth, I need to tell you my story regarding George Wickham, but I do not know quite where to start," he said.

"How about at the beginning. Then, when you are finished, I will tell you my story," she replied.

"That is fair enough," he answered.

Darcy talked slowly and without anger or resentment. He told Elizabeth every detail regarding George Wickham's involvement with the Darcy family and how he had been banished from Pemberley. By the time he was finished, evening had begun to settle upon Pemberley. Elizabeth felt exhausted and sick after hearing the story of how her husband had attempted to ruin the Darcy name and had caused the deaths of Fitzwilliam's parents. How ashamed and overwhelmed she felt. Darcy, concerned for her welfare, poured another glass of whiskey and ordered her to drink it to calm her nerves. She accepted the glass humbly.

"Elizabeth, do you know we have met before? You asked me for directions while you were walking across London in search of your family's house. You were exhausted, had been beaten, and were near starving."

"Yes, I recognized you also, but I was too embarrassed to say anything to you. You have seen me at my worst—the lowest I have ever been in my life. Oh, Fitzwilliam, I do not know what more to say. This is a terrible situation, and I am ashamed and overwhelmed," said Elizabeth quietly.

"Elizabeth, I know this is overwhelming for both you and me, but believe me; we will survive this."

The words told to her by the woman at the tavern about survival returned to her. She had her doubts, and an incredible sadness overcame her. Unable to continue the conversation, she politely declined a dinner invitation with Darcy and quietly returned to her room in the servants' quarters.

Mr. Darcy looked at her with sorrow and regret as she walked away. Initially he wished he could take back his words of admiration for her. She was a married woman, and his words of affection were inappropriate and scandalous. If his words of affection were repeated by any of the servants to the townspeople, her reputation and the futures of both their families would be ruined. Her family would be outcasts, and his sister would be shunned from society. He felt torn between two worlds—two worlds so very different.

29

Darkness had nearly descended when she lit the single candle in her room. She sat quietly gazing out onto the open meadow, which was now covered with snow. She heard a faint knock on her door but was unsure as to whom it could be. She cracked open the door and saw Mrs. Bergman with a dinner tray of bread, cheese, hot soup, and tea. "Please, my dear, may I come in?" she said. "Mr. Darcy is quite worried about you and asked me to bring your dinner and make sure you are all right."

"Yes, please come in," she said sadly while opening the door fully and stepping back to allow Mrs. Bergman to enter.

Mrs. Bergman set the tray on Elizabeth's dresser and asked, "May I sit down?"

"Yes, please do," Elizabeth replied slowly.

"Miss Bennet, I know Mr. Darcy told you about George Wickham and what he did to the family. It was a terrible time for all of us. George Wickham was proved wrong about Mrs. Darcy, and he never set foot upon Pemberley again."

"Yes, I know," Elizabeth answered. "But Fitzwilliam's parents died because of my husband."

"Yes, dear, but he wasn't your husband when all this happened."

"I know, but I still feel responsible for Mr. Darcy's heartache now," Elizabeth said.

"Miss Bennet, I must tell you, the master loves you very much, and I can see you love him also."

"Yes, I do," Elizabeth said as a tear trickled down her face.

"Trust me, dear; this will work out." Mrs. Bergman nodded. "Now please eat some dinner," she said finally.

Elizabeth smiled and nodded in agreement.

Early the next morning, Mrs. Bergman arrived at Elizabeth's room to escort her to the breakfast room she so enjoyed. Mr. Darcy was waiting for her. Coffee with sugar added had already been poured for her. She wore the gray servant's dress without the white apron. She only had one dress to wear other than the one she had arrived to Pemberley in. She was thankful this one was clean and not torn.

"Good morning, Miss Bennet," he said cheerfully.

"Good morning to you, sir," she replied. He helped her with her chair before sitting down across from her. She took a sip of coffee, smiled at him, and said, "Perfect."

"Good," he answered. Their breakfast was served by the attending servants, who thereafter dismissed themselves from the room.

"Where is your sister this morning? I thought this was her favorite room," Elizabeth stated.

"It is," he answered. "She will be very busy this morning. We are expecting guests today for the start of the holiday season." He started to eat breakfast and continued speaking while looking at her. "Yes, well, my aunt, my uncle, several cousins, and one of my best friends should be arriving by midday. I should tell you it is not unusual for guests to stay several weeks to several months here at Pemberley. As you know, traveling can be dangerous in the winter months. Georgiana loves this time of year and has become quite the hostess."

"You are very generous hosts indeed. My uncle, Mr. Gardnier, told me that before I came here to Pemberley."

He smiled back but did not comment. While staring at his plate, he said, "Elizabeth, you look so sullen."

She took a deep breath, returned her coffee cup to its matching saucer, and said to him, "Fitzwilliam, you told me your family's story regarding my husband; now you should also know my story. It is difficult to repeat, so please be patient with me." She had eaten only a few bites and had no appetite to continue. She stated, "I had never been with a man before I was married to George and did not know what to expect from the marriage bed. I had heard stories of lust and force from men, but I never understood or believed them." As she told her story to Mr. Darcy, she needed to stop frequently to catch her breath before proceeding. Even after months away from Wickham, she still had difficulty in speaking about him.

"He took me suddenly and violently with no thought of love or affection. His love was savage and hard. It was most uncomfortable and unpleasant. I am deeply embarrassed to speak of it even now." Her face had turned crimson and hot with a tear-streaked, saddened look. She turned her body away from his look of hurt and discouraged stare.

She described the house he had acquired for them and its location. "I must have displeased him greatly for him to treat me as he did, though I do not even know how I could have." She could hardly speak in between sobs.

Darcy put his hand on her shoulder and turned her toward him. He lifted her chin to meet his face. His eyes were intense yet reassuring when he spoke to her.

"Elizabeth, you did nothing wrong. A man like Wickham knows nothing about love; he only understands how to scheme, hate, and manipulate women to gain what he wants. Unfortunately, you are not the only innocent woman he has mistreated, and before he dies, you will not be the last. Elizabeth"—he placed his hands in hers—"it pains me deeply to hear how he mistreated you. I promise you it will never happen again." His voice was soft and gentle, and for the first time in many months, she felt secure and safe.

"He lavished me with expensive gifts. He said he had great affection for me and seduced me with his words. I was overwhelmed with his seductive attention and admiration for me. I later found that the gifts given to me had been confiscated from other female acquaintances. I know now that all of his attention, his words of love and affection, was only to obtain my family home, Longbourne. Once he realized that my family's home was not the huge estate he thought it was, and he would not inherit any of it, he left me alone with his debts and threats. How embarrassed and humiliated I was when I discovered his deception. Maybe I deceived him with my initial thoughts and feelings; maybe this was all my fault."

"No, you did not and could not. He deceived you with his lies and actions. He is a cruel and evil man," Darcy said. "He's a drunkard, a gambler, a womanizer, and a fortune seeker. He beat you and committed the worst violence a man can inflict upon a woman."

Elizabeth turned her head away from him, tears spilling down her face. "After he left me bruised and wounded, the anger and hurt I felt welled up inside of me. I experienced shaking chills from both fear and disgust for the man I had married. I still do. How could this have happened? How could I have had misunderstood his intentions?" Darcy listened intently with little expression.

"Elizabeth, look at me. George Wickham is an expert in deception. Outside of the military, he makes his living deceiving innocent people, attempting to rob them of their civility and money. He truly is one of the most undesirable people I have ever met."

When Elizabeth was finally finished with her story, tears were running down her face.

Darcy moved his chair closer to her and clasped both of her hands. "Look at me, Elizabeth; you are beautiful. I love you; in fact, I love you more now since you have confided in me."

"Fitzwilliam, I love you too, but we must face the realization that I am a married woman, despite who my husband is. I am not free of my marital vows, no matter what we may wish or want. That bond will always hold us back."

"Yes, dear, I know. We will keep our thoughts and wishes a secret for now, or at least until I decide what to do. Do you agree?"

"Yes, I do," Elizabeth answered.

"Elizabeth, I promise you we will prevail with this situation. I will not let George Wickham or anyone else come between us."

"Fitzwilliam, what about the upcoming weeks, the holidays, your guests? What will we do?"

"Elizabeth," Darcy said, "I will talk with Mrs. Bergman. Would you be willing to accompany her about the house—be her assistant? I feel this will hold down the gossip. Besides, if you are going to be the mistress of Pemberley, you will need to know the household workings of the mansion and how to manage its staff."

"The mistress of Pemberley? I can hardly believe these words, but if that is what you wish me to do, and if it will help resolve our situation, I will do whatever it takes."

"It is not what I wish, but it is what we will need to do for now. Will you be all right?"

"Yes, I will," she said.

"Now," he exclaimed as he slammed his hands on the table, "The first and most important task today is to get you some decent clothing." She laughed for the first time in months.

30

Guests started to arrive at Pemberley by midday. Carriages with ladies and gentlemen dressed in fine traveling clothes were greeted by Mr. Darcy and Georgiana. Elizabeth and Mrs. Bergman observed their exchange of greetings from within the front hallway. Both women exchanged glances, reading each other's thoughts; this was going to be a stressful visit. An acquaintance of Darcy's aunt, Mrs. Jeffery, had also been invited, but neither Mr. Darcy nor Georgiana knew her. She was elderly, well-dressed and presented with a stern demeanor. Her unsmiling face immediately caused some concern with the other guests, though Darcy's aunt had never shown any interest in her friends' indifference.

The guests entered the mansion and removed their wraps, handing them over to the butler. Georgiana agreed to provide a tour of the mansion. She was proud of her endeavors with the holiday décor and eager to display her talent. While the group toured the mansion with Georgiana, Darcy walked slowly behind the group, allowing his sister to speak freely. He was proud of her confidence, presentation, and appearance while speaking with their guests. She reminded him of their mother—always the perfect hostess. He also knew Elizabeth would be close by, as Mrs. Bergman always was when guests were at Pemberley.

As evening approached, the guests retreated to their rooms for rest and toilet before gathering again for a glass of wine prior to the evening meal. Mrs. Bergman and Elizabeth were quietly speaking in the hallway just outside of the library as the guests started to gather for five o'clock cocktails. Darcy and Georgiana were seated in the library when they heard loud voices coming from the hallway. Both rose from their seats to see to the disturbance, only to find Mrs. Jeffery shouting at Elizabeth. Darcy approached, quietly asking, "Excuse me, ladies; what is this about? Is there something wrong?"

"I would certainly say so, sir," exclaimed Mrs. Jeffery. "Your servant is rude. You need to control your help and put them in their proper place when needed. I certainly do." She then walked into the library. Darcy stared after her as she walked away, only to turn back to Elizabeth with a questioning look.

Elizabeth whispered to Darcy, "I was only complimenting her on her lovely brooch, and she accused me of wanting to steal it! Fitzwilliam, I would never—"

Darcy held up his hand and put his fingers to her lips.

"I know, my love; I will take care of this. I am so sorry this happened," he whispered. Elizabeth was only able to nod briefly to Darcy before turning from him and walking away.

Infuriated, Darcy walked back into the library to find Mrs. Jeffery speaking to the group about the importance of servant loyalty. "You need to keep a firm hand with any servant," she said. "You can never let them think they rule the house, and never let them have too much responsibility. The next thing, they start lying and stealing from you. Remember this, young lady of the house." She pointed her crooked finger at Georgiana.

"Yes ma'am, I will," answered Georgiana reluctantly. She looked up from Mrs. Jeffery's stare and saw her brother staring back. His look of silence and anger frightened her.

Darcy turned to Mrs. Jeffery and said to her, "Ma'am, you are a guest in this house, and because of that, you do have some privilege, but speaking to members of my household in an inappropriate manner is not acceptable. You will honor the wishes of me and of my sister regarding this. From now on, you will speak to either myself or Miss Darcy regarding any concern with our staff."

Mrs. Jeffery made no further comment and looked away, not heeding his words. The other guests in the room were silent and did not know how to read the scene they had just witnessed. It was Darcy's uncle who broke the silence, offering to pour a glass of wine for everyone. Georgiana, not used to drinking wine, accepted a glass with a shaking hand. Darcy thought, refused the wine, and instead poured himself a whiskey. He drank the contents while facing away from the group. He had no more to say. A light conversation started, centering on the winter weather, the upcoming holidays, and the latest news from London. Georgiana and the others, eager to engage in the exchange of news, soon forgot the altercation between Elizabeth, Darcy, and Mrs. Jeffery. Unfortunately, none of those involved forgot the incident.

The evening progressed without any further confrontation. The evening meal of roasted pork, potatoes, and vegetables was complemented by a dessert of custard and a glass of port. By midnight, the guests had retired to their rooms, leaving Darcy alone with thoughts of Elizabeth. He missed her terribly and wished she could join him as mistress of Pemberley. Tomorrow he would correct their situation, gossip be damned.

31

The next morning brought a light snowfall with bright, clear skies and the promise of a temperature above freezing. After breakfast, Darcy and his cousin promised the ladies a carriage ride about the estate, with the men accompanying on Pemberley's prized thoroughbreds. The weather forecast proved to be true, and the day progressed without any further incident from Mrs. Jeffery. Upon the group's return to the mansion in the late afternoon, a light meal was served. The men retreated to the library for conversation and whiskey, while the ladies left for the music room. Georgiana was anxious to show her aunt and cousins her new pianoforte, just purchased by her brother for a holiday gift. She played for them briefly and promised a presentation of a more difficult piece later in the evening.

It was when Mrs. Jeffery again saw Mrs. Bergman and Elizabeth pass by in the hallway that she called out to them. "You there—yes, you. I am talking to you. Come in here immediately." She pointed to Elizabeth. "Your service is required now. Do you hear me, or are you deaf, girl?" Elizabeth stopped, turned, and faced Mrs. Jeffery from the hallway.

"Excuse me, ma'am; did you call for me?" Elizabeth asked with puzzlement and growing resentment.

"Yes, I did; get in here. I said your services are required in here."

Elizabeth walked into the room, never taking her eyes off Mrs. Jeffery. A growing fury was starting to build in her. She was tired and homesick, and her hatred for George Wickham was becoming too much for her to bear. Her underlying fury was causing her to shake with both fear and resentment toward this woman who was intent on embarrassing and ridiculing her in front of guests.

"Clear away these glasses now. Do your job, for God's sake, and don't be so glum about it. Hurry up, and don't be lazy!"

Elizabeth stared at Mrs. Jeffery. "No, I will not!"

All was quiet for a moment until Mrs. Jeffery shouted back, "How dare you speak to me in such a manner. You are a servant and nothing more. You have no right to refuse a direct order."

"I told you *no!* I have no intention of doing anything for you. You are a mean, stupid old woman. It is you who has no right to talk to me or anyone else in this house with your irate and disrespectful tone. Being a guest here gives you no favor for bad manners!"

Meanwhile, Mrs. Bergman, upon hearing the verbal encounter, rushed to the library to find Mr. Darcy.

Mr. Darcy was in a pleasant conversation with his uncle when Mrs. Bergman called him aside. "Yes, Mrs. Bergman, what is it?"

"Mr. Darcy, sir, you must come to the music room immediately," she said. "Mrs. Jeffery and Miss Bennet are shouting at each other. I'm concerned there will be a fight!"

Darcy rushed past the bewildered Mrs. Bergman and ran toward the music room. Upon entering the room, he indeed found Elizabeth and Mrs. Jeffery staring at each other and shouting about the poor manners exhibited by both ladies. Georgiana was speechless and pale, never before having had to address a domestic situation between guest and servant.

"Ladies," Mr. Darcy said, "what is happening here?" He quietly came up behind Elizabeth, gently placed his hands upon her upper arms, and moved her slowly aside, moving between the two women. "Please, ladies," he said while glancing back and forth at the women but spending more time looking at Elizabeth.

"My apologies, sir," Elizabeth said to him while curtseying to him. She turned and quietly left the room without a look back or further acknowledgment of Mrs. Jeffery.

"Mr. Darcy," said Mrs. Jeffery, "That woman is disrespectful and brazen. You should discipline her and then release her from this house immediately. I demand an apology for her atrocious behavior."

"Mrs. Jeffery," said Darcy, "I will apologize for your discomfort here, but if Miss Bennet spoke to you in a disrespectful way, you must have deserved it."

"How dare you, sir!" Mrs. Jeffery shouted. "Your manners are as poor as those of that awful servant. I will not stay here and be insulted by this company."

"Mrs. Jeffery," Darcy said, "if you wish to leave, I will gladly arrange transportation for your journey to wherever you wish."

"Gladly!" she shouted. Mrs. Jeffery stood, and as quickly as she could, she left the music room. As she passed down the hallway, the other guests could hear her shouting to any servant who would listen. "Get my bags packed and delivered to any awaiting carriage immediately," she demanded. "I have never been so rudely treated. You can be sure others within our circle are going to hear about this!"

Within the hour, Darcy and Georgiana stood on the portico, arm in arm, and watched the carriage pull away with a still seething Mrs. Jeffery inside. Darcy had tried to soothe his still upset sister, assuring her that her hostess skills were still impeccable and she had done nothing wrong. After the carriage left, Darcy and Georgiana rejoined their guests in the music room. A glass of wine was poured for all, while Georgiana demonstrated her skills at the pianoforte. With the absence of Mrs. Jeffery, the general mood heightened, and soon Christmas carols were being sung by the increasingly inebriated guests.

The remainder of the evening progressed uneventfully and without any further incident. No more was mentioned about the confrontation between Elizabeth and Mrs. Jeffery. Even Darcy's aunt and uncle discussed Mrs. Jeffery's abrupt leaving as necessary. After the evening meal, the guests again retreated to their rooms, and Darcy could now concentrate on the earlier event that had caused Elizabeth's upset and departure. It surely was not the mean Mrs. Jeffery's comments that had caused such uproar. He needed to find Elizabeth to be sure of her well-being. After ensuring Georgiana was secure for the night, Darcy started to walk to the servants' wing. Before going too far, he was intercepted by Mrs. Bergman, who was also heading in the same direction.

"Mr. Darcy, sir, I know where you are going, but you should not go there. Sir, there has been enough talk for one day; you do not need to add more. Miss Bennet is fine, sir; I have spoken with her several times tonight."

Darcy quietly listened to her words and simply said, "Thank you." He turned slowly, his head down and hands clasped behind his back, and walked back to his study. He poured a snifter of brandy and sat heavily in his chair behind the desk, removing his cravat and loosening the top buttons on his shirt. He turned his back away from the door and put his feet on the desk. He was sitting quietly, thinking about the day's events, when he heard a soft knock at the door.

"Brother, may I come in?" Georgiana asked. He turned around to face her and sat up.

"Of course, sweetheart; please come in," he said without any significant expression. "I thought you were settled for the night. What's wrong? You cannot sleep?"

She dared not look at her brother directly but said, "Fitzwilliam, what happened today? What went wrong? The shouting and accusations were so terrible."

"Yes, I know," he said sullenly while looking at the contents within his glass. "Mrs. Jeffery is gone now, and we do not have to deal with her again, so I do not want you to worry any more about today."

Georgiana kept her head downcast but was able to raise her eyes to look at her brother. "Will she spread rumors about us?"

"Oh, probably," he said slowly. "But it is nothing to be concerned about. Now please, Georgiana, go back to bed. Tomorrow is another day, and you should be rested when it greets you.

"Yes, brother," she said. She turned slowly and walked to the door. Before she left, she faced her brother and asked, "Fitzwilliam, is Miss Bennet the woman you spoke with me about yesterday?"

He did not answer he immediately but finally said, "Georgiana, go to bed, please." Neither made any further comments, and she left to the room and went directly to her bedchamber, uncertain what the next day would bring. Darcy finished his brandy and also retired for the night.

Early the next morning, Georgiana, Darcy, and their guests met in the yellow breakfast room that Elizabeth and Darcy had dined in recently. It was the same room, just the day before, in which they had confided to each other regarding George Wickham. The sideboard was spread with breakfast foods seen typically at an English countryside estate. These consisted of eggs, thickly sliced fried bacon, sausages freshly made, pancakes, toast, fruit, tea, and coffee. Coffee with sugar had never been served before at Pemberley, and few of the guests knew of the drink, but Darcy had insisted it be available. The conversation during breakfast was light and cheerful. The young adults laughed and talked, making the events of the prior day forgotten. The adults talked of local historical events and repeated stories of family exploits told many times before. Everyone was at ease except for Darcy, whose thoughts drifted to Elizabeth. The room, her face, and their conversation gave him both pleasant and sad memories. Maybe he was wrong about his feelings. Maybe she was correct in thinking they should not be together. Maybe their differences were just too much for them to conquer. While his thoughts shifted toward yesterday, he drank his cup of coffee with sugar, remembering how she liked this so much. He was not fond of its taste but drank it while still thinking of her. For the first time in his life, he did not know what to do.

After breakfast, the men gathered for a morning of driven game shooting. It was a sport that was becoming quite popular among the English countryside estates. Since its introduction to the area, driven game shooting had become a favorite at Pemberley. Many of the boys who lived at Pemberley drove the birds from the open fields and woodlands. The birds were then shot by the sportsmen. Snipe and woodcock were some of the prey seen at Pemberley, but pheasants remained the chief game fowl. It was well known throughout Pemberley that no fallen bird was wasted. The game birds were always collected and used for food for the farmers and tenants living on the estate.

Today, while the men engaged in the hunting for game and sport, the ladies enjoyed a day of shopping locally and a midday meal at a popular pub. The ladies were well chaperoned by loyal and trusted members of the household and stable staff. The local and popular pub they entered was bright and cheery. Patrons were enjoying their holiday shopping and luncheon. It was after their luncheon was served that Georgiana saw Mrs. Jeffery also enjoying a meal with several other older women. They were talking loudly and occasionally glancing in Georgiana's direction. She tried not to be bothered by their stares, but she would remember to mention their obvious rude gossiping to her brother when she returned home. It was on days such as this that Georgiana missed her mother.

The rest of the day progressed without any further incident. The mood was lively, and Christmas Day was rapidly approaching. The Pemberley guests were expected to leave within the week, leaving Christmas Day open for Darcy and Georgiana to attend to the farmers and tenants of Pemberley. It was the tradition of their parents to visit each of the tenants' homes and present them with a holiday dinner of ham, turkey, and fowl. The children received gifts of toys, clothes, or sweets collected and prepared by the Darcy family. It had always been a very joyful occasion that centered on the true thought of Christmas giving.

Christmas morning was a cold, snowy day with winds blowing from the north. Darcy and Georgiana enjoyed a simple early breakfast and then collected the foods and gifts for the tenants of the estate. They left the mansion by midmorning and traveled to the many homes located on Pemberley. They returned to the main house by late afternoon, feeling comfortable with the day. Both Darcy and Georgiana were chilled from their day being in the outdoors, but both were also excited and satisfied with the completion of their special day. Meeting the many people whose lives depended on Pemberley had always been important to the Darcy family. Upon returning to the manor, they removed their outer cloaks and retreated to the library. Darcy poured himself a whiskey and a small glass of sherry for Georgiana. He allowed her to have a glass of spirits occasionally, but he did not approve of her drinking on a daily basis. Their mother did not partake of spirits, and he wanted Georgiana to follow her lead.

"What a wonderful day, brother," Georgiana said. "How I love the Christmas holiday, when we visit everyone and deliver the food and gifts made by everyone here. Everyone is so happy, and no one is cross on this day."

"Yes, I agree," Darcy answered.

"Brother," she asked quietly, "please tell me what went wrong the other day. Please tell me again—was it something that I did wrong or something that could have been prevented? I certainly would not want something like that to ever happen again."

"No, sweetheart, it was not something you did. Mrs. Jeffery is just a mean old woman who has forgotten her decent manners." He hesitated. "She had no business speaking to Miss Bennet the way she did. I will not tolerate her or anyone else speaking to someone in our employ the way she did." Georgiana smiled back at her brother but made no further comment.

They finished their drinks, and Darcy said, "Come, now; let us have Christmas dinner; then I have gifts for both Mrs. Bergman and Mr. Hickey."

A small dinner had been previously prepared for them. The servants had been dismissed earlier in the day to spend time with their friends and family. Mr. Darcy's favorite dessert of chocolate cake was being served by Georgiana when Mrs. Bergman and Mr. Hickey entered the room. They had been asked to join the Darcy siblings for the Christmas dessert so Mr. Darcy could present them with their gifts. Both sat at the dining table with Darcy and Georgiana to share the end of the holiday with the master and mistress of Pemberley. It was one of the few times everyone was relaxed and able to enjoy each other's company. After all, both Mrs. Bergman and Mr. Hickey had been with the Darcy family for many years and had been very loyal to them. They were considered part of the family.

After the dishes were cleared, Mr. Darcy presented Mrs. Bergman with a pink coral necklace. She loved colored jewelry and had made mention to the late Mrs. Darcy that pink coral was a favorite of hers. Unfortunately, nothing like this had been available until recently, when Georgiana had seen one while shopping with her aunt in London. She had bought the necklace with Mrs. Bergman in mind.

"Oh, how beautiful," she said, near tears. "I have never had anything as beautiful as this. Thank you so much. It must be very expensive."

"Never mind how expensive it was; it is beautiful, and so are you, Mrs. Bergman. We could never mange this house alone, and we cannot thank you enough for all you do for us," said Georgiana.

Next Mr. Darcy gave Mr. Hickey a shotgun to be used specifically for bird hunting. He knew Mr. Hickey enjoyed hunting whenever his duties allowed him. Occasionally he would accompany guests when they participated in the driven game hunting.

"Thank you, sir; this is very generous and kind of you," he said with his heavy Irish accent.

"You are very welcome, sir," said Darcy. "Like my sister said, we could never manage this house without help from the two of you. Loyalty like yours is rare and well appreciated."

The next gift was to Georgiana. "Sweetheart," Darcy said, smiling, "this is for you. You are becoming a proper young woman now, so you will need a proper ball gown."

She took the large package with anticipation from her brother's hands. With her eyes wide and glistening, she opened the box carefully and lifted the cotton sheet protecting the silken gown. She lifted the gown from its box with squealing delight under the watchful eyes of both Mrs. Bergman and Mr. Hickey. They so loved Miss Darcy, and thought of her as their own child. They had seen her grow from infancy to the beautiful and smart young woman she was today. *Oh, how proud her parents would be to see her as she is now*, they both thought. They were very happy to see their young woman so excited.

The gown was a dark blue silk with long sleeves and a modest neckline. It was fitted at the waist, with a full skirt, following the change in style from the previously favored high-waisted fashion dresses. Bright sequins decorated the bodice and upper sleeves, giving an adult eloquence to the dress that had not been previously seen in her clothing.

"Oh, Fitzwilliam, how beautiful. How can I ever thank you?" she exclaimed.

"Your beautiful smile and understanding will give me your thanks," he answered.

"My understanding?" she asked. "Brother, what do you mean?"

"Just be patient with me, sweetheart, and you will soon comprehend my meaning." Both Mrs. Bergman and Mr. Hickey smiled at each in quiet recognition.

The evening was late, and after the busy day, everyone was tired except Fitzwilliam Darcy. He had not seen Elizabeth in several days and was anxious to speak with her. He knew it would be impossible to go to her room to see her, so Mrs. Bergman gladly agreed to fetch her for him.

When a quiet knock sounded at her door, Elizabeth opened it, allowing Mrs. Bergman to enter. "Miss Bennet, the master would like to see you; please come to the main house with me. Everyone is in bed and asleep. It is safe; believe me."

"Oh, Mrs. Bergman, this is wrong. I am a married woman, and someone will find out. I am not properly dressed and have only my nightclothes on," she pleaded.

"Child, it will be all right; now please come with me. Hurry."

Holding a single candle and walking quietly down the servants' hallway, Mrs. Bergman and Elizabeth walked to the main house. Little did they know that two servant girls were hiding in the hallway closet, listening to their conversation and watching them proceed to the main house and the waiting Mr. Darcy. The girls knew that what they saw and heard would be a valuable commodity sellable to someone.

Mrs. Bergman took Elizabeth to Darcy's study and smiled at the two of them before quietly shutting the door. The room was illuminated by only two candles and a low fire, leaving the room warm and comfortable, though poorly lit. Darcy walked slowly to Elizabeth and took her hands in his.

"Elizabeth, I must tell you, I cannot get you out of my thoughts. These past few days have been intolerable for me. Today is Christmas, and you have not been by my side until now. I will make amends for this, I promise you. I love you," he said with deep passion. He raised her hands to his lips and kissed them softly.

"Oh, Fitzwilliam, we must stop this; you must release me and forget about me. This cannot happen to us."

"But it is happening to us; you cannot deny what we feel," he answered.

"You have charm, money, and a pedigree, none of which I possess. Your guests so loudly and rudely pointed that out to me, you, and everyone else here. I have tried to fight my feelings, but I cannot; they are too strong." Anxiety showed on her face as she spoke. "I love you also. I have tried to keep you away from my thoughts, but it is no use. My feelings for you are too strong now. Fitzwilliam, I have never felt like this before."

"Oh, Elizabeth," he said, "I love you so much. I promise you we will survive this." He continued to hold her hands in his.

"But what if George Wickham finds me or returns here and discovers I am here in your employ? He will take me away. What will we do then?" she asked, becoming tense.

"If he finds us, we will manage; he will not prevail in this," he answered.

"But you do know him; you know how awful he is. He will be angry, and with his violent temper, who knows what will happen. He could draw a sword or a pistol and kill you, me, or both of us!" She was near hysterics and starting to tremble.

He gently held her hands tighter in his. "Elizabeth, I promise you that will not happen," he replied slowly. "Look at me, Elizabeth; we will get through this. I love you, and I will take care of you. Elizabeth, we can work this out, I promise you."

"I believe you." She smiled. With his soft touch and reassuring words of comfort, she immediately calmed herself.

"Now, Elizabeth, I have a gift for you," he said while looking at her face. The low illumination of the room made her eyes dance and sparkle with beauty. He let go of her hands and quickly walked to his desk. He unlocked a side drawer and retrieved a small wrapped box. He returned to her side and presented the box to her. She had been holding her hands close to her face, and her anxiety started to rise again. "Here, I would like you to have this—my Christmas present to you," he said.

"Fitzwilliam, I cannot and should not accept a gift from you. It is not proper," she said reluctantly.

"Yes, you can and should accept this," he answered.

She cautiously took the box from his hands and pulled the ribbon that secured the wrapping. She slowly lifted the top off the box to see a beautiful, large white pearl drop capped in gold and attached to a gold chain.

"Oh, Fitzwilliam, this is exquisite," she said while lifting her eyes from the box to his face.

"It was my mother's, and she told me once that she would like the woman I love and marry to have this." He removed the necklace from its box. "Here, please pull your hair aside and allow me to put it around your neck." She smiled at him, collected her hair up into her hands, and held it up, exposing her thin neck. He opened the clasp, lifted the necklace over her head and placed the chain on her neck. He closed the clasp, never taking his eyes away from hers. He then adjusted the chain so it lay perfectly around her neck.

She let her hair back down, and he said, "There, absolutely beautiful. That is where this necklace belongs."

"I do not have anything for you," she said quietly.

"Your just being here is gift enough for me," he answered.

"Fitzwilliam, I am ashamed of the way I feel. I should not return your affection; I am a married woman."

"Elizabeth, our secret is secure here."

"Oh, Fitzwilliam, I truly hope so." She stood on her toes, lifted her arms to him, and grasped him about the neck and shoulders, slowly caressing the hair at the back of his head. He simultaneously put his arms around her, holding her close to his body. Embracing each other tightly, they searched for one another and kissed deeply, their tongues exploring for several minutes. Reluctantly, they pulled apart, knowing that their current feelings could carry them too far.

Looking at Elizabeth, Darcy held her face in his hands, stroking her face with his thumbs, saying, "It is late; I will walk you to your door." She nodded back to him.

He walked her as far as the entrance to the servants' quarters hallway, kissed her hand, and watched her open the door to her room and disappear inside. Little did they know that two pairs of eyes had been watching them secretly.

By morning, word of an affair between Mr. Darcy and a married servant woman had spread throughout the Pemberley staff and even reached the outskirts of London. The two servant girls had passed word of what they had heard and seen between the master, Darcy, and a servant woman named Elizabeth to several boys who regularly came to Pemberley to deliver food and any other supplies not grown, harvested, or made at the estate. The girls knew the boys would pay money for news that they could pass on to whomever was willing to pay for such information. Recently the boys had learned of a man looking for his missing wife, and they hoped this might be the sellable information he was looking for. The exchange of stories regarding master and servant girl were not unusual, but gossip concerning Mr. Fitzwilliam Darcy, the proper and proud master of Pemberley, having an affair with a married servant woman was extraordinary. That combined with Mrs. Jeffery's account of her ill treatment by the same servant woman was worth repeating. Mrs. Jeffery's narration and gossip had spread throughout London's society rapidly, like a fire in a dry forest.

The day after Christmas brought a warm day with the temperatures above freezing. The snow from the day before had melted, leaving the air fresh and comfortable. Elizabeth had awoken early, dressed, and left her room for a walk about the outside of the Pemberley mansion. She would be meeting Mrs. Bergman soon to continue her lessons regarding the management of the mansion. The holiday had come and gone without correspondence from her family. She continued to worry about them—their health, their finances, and the status of their home. She missed her family and wished she could see them again. This was the first Christmas holiday she spent away from her family, making her feel sullen. She wanted to talk to them about Fitzwilliam Darcy and tell them she had found love again.

She avoided breakfast and even her favorite sugared cup of coffee to get an early start on her journey. She put on her warmest clothes and cloak, and then set out on her walk. She missed walking and always felt her spirits lift when in the fresh air. She left Pemberley through the side door by the servants' quarters that she knew so well and strolled past the well where she had fallen many weeks before. She was thankful that there was no ice today and that, to her understanding, no one else had been hurt while pumping water from the well. She continued her walk past the stables and the main path, toward the lake. Of course there would be no birds singing this time of year, but geese and several swans remained at Pemberley during the winter months. She enjoyed watching and listening to them chatter with each other as if they were having a pleasant conversation. Occasionally she would hear loud screeching, as if an argument was taking place. She was lost in thought when she heard the soft sound of hooves and a single horse neigh. Startled, she turned and saw Darcy approaching astride his horse.

"Good morning," he said. "I looked for you this morning. When I could not find you, I assumed you would be out here walking. I know this is one of your favorite spots at Pemberley."

"Yes, it is. It is so beautiful and quiet," she said while looking out over the lake and fields.

"I know; I came here often as a child when I wanted to hide from my parents or Mrs. Bergman," he said, smiling. He dismounted from his horse and walked over to her. He then took her hand and gently kissed it.

"Fitzwilliam," she said anxiously, looking around, "are you not afraid someone will see us?"

"That is what I came to tell you. I have thought about this since last night. I am the master of Pemberley, and I will not let idle gossip keep us apart. We will not have secrets at Pemberley anymore," he said sternly.

"Do you think that wise? After all, my husband is close by. Word will surely get to him soon."

"I am sure it will, and we will do what is necessary. As I said before, I will take care of you."

"Fitzwilliam, you know he is a dangerous man capable of anything. You must not underestimate him. You know he is an insecure and unpredictable man."

"Yes, I know," he answered back quietly, hoping to calm her heightening voice and growing fear. "Enough of that now." He changed his expression to one more animated. "It is a beautiful day; let us enjoy it. Please, let us continue our walk." He extended his arm for her to take, but when she reached out to take his arm with both of her hands, he noticed that her gloves were old and worn.

"Elizabeth," he said, looking down at her hands, "your gloves are torn."

"Yes, I know," she said with seeming apology. "These are the only ones I have left. I sold just about everything I had to help pay George's debts."

Darcy remained quiet and covered her hands with his own, both to hide her shame and to keep her warm.

They continued walking down the graveled pathway, careful not to step into any melted snow. He worried that her shoes may be worn, allowing her feet to become cold and wet. She, however, did not seem to worry about such things. She walked along with him, his horse trailing behind, while looking attentively up at the bright day and sunshine.

"I love walking, I always have. My mother always disapproved of me walking out of doors. She was concerned about me getting too much sun and developing freckles upon my nose. I never concerned myself about that, though. I think that is silly and always did. I love the sun. The sunshine feels good on my face; it somehow makes me feel happy and takes away sadness."

He smiled. "Then I shall cork the sun in a bottle for you so you can drink it in whenever you are sad."

She smiled back. "You know, I think you can do that."

He looked down at her and said, "I love your smile, the curves of your face, and the sparkle in your eyes. The sunshine makes you glow."

"Oh, Fitzwilliam, we will be all right, won't we?"

"I promise you we will."

They remained quiet for several minutes while continuing to walk, both lost in their own thoughts and enjoying the day. They reached for each other's hands and held each other as they walked. The gravel path ended at the edge of a wooded area, not allowing them to proceed any further. The ground was wet, but Darcy noticed a dry fallen log that had been protected from the winter weather.

"Please let us sit for a while; I brought some apples for us to eat." He smiled. "Actually, they were for my horse, but I am sure he can spare one or two for us."

Elizabeth laughed and nodded to him. He raised her hands to his lips and kissed them again before she sat on the log. He turned toward the horse, opened a small bag on his saddle, and returned with a large red apple. He started to give it to his horse, but Elizabeth called out, "Please. Allow me." She got up from her seat, took the apple from Darcy's hand, and approached the horse. She was not used to being close to horses but was not afraid of them. She reached out to give the apple to him, but Darcy stopped her.

"Wait; not that way. Open your hand out flat to him; otherwise, he may accidentally bite your hand while taking the apple from you." He took her hand, removed her glove, and opened her fingers. He then placed the apple into her open palm. "Now you may give it to him."

Elizabeth's eyes moved from her hand to Darcy's face, and she then turned to the horse with the apple balanced in her hand. The horse eagerly took the apple into his mouth, backed away slowly, and shook his head with apparent delight. Both Elizabeth and Darcy laughed and returned to the fallen log with their own apples to eat. They bit into the ripe apples and ate them slowly, with juice running down their faces. Elizabeth remembered she had not eaten breakfast and realized she was quite hungry.

After they finished the apples, both threw the cores into the wooded area. It did not take long for two deer to approach the treats and leave quickly with them. Again Elizabeth and Darcy turned to each other and laughed.

"This reminds me of a class required during my days at Cambridge," Darcy said. "It was a languages class in poetry. I thought the class pathetic at the time; I now appreciate it. I specifically remember a poem which fits today perfectly. I would like to recite it for you."

"Please do; it has been a long time since I have read or heard poetry," Elizabeth said. She held her head down while he spoke.

"This poem was written by a Scottish poet, Robert Burns, in 1794, and it says what I need to say to you now."

O my Luve's like a red, red rose
That's newly sprung in June;
O my Luve's like the melodie
That's sweetly play'd in tune.

As fair art thou, my bonnie lass,
So deep in luve am I:
And I will luve thee still, my dear,
Till a' the seas gang dry:

Till a' the seas gang dry, my dear,
And the rocks melt wi' the sun:

I will luve thee still, my dear,
While the sands o' life shall run.

And fare thee well, my only Luve
And fare thee well, a while!
And I will come again, my Luve,
Tho' it were ten thousand mile.

After he was finished, she looked up slowly with wet eyes and said, "Oh, Fitzwilliam, that was beautiful, but I do not deserve such words." She spoke slowly, being careful not to cry.

"Elizabeth, you do deserve these words and more, and I will repeat these words for the rest of my life if it makes you happy."

Both were silent. They simultaneously reached for each other and engaged in a deep embrace. Elizabeth rested her head on Darcy's shoulder while he held her head to his chest. It was not until they both heard the sound of horses coming near that they separated. Darcy's own horse became restless with the oncoming strange sound. Darcy stood and turned toward the approaching hoofbeats, which were growing louder. Elizabeth became frightened, unsure of who was approaching. Despite Darcy's assurances of security and safety, she continued to be concerned about George Wickham—especially now that she had learned that he had recently been seen in nearby London. George Wickham still bought back thoughts of fear, anger, and disgust to her. Now that she knew what love, caring, and even passion were, she could not understand her husband's vicious actions. How could he treat her the way he did? He was an evil man. Fitzwilliam had been correct when he called him undesirable.

"You there, who are you? What is your business here?" Darcy called out.

"Excuse me, sir; my name is Adam, and this is my cousin, David. We are in search of Pemberley, sir."

"This is Pemberley. I ask you again, What is your business?"

"Sir, we have a delivery for Pemberley. It is for the upcoming ball scheduled there. We have fruits, vegetables, and spirits that have been requested by your cook, Mrs. Enders. We must get these to your cook immediately, sir. If you allow us to continue our delivery, the she will not be angry with us."

"Yes, very well then; you may proceed, but do not linger. You will need to turn your wagon around and take the next road to your right. That will lead you directly to the Pemberley kitchen."

"Thank you, sir," said the young delivery boy named Adam. Little did Darcy or Elizabeth know that they were the same delivery boys who had received the reports regarding the master of Pemberley and his servant woman. The delivery boys expertly turned the wagon around and proceeded back in the direction they had come, down the gravel path.

"That's her all right, with the master of Pemberley himself. Mr. Wickham will be glad to get this news. It should pay us a good amount too," said Adam.

"Sure will," answered his cousin David.

"They think they are fancy folk, but they no better than you or me," David chuckled. "Let's get going so we can get our money."

"Yes, sir, we will," David agreed.

Once they were out of sight, Darcy turned back to Elizabeth and saw the frightened look on her face. "It is all right; they are gone now."

"Fitzwilliam," she called out to him, "those boys—they look familiar to me. I am sure I have seen them before."

"Well, they are local delivery boys, and you have probably seen them before at the kitchen."

"I am not sure; something is different about them. I do not think they are our usual delivery boys."

"All right," Darcy said. "When we return to the main house, I will inquire about them with Mrs. Enders. If they are who they say they are, she will certainly know."

"I am being foolish, aren't I?"

"No, you are not. You are just confused and tired; that is all." He paused and then said, "It is getting late, and we should be getting back." She smiled to him and nodded in agreement.

They walked back to Pemberley with Mr. Darcy's horse in tow. They were not holding hands, and to anyone's eye, they appeared to merely be friends taking a stroll. Their conversation was light and almost nonmeaningful. When they approached the manor, Darcy handed his horse to a groomsman, tipped his hat to Elizabeth, and proceeded to the main portico, where she curtseyed his acknowledgment and walked to the servants' wing without looking back.

32

When Darcy entered the mansion, he handed over his hat, coat, and gloves to an awaiting butler. He went to his study, only to find Mrs. Bergman waiting for him. "Good morning, sir; did you have a pleasant walk?"

He looked at her hesitantly while walking to his desk and responded, "Yes, I did. Is there something on your mind, Mrs. Bergman?"

She walked to the door and shut it quietly, leaving them alone. She hesitated momentarily and said, "Yes, sir, there is. Sir, word is circling among the staff about you and Miss Bennet. I don't believe anyone knows about Mr. Wickham, though, but, sir, it's only a matter of a short time before someone finds out. You know what that will mean. Two delivery boys have been here twice this week."

"So? Is that so unusual?" he said with attitude.

"Not with these two boys; they're trouble. Sir, these two have been known to seek out and even receive pay for any information they acquire."

"What do you mean?" he asked, now with a hint of anger.

"I mean these boys have a repetition of being bad. They hear of gossip that may be valuable on the market, confirm it, and then pass it on to an interested buyer, for a price. You and Miss Bennet are the information they are looking for. Sir, I am very concerned it may be Mr. Wickham buying the information, looking for his wife, Miss Bennet. I fear for her life if he hears of any folly."

"How did you find this out?" he asked in a more civil tone.

"I may be the housekeeper here, sir, but I still have connections with the staff, and this is what they are telling me."

"What do you think it means?"

"Sir, I believe it means trouble for both you and Miss Bennet," she said, walking up to him closely. "I fear George Wickham is the one asking for and buying information. If he is, then it is only a matter of time before he finds her here. If he does, sir, I fear the worst."

He paused for a moment and said, "With that said, you may be correct. I must meet with Mr. Hickey and several of our loyal groomsmen soon. They may know something also. Would you please have Miss Bennet moved over to the main house immediately. I would like her nearby—away from the other servants and their talk."

"Sir, that is wise, but wouldn't bringing her here just confirm the rumors?"

"Rumors be damned! Her safety is more important. I want her in one of the rooms upstairs, next to mine."

"Sir, that would be scandalous and unforgiving—especially for Miss Darcy," Mrs. Bergman answered in a calmer voice.

In a now more controlled voice, Darcy replied, "Yes, I understand the consequences, Mrs. Bergman, but she is important to me, and her safety is crucial. I will not allow vicious gossip, threats, or possible physical assault invade this estate, its people, or its functioning."

"Very well, sir; I'll fetch her immediately."

While Mrs. Bergman went to fetch Elizabeth, Mr. Darcy himself went to the kitchen and spoke with Mrs. Enders. "Those boys," Mrs. Enders said when questioned, "they're evil, they are. If they are the ones sneaking around, it wouldn't be the first time." She shook her head. "Yes, they are evil, they are. I knew they was no good." With that she walked away from Mr. Darcy while still shaking her head.

Mrs. Bergman walked quickly to the servants' hallway. Just as she entered the corridor, Elizabeth was leaving her room, ready to resume her duties in the main house with Mrs. Bergman.

"Miss Bennet," Mrs. Bergman called out. She reached her door and then pushed Elizabeth back into her room. "We must talk, my dear."

"Mrs. Bergman, what is wrong? What has happened?"

"Listen to me, child; word of your relationship with the master has reached London. I suspect someone has been asking for information regarding you, and Mr. Darcy fears trouble is imminent. You must pack your things; I am taking you to the main house to stay. Hurry now; the master is waiting."

"Mrs. Bergman, I was afraid this would happen. I saw those two boys today, and I knew something bad was going to happen."

"The boys saw you?"

"Yes, today, while Mr. Darcy and I were walking." Mrs. Bergman hesitated before speaking and then said, "Come now, child; let's go now." Elizabeth packed the few possessions she owned into the same tapestry bag she had arrived at Pemberley with. It took only minutes for Elizabeth to finish packing, and the two ladies then walked back to the manor house. She was escorted to the study by Mrs. Bergman and into the company of Mr. Darcy and Mr. Hickey. Together the three of them quickly agreed the delivery boys were the guilty informers, and if seen again at Pemberley, they were to be arrested by the local constable. Mrs. Enders was also notified of their decision and agreed.

When Elizabeth arrived to the study, she was pale and shaking. As soon as Darcy saw her, he immediately walked to her side and hugged her tightly, despite Mrs. Bergman and Mr. Hickey present. "Elizabeth," he whispered to her, "It is going to be all right. You are here now and with me. There is no danger. I want you here with me, to stay here with me. Is that all right?"

"Yes," she whispered back to him.

Mrs. Bergman and Mr. Hickey left the study, leaving Darcy and Elizabeth alone. He escorted her to the settee to calm herself and then walked to the sideboard, poured two glasses of whiskey, and presented one to her. "Here, drink this," he said.

She took the glass and glanced at it briefly before looking up at him. "I have noticed, Fitzwilliam, that it is your habit to give me a glass of whiskey prior to a conversation that will be difficult. What is it that you have to say to me?"

He chuckled for a brief moment and then said, "You are very astute, Elizabeth. That is part of why I have grown to love you so much." He paused to catch his breath and then noticed something amiss. "I thought you were bringing your belongings with you. Is all you have in this one bag?" he asked, nodding to her tapestry bag.

"Yes, it is. Remember? I told you I sold everything I owned."

"Yes, you did. I apologize for asking you that. I should have remembered." He walked to the settee and sat closely to Elizabeth. "It pains me terribly what you needed to do because of George Wickham. The man is horrendous and does not deserve to be alive," he said severely.

"Fitzwilliam, please do not say that. It frightens me to hear you say those things. If something should really happen to George Wickham, you could be accused and charged for something you did not do." She stopped to catch her breath and took a sip of whiskey. "Now tell me what has happened."

Darcy drank his whiskey down with one swallow, cleared his throat, and then stated, "Elizabeth, it has come to my attention that word has reached London about us. You were correct about the delivery boys we saw. Apparently they are informants who came to Pemberley brokering for someone in London to collect information concerning us. Someone here has contacted these boys, who have a reputation for gaining information in exchange for money. I assume this started as idle gossip from Mrs. Jeffery and now exploded to this." Darcy stood up from the settee and threw his glass against the fireplace, shattering it into hundreds of shards of glass. Elizabeth was startled by his quickness, but otherwise she felt apathetic. He started pacing the floor with his hands clasped behind his back. She knew he paced when he was deep in thought and very upset.

She finished her glass of whiskey and said to Darcy, "Fitzwilliam, I need to leave here. I need to go back to Longbourne—back where I belong, and back to where my family live. I knew our connection was a mistake, and now I have ruined both of our lives and our families' lives."

He stopped and quickly turned to her and said loudly, "Absolutely not! You will not leave her. Remember: I told you no more secrets at Pemberley. We will not let anyone destroy what we have. It has taken us both years and suffering to find each other. I will not lose you now."

She sat silently, sad faced, and then she tilted her head back and closed her eyes. He walked over to the settee and sat beside her, first clasping her hands and then embracing her.

"We will continue with this, Elizabeth; we will endure, and we will survive."

"I believe you, Fitzwilliam. It will be a struggle, but I believe you," she answered.

They walked slowly up the grand staircase. He carried her one tapestry bag and showed her a spacious and finely decorated bedchamber next to his. "I hope you will be comfortable here," he said as he opened the door for her.

"My goodness, I have never seen a bedroom like this before." Even with the room illuminated only by several candles, she could see the enormous bed, dresser, mirrors, and fine wall hangings. "I have always had to share a bedroom with two of my sisters; I even had to share a bed with one of them until I left Longbourne when I married George."

Darcy smiled at her, remaining silent and shaking his head in regard to her modest past.

She then turned to him and said, "Oh, Fitzwilliam, I am so afraid."

He continued to smile and said, "Do not be afraid; there is no adjoining door between these rooms." She stared at him for a brief moment and then laughed.

"That is not what I meant."

"I know, but it helps." He smiled.

33

Early the next morning, Mrs. Bergman knocked softly on Elizabeth's door to inquire as to whether she had awakened. Mr. Darcy would not be so bold as to enter her bedchamber and communicate with her himself. Elizabeth was awake but had not yet dressed.

"Good morning, Miss Bennet. The master asked me to fetch you and ask of your health. Did you sleep well, ma'am?"

"I am well, Mrs. Bergman, but I admit sleep was difficult. Mrs. Bergman, so much has happened. It makes my head spin."

"Yes, I know, dear. The master—he is most distressed. He was awake early this morning and has gone down to the kitchen, inquiring as to who may have spoken ill of you to those awful boys. When he finds out, and he will, there surely will be consequences. My master demands loyalty from all his employees."

"Mrs. Bergman, I have caused such trouble here. I did not mean for any of this to happen," she said sadly.

"I know, dear. Now let us get you dressed and ready for breakfast. Mr. Darcy is most anxious to see you."

Georgiana and Mr. Darcy were seated at the round dining table, she drinking tea and he coffee, when Elizabeth entered wearing one of the new dresses Mr. Darcy had recently purchased for her. It was not custom made, so the fit was not exact, but the dress was suitable and flattered Elizabeth's petite form. The dark green color complemented her red hair and dark hazel eyes. It was a simpler style and a darker shade of green than the one she had borrowed for the Meryton ball, which pleased her. Anything that reminded her of those earlier days needed to be lost. Both

Georgiana and Darcy rose from their chairs when Elizabeth approached the table.

"Good morning, Miss Bennet." Georgiana curtseyed.

"Good morning to you. It appears to be a very pleasant day outside, does it not? The sun is shining, and the sky is blue, and hopefully there are no storm clouds brewing," Elizabeth answered.

"Yes, it does," Georgiana responded.

Darcy motioned Elizabeth to sit between himself and his sister, but at a comfortable distance. The round table allowed them to see each other and converse with ease. Elizabeth always preferred a round dining table for this reason.

Darcy smiled at Elizabeth and asked without embarrassment, "Did you sleep well, my dear?"

"Yes. Yes I did, sir," she replied hesitantly. His use of "dear" in the presence of his sister embarrassed and surprised Elizabeth. Darcy had informed her that there would be no more secrets at Pemberley. This was only the start of his promises.

"Good. I believe you ladies, with the input of both Mrs. Bergman and Mrs. Enders, have plans to complete for our New Year's ball."

Elizabeth shot Darcy an angry look but did not comment immediately.

"Please, let us have breakfast," said Darcy. "I myself have had a busy day. I must confess to you both, I have neglected some of my duties around here. So I will need to attend to them. Georgiana, I will be around if you need me though."

"Thank you, brother, but I am sure we will be fine. In fact, today will be a wonderful opportunity for Miss Bennet and me to get to know each other; do you agree, Miss Bennet?"

"Yes, I do; thank you, Miss Darcy," she replied with a nod.

They ate their breakfast in relative silence, the servants leaving immediately after the food was set out on the sideboard. Georgiana finished her breakfast quietly and excused herself for the morning. Darcy stood, kissed her cheek, and walked her to the door just before she left the room. He then quietly closed the door. When he turned toward Elizabeth, he knew immediately she was upset.

"Fitzwilliam, I do not appreciate you telling me what I will be doing—especially without my consent," she said while looking at him directly.

"Yes, I have no doubt regarding your distress about my comments, so please, let me explain." He poured himself another cup of coffee and offered one to Elizabeth also. She looked at him patiently and then accepted his offer. He added a teaspoon of sugar to his cup and again offered to add the sugar to hers. She accepted with a nod of her head. After stirring the contents of the cup, he silently placed the spoon on the saucer and continued his conversation.

"Elizabeth, I am sure you are aware of the vast underground gossip and message exchange scheme that exists at Pemberley. I am sure it is no different than at any other large estate. You must have heard some of the small talk while living in the servants' quarters and working in the kitchen. Elizabeth, I do not mean to upset or humble you in any way, but you must realize the importance of our situation." He took her hands and held them tightly while appearing to be deep in thought. They looked up at each other, both with desire in their eyes. They smiled, and then, together, they leaned toward each other and kissed lightly, both eager for more.

"Elizabeth, I need to keep you safe, and since my acquisition of the more recent rumors, I am concerned for your safety—whether they are from the servants' gossip or George Wickham. Your being in the company of someone, even in the confines of the mansion, will assure me of your safe keeping for now. I hope you understand this."

"Yes, I do," she said quietly. "I understand your concern, and I love you for it, but Fitzwilliam, I must tell you …" She paused to catch her breath and took her eyes away from his face before she could continue. Looking back to his face, she said, "I find you the most wonderful man I have ever met. You have aroused me deeply, like no other ever has—even the man I thought I loved and married. You have shown me what love really is and what it can be." She stopped, picked up her coffee cup with a shaking hand, took a sip, and set the cup back on the saucer with a loud sound. She was afraid she may have chipped the china, knowing it would be impolite if that happened. She took a deep breath, sighed, and then continued. "I never thought I could love again, but you have proved to me it is possible. I love you deeply, and I want to be your wife." Tears flowed down her cheeks. "I do not know what else to say."

Darcy got up from his chair and walked to Elizabeth and knelt by her side. He pulled her off her chair so she too was sitting on the floor. They embraced and kissed deeply. He started to grasp for the buttons on her dress, while she reached for his jacket.

She suddenly said, "Stop! We cannot do this. Oh, Fitzwilliam." She rested her head on his chest.

All Darcy could say was "I know." He stood first and then helped her up, both of them being careful not to step on her skirts. They held each other closely before separating. He brushed her hair away from her face, searching her eyes, while she touched his lips with her fingertips.

Elizabeth felt her legs shake slightly when Darcy said, "Elizabeth, We need to attend to our duties before this goes too far."

"I know," she answered, looking at the floor and smoothing his shirt. "I do not think we should be alone anymore."

"I agree," he said. "Let me walk you to the main room, where I am sure Mrs. Bergman and Georgiana are waiting for you. I am sure the preparations for the ball are not yet finalized." He took her elbow and guided her out of the breakfast room and into the main ballroom.

"Fitzwilliam, I do not think I should attend the ball. It will just be more talk among your guests," she said.

"*Our* guests. And remember: no more secrets."

"All right, I am not sure I am ready for the challenge, though," she answered.

"I am not either, but we will face it," he said with confidence.

When Elizabeth and Darcy reached the main ballroom, they settled themselves and appeared calm and appropriate in appearance. Mrs. Bergman and Georgiana were talking, discussing the menu and decorations. Georgiana rushed to Elizabeth, eager to share her plans made so far.

"Miss Bennet, please see what we have decided," she said.

"Yes, I would love to be part of your plans—part of your ball. It will be a lovely party, and I am sure you will be the most beautiful woman and hostess attending." Elizabeth smiled at her while seeing those smiles shared by Mrs. Bergman and her brother.

The day of planning passed quickly. Darcy had retreated to his study to attend to the business of the estate, while the ladies kept to themselves busy with linens, tables, dishes, and glasses. The guests would be arriving in two days, and the staff remained laboring and anxious to receive Miss Darcy's visitors. It had been several months since the last formal gathering, though that had not as spectacular as this ball was expected to be. The servants were anxious to demonstrate their talents to those expected to attend. There was no doubt that even those who did not attend would hear details of the ball.

Elizabeth and Darcy saw little of each other during the day but managed to have a quick dinner together in the late evening. They enjoyed a glass of wine together while sitting next to the fire in Darcy's study.

"It has been a long day, Elizabeth, but knowing you were close by made me feel comfortable today. This is how we should be and will be soon," he said to her.

"Fitzwilliam, I feel so comfortable here. When I first came here, I was so nervous and already homesick, but now it is so different. It is hard to explain."

"I am glad you are happy here, Elizabeth. I will always want you to be happy, but come; it is late, and tomorrow will probably be a very hectic day."

"I know, but I hate for this day to end," sighed Elizabeth.

"I love you, Elizabeth."

"I love you also," answered Darcy.

"Elizabeth, I have been doing some reading regarding our situation. I would like you to consider obtaining an annulment from Wickham. I will contact my solicitor in London, Mr. Fellows, in the morning to inquire into this. I think this is a reasonable and realistic solution for us. What do you think?"

She was quiet for a moment and then responded, "I also have read about the annulment document, though not recently. I overheard my father discussing it with one of his clients. I think it will be difficult for us to obtain, and George will be quite resistant to the thought, but it is certainly something we can contemplate. I certainly would not reject the idea of an annulment from my marriage."

"Good. I will proceed with inquiries in the morning." Without further discussion, they finished their wine, strolled upstairs, said a polite good evening to each other, and retired for the night in their separate bedchambers.

The next day again brought a busy household together, with the servants and staff cleaning, polishing, and cooking. The linens were spread on the tables, and the china, crystal, and silver were laid out. Centerpieces of candles, greens, and ornaments reflected the shine and sparkle of the table settings. Georgiana anticipated the arrival of tomorrow's guests with the hopefulness of a young child at Christmas. Darcy watched her from across the large room, seeing her excitement fill the room with sunshine and fair weather. He smiled and walked over to her, placed his arm around her, and brought her close.

"Oh, brother, how exhilarating this is," said Georgiana. "I am so excited! This will be the most wonderful party we have ever had. I just know it."

"I am sure it will be. You, Mrs. Bergman, and Mrs. Enders have been planning for months for this ball. It will be wonderful. You are very anxious to see your friends again—especially because it may be the last time you will see some of them for a long time."

"Yes, it will be. That is the only sad part of this ball; so many of my friends will be separating from their families and leaving home."

"It is part of growing up, sweetheart," Darcy said quietly.

Georgiana's demeanor changed to a more serious tone when she asked her brother, "What is going to happen to you and Miss Bennet?"

"Georgiana, you do not have to worry about us. Tomorrow is going to be a wonderful night for you. Please just think about the ball and how delightful it will be." As he spoke, he sounded somewhat annoyed with her persistent questions about Elizabeth. "Now please, no more questions about this."

"Brother," she said, now becoming agitated herself, "I deserve an answer to my question. After all, I live here also, and if Miss Bennet is going to join our family, I should be like to be engaged in the conversation. I understand there are complications with your possible union, but I still deserve to know what is going on."

Darcy looked at his sister for several moments, shifted his gaze to the ceiling, and said, "Yes, I suppose you do deserve an explanation. Please come with me to my study, and we will talk." He lowered his eyes to her again, stepped back, and allowed her to pass in front of him, and then they left the room, allowing the staff to continue with their preparations.

Once Darcy was seated at his desk and Georgiana was facing him from an opposite chair, both stared in silent thought. It was Darcy who broke the silence. "Georgiana, dear, I know you have been curious about my relationship with Miss Bennet and I have been reluctant to discuss her with you. You mentioned there are complications, and you are correct about that." He paused before continuing his discourse, now mindlessly looking at the ceiling and rolling a pen between his fingers. He took his eyes off the ceiling and looked directly at his sister. "Miss Bennet is currently married to a most disgusting and dangerous man. He is violent, savage, and desperate for money. He is a gambler, a cheat, and a liar. He is rumored to have killed men for his own gain. Now rumors have spread to London that Miss Bennet is here, under my protection, and I fear he may come here looking for her. Do you understand now my reluctance to discuss this with you? Georgiana, I fear for Miss Bennet's safety and for the safety of all who live and work here."

He paused again before continuing, shifting his gaze back to the pen and desktop. "Sister, I know this man personally. In fact, he once lived here with our parents, you, and me for a short time. His name is George Wickham." Darcy's eyes now stared directly at Georgiana.

Georgiana was silent, absorbing the words spoken to her by her brother. She then said, "I have heard of this man, though I barely remember his name and him being here. He left suddenly—to enter the military, I think. Is this the same man?"

"Yes, it is."

"But how could Miss Bennet marry such an awful person? She is very sweet and kind. I do not understand how she could be associated with such a person."

"George Wickham is a master of deceit," Darcy continued. "He misrepresented himself to Miss Bennet and her family for personal financial gain. Once he realized she had no money, he left her alone to pay his debts. That is why she came here—to earn money to satisfy his creditors."

"Oh, brother, how awful this must be for you both. What will you do now?"

"We must wait for Wickham to present himself here, and I am sure he will. I have made an appeal to Mr. Fellows, our solicitor, to file the documents necessary for an annulment of their marriage."

"An annulment, what is that?" she asked.

His eyes were downcast as he answered her question. "An annulment is a statement from the church's perspective that a marriage ceremony is invalid and the marriage vows were never exchanged. It means a marriage has not occurred or existed. Since no children are involved, Miss Bennet and I feel this is a reasonable and achievable solution to our 'complication,' as you call it. A valid reason does exist for granting the annulment. Miss Bennet was deceived by Mr. Wickham in order to gain her trust. If she had known about his intentions, she would not have agreed to marry him. According to the church's rule, an annulment can be granted. Do you understand?"

"Yes, I think I do," she said slowly.

"Now, if this annulment is not granted, then a divorce will need to be arranged."

"A divorce!" she called out loudly. "Brother, that would be scandal and unheard of. That awful Mrs. Jeffery would love to hear of this. Is there anything else that could be done?"

"Short of George Wickham dying, no, there is no other choice." Both again were silent for several minutes. "Georgiana, I want you to understand that this will not affect your ball tomorrow, but I am sorry to say that I cannot guarantee it will not negatively affect you or your future prospects for marriage."

"Brother, your happiness is as important to me as mine is, and together we will beat Mr. George Wickham at his own game. I am sure of it."

"Yes we will, sweetheart. Now, please, finish your preparations for the ball. Tomorrow will be a long and exciting day for you."

"Thank you, brother. I know all this has been so difficult for you, and I love you for it."

As they finished their conversation, Elizabeth entered the room. Darcy rose quickly from his study chair and walked to her, taking both of her hands into his. Georgiana, embarrassed by their outward affection for each other, lowered her eyes but still managed a smile. Elizabeth glanced to her and then returned her attention to Mr. Darcy.

"It is all right, Elizabeth; I have told my sister everything. She understands."

"I see," she said quietly, obviously embarrassed that her future sister-in-law knew of her marriage to George Wickham.

Georgiana rose from her seat and walked toward the door. She turned back and said, "I will leave you two alone. I wish the best for you, I truly do, and I hope your situation can be resolved quickly." She turned away for them and left the room, closing the door behind her. Elizabeth and Darcy looked at each other.

"Elizabeth, are you well? You look tired. Please come and sit here with me," Darcy said as he guided her toward the settee.

"I am well, but I do admit I am tired—a tired much different from when I worked in the kitchen. All of this has happened so fast and has left me worried about the future for us and our families. George Wickham is out there somewhere, lurking, just waiting to attack like a rabid animal."

"Elizabeth, I feel the same, but George Wickham will not hurt us; that I can promise you."

She smiled slightly while they hugged gently.

After Georgiana left Elizabeth and her brother in the study, she found Mrs. Bergman supervising the final preparation for tomorrow's festivities. Her anticipation continued to be present, but the conversation with her brother left behind a cloud of doubt and worry. As she told her brother, she had heard the name of George Wickham before, but she could not immediately remember where or when she had heard it. She was sure it was nothing, but something regarding his name was uncomfortable and nagging at her.

The annual New Year's ball promised to Georgiana by her brother had been planned for months. The menus, music, decorations, and guests had been discussed and agreed upon by both Mr. Darcy and the senior staff of the manor. At this ball, many of Georgiana's friends from the school she had attended several months prior had been invited and had agreed to her invitation to attend. Family members and friends she knew from London had been invited and responded that they would attend. She had continued to keep up correspondence with her friends and was quite anxious to see them again. Even the staff was eager to see the young men and ladies once more. Their presence always brought life back into the Pemberley estate. Since the death of the elder Mr. Darcy and Lady Anne Darcy, the manor had seemed cold and lonely. The company of so many young people dancing, talking, and laughing always made the rooms of Pemberley come alive again. The orchestra playing lively music after dinner seemed to awaken the quiet walls of Pemberley. The gowns worn by the young women, with their jewelry sparkling, always added elegance to the occasion. The young gentlemen practicing their manners and parading for the ladies brought humor to the adults watching. Approximately one hundred guests, young and old, were expected to attend. Oh, how Mrs. Bergman and Mrs. Enders had planned and looked forward to this yearly occasion.

"Brother, may I speak to you?" Georgiana asked.

"It is late, Georgiana. You need to retire for the night," he said impatiently.

"Fitzwilliam, I need to talk with you, and you need to listen to me," she answered, also with impatience.

"All right, sweetheart, what is it? What is so important that it cannot wait until morning?" he said.

"This afternoon you spoke of a man named George Wickham. I told you then that I have heard the name before. I know I have. I could not recall where or when I heard it, but now I remember."

"Georgiana, come into my room and tell me what you know about George Wickham," he said anxiously. He took her hand, and she followed him into his sitting room adjacent to his bedchamber. A fire was burning, providing just enough heat and light to keep the room comfortable. She sat in a large chair opposite his.

"Sister, now tell me what you know about George Wickham."

She took a deep breath before continuing. "Several weeks ago, when the ladies went into London for shopping—it was the same day you gentlemen went hunting—I saw Mrs. Jeffery. She was dining with several other ladies. She made a point of turning, staring at me, and then talking again with the others. They also turned and stared before returning to their own conversation."

"That, Georgiana, does not imply George Wickham is involved."

"Yes, I realize that, but I also saw her talking to two young men. They were the same young men who were here making a delivery for Mrs. Enders. I overheard Mr. Wickham's name mentioned. Brother, I think they were trying to obtain information about Miss Bennet from Mrs. Jeffery. She is such an awful person; she would gossip to them."

"I see." He paused. "Georgiana, would you recognize these boys again if you saw them?"

"I do not know. I tried not to listen or interfere, but I do remember the name George Wickham was mentioned. Brother, what does this mean?"

"I do not know, sweetheart, but thank you for telling me. Please let me walk you to your bedchamber." He rose from his chair, reached out for her, and hugged her sincerely. He kissed the top of her head, released his hold, and reached for a candle.

"You do not need to escort me to my room, brother. I am fine. Good night." With that she turned and left the room.

Darcy turned back to the fire, his hands clasped behind his back. He sat deep in thought, staring at the flames. He heard a noise, turned, and saw Elizabeth standing at the doorway in her nightclothes.

"So he definitely knows I am here," she said matter-of-factly.

"Yes, it seems so. Did you hear?" he asked.

"Yes. The walls are thinner than you think. What do we do? You know he is going to come here. He will make accusations, repeat scandalous stories, and probably request money or, worse, demand satisfaction."

"George Wickham is too much of a coward for dueling, so please do not think about that. There is nothing we can do now, Elizabeth, except wait. I suspect he will come here and demand money. I am sure we will know soon enough about his intentions."

"I am sure you are right." She turned and started to go back to her bedchamber.

"Elizabeth, I love you," he said quietly.

"I love you too." That was all that needed to be said.

The excitement and anticipation of the New Year's ball started to escalate by midday. The invited guests started to arrive by carriages coming through the gates, anxious to enter Pemberley's open doors and enjoy the conversations they had missed over the past several months. Some of the guests had traveled for days and over several hundred miles to attend the Pemberley ball. Many of those invited were expected to spend the night at Pemberley because of the long distance they had traveled. The servants were well prepared for their guests. As they arrived, the guests hugged and kissed each other with happy greetings. The young ladies laughed and giggled, while the young men boasted of recent heroic adventures. All knew that this could possibly be their last time together before the ladies had their coming-out debuts with promises of marriage and financial gain, while the men would go off to colleges or to fulfill their obligations to the military. Either way, most of them likely would not return to their innocent youth in the next several years.

The evening progressed with dancing and gaiety. Happiness surrounded the young couples with laughter and singing. The accompanying orchestra played music that was enjoyed by both the adults and the younger guests. Darcy and Elizabeth stood apart, admiring the dancing but making no attempts to talk or acknowledge each other. Darcy was dressed in his formal best, while Elizabeth wore a simple, plain gray dress, hoping to elude notice. To an unknowing eye, she resembled a common servant acting as a chaperone while Darcy, the ever vigilant older brother, watched his sister.

Mrs. Bergman, Mr. Hickey, and Mrs. Enders, dressed in their finest clothes, also acted as chaperones, admiring the young ladies and gentlemen enjoying themselves.

Individual conversation among the clusters of guests occurred throughout the afternoon and evening. Georgiana had forgotten about George Wickham for much of the day and evening but was quickly reminded when she again overheard gossip among several of the young guests:

"Is that her, standing next to Georgiana's brother? She is not very pretty."

"Look at that dress; how ugly."

"I heard they were sharing the same bedchamber."

"I know she is still married and that her husband is still living locally."

"My aunt said her husband left her because of her association with Mr. Darcy."

"Her family probably does not want to associate with her either."

"She is just the maid; my uncle regularly visits the maid, if you know what I mean."

They all started to laugh until one of the boys noticed Georgiana watching them. He assumed she had heard the comments but made no immediate interaction to stop the gossip. Georgiana was hurt and disappointed with her friends, but she felt prepared for such an occurrence. She left the gossipers to themselves and proceeded to join others already dancing. One of her favorite friends had asked her to dance, and she eagerly accepted.

"Your gown is beautiful, Georgiana," he said. "You must be the loveliest lady here tonight."

"Thank you," she replied. "My brother gave it to me as a gift for tonight's party."

"Your brother is a very kind and generous man. We all know that. He is honest and takes care of his servants and tenants. No one who lives or works on your estate goes hungry or goes without work or pay."

"Thank you for saying that."

"Georgiana, I know there has been gossip about your family lately, but I must tell you I have never trusted or believed idle gossip. I want you to know that."

"You are a very kind and good friend for saying that."

"It is true, Georgiana. I want you to believe in me and what I say to you. People who talk do not understand you or your family. I want you to know that." She did not reply but smiled and nodded to him.

When they finished their dance, he kissed her hand, stepped back, and slowly turned to walk away. Neither said anything more to each other for the rest of the evening.

The orchestra stopped playing about four in the morning, and the food and dishes were cleared away. Some of the overnight guests had already retired; some had changed their clothes from their formal wear to traveling clothes. When it was time for the guests to leave, both Georgiana and Darcy personally thanked and recognized the carriages as they approached the portico and then pulled away. After all the guests had left, Darcy hugged his sister and asked her how she felt.

"I am tired, brother, but otherwise it was a wonderful party. Thank you so much. You are so kind and generous to me."

"You, sweetheart, are worth whatever I have and more, but I do think we all need to get some rest. You should go upstairs and get some sleep. I will see you to this evening or when you awaken."

"Yes, I am tired." She left her brother standing on the porch and retired to her bedchamber.

Mrs. Bergman was waiting for her upstairs. This was quite unusual, as her personal maid was not in attendance.

"Miss Darcy, did you have a nice time? It was a lovely party, and everyone seemed to be in high spirits."

"Yes, everyone seemed to have a wonderful time," she responded as she was removing her formal attire. "I did hear a few comments regarding my brother and Miss Bennet, but otherwise the evening was perfect."

"Did you ignore the comments?" she asked.

"Yes, I did," Georgiana answered.

"I'm so glad, my dear. Now get yourself into bed for a good rest; you deserve it."

"Thank you, Mrs. Bergman; thank you for everything, and good night."

Once Darcy knew his sister had retired to her bedchamber, he sought out Elizabeth. Despite his having seen her throughout the evening, he had been unable to acknowledge or talk to her. He was frustrated about that but knew their secretive public relationship was necessary for now. Once he knew they would be alone, he searched for her. He found her in the kitchen pantry, putting away dishes and foodstuffs that had not been used. After the party, Elizabeth insisted upon helping in the kitchen and continuing her masquerade as a servant, despite Darcy's protests.

"Elizabeth, I must talk to you," whispered Darcy when he entered the kitchen. Mrs. Enders with the other maids and assistant cooks stared at both of them but quickly turned away when Darcy returned their stares. They stepped out into the cooler hallway. The heat from the kitchen had made Elizabeth's skin red. Her face was damp from sweat.

"Elizabeth, look at me," he said. "We cannot go on like this. I cannot live like this. Tonight's party proved that to me."

"Fitzwilliam, what can we say to each other that will make any difference now?" she asked.

"Elizabeth, what are you talking about?"

"I overheard some of your guests, Georgiana's friends, talking about us—about my marriage and our inappropriate relationship—and saying that I am just the maid so it is acceptable that you have an association with me. They said my family will no longer see me because of all this. There were more comments, but I will not repeat them to you." She spoke flatly, as if her comments were rehearsed. "Fitzwilliam," she said sadly, "I am embarrassed by my behavior both within and outside my marriage vows. My family should be mortified by my conduct. Those children had every reason to say what they did."

"Elizabeth," he said suddenly, holding her upper arms and shaking her slightly. "Those who gossip and spread their evil talk can go to hell! We will not succumb to or be victims to them. Do you understand? I cannot and will not listen to them or have them insult you. Do you understand?"

She was quiet but examined his eyes with intent. "Fitzwilliam, I love you more than any man I could possibly conceive of, despite my underlying concerns with infidelity. I want to be with you. I mean I want to be with you as your wife, not as your companion or mistress. Do you understand?"

"Yes," he said slowly, watching her expression. "Yes, I do. Will you come with me to my bedchamber now?" he asked quietly.

"Yes, I will," she replied without hesitation in the same quiet voice. While holding hands, they ascended the staircase to the third floor, where his bedchamber was located. It was adjacent to the room she had been occupying, but no recognition was made of that. They entered the room, and he quickly closed and bolted the door. It was obvious that the nearby servants were staring in complete astonishment, but neither Darcy or Elizabeth acknowledged them.

"Elizabeth," he said, "you are the most beautiful woman I have ever seen. When you are near me, my heart stops beating and I cannot breathe."

"Fitzwilliam, I am scared. We both know this is wrong."

"Yes, I know, but my heart tells me it is right."

He held her face in his hands and started to gently kiss her lips, eyes, nose, cheeks, and, eventually, her mouth. Her initial impulse was to hold back her desires, but their feelings were strong and undeniable. She responded to his advances, though her guilt was consuming her lust. His touch was strong and not the hard or forceful consuming touch she had suffered at the will of George Wickham. She did not want to compare the two men, but she felt safe and comfortable within the intimate company of Mr. Fitzwilliam Darcy, master of Pemberley. He ran both of his thumbs over her face. His hands then spread across her neck and her shoulders, and eventually down her arms. She shuddered in response. He took both of her hands in his and kissed them.

"Elizabeth," he said, "we must not go any further until we are man and wife, but if we do, we cannot go back. I will not allow anyone to call you a whore or my mistress. I will not let them seduce us with their vulgarity."

"Oh, Fitzwilliam," she said while laying her head against his chest. "I love you, and I trust you."

"Yes," was all he could say. He kissed the top of her head as she continued to lean against him. Several minutes later, he whispered, "I will walk you to your door."

Most of the household members slept during the day after the party, overtired from the evening's ball, but they reconvened by late afternoon. Darcy was first to enter the library at five o'clock. He felt refreshed and animated—ready to face any problems that might lurk ahead regarding George Wickham, but little did he know those problems would soon be at hand. He dressed casually, but not in morning riding attire. He wore dark trousers and boots with a pale yellow silk shirt, buttoned and without a cravat. He also wore a dark green velvet vest without a dinner jacket. He felt comfortable and confident. Thoughts of Elizabeth resurfaced while he read correspondence regarding the estate, making it difficult for him to concentrate. How wonderful it would be if she could be at his side, managing this massive estate. He did not notice anyone else come down the stairs, leaving Darcy alone with his passion for Pemberley and Elizabeth. This was always his most favorite time of the day. He always enjoyed a predinner cocktail, so he poured himself a small whiskey.

34

After several years of absence from Pemberley, George Wickham's single carriage pulled into the main entrance and up Pemberley's long drive to the front gates of the huge mansion estate. The longtime and loyal stableman for Mr. Darcy, Mr. Patrick Hickey, recognized the carriage driver as George Wickham, a man well known by the Darcy family as the deceitful and murderous man who had plagued the Darcy family many years ago. Mr. Hickey knew he was the estranged husband of the woman known to Pemberley as Miss Elizabeth Bennet, the former kitchen maid and current lady friend of his master, Mr. Fitzwilliam Darcy. Remembering the last altercation the elder Mr. Darcy had with George Wickham, Mr. Hickey immediately went to the mansion to alert Mr. Darcy of George of Wickham's expected arrival. It was well known that George Wickham would eventually locate Elizabeth Wickham at Pemberley, but when he actually set foot on Pemberley soil, the immediate notification of his arrival was needed.

Mr. Hickey ran as fast as his short legs could carry him through the kitchen door of the manor. He immediately saw Mrs. Bergman leaving the kitchen and asked her if her could speak to Mr. Darcy concerning a very serious and grave matter. Despite Mr. Hickey's long association with Pemberley, Mrs. Bergman was reluctant to allow him into the kitchen. Mrs. Enders did not allow anyone working in the stables to enter her kitchen for fear of soiling her floors, but Mrs. Bergman could see on Mr. Hickey's face his look of worsening distress.

"Please come in, Mr. Hickey; the master is in his study."

"Thank you, Mrs. Bergman. I must see him immediately. I think you should come too and hear this."

Mr. Hickey rushed past the housekeeper, up a flight of stairs, and down the long hallway to the master's study. He knocked hard on the door, which was immediately answered by Mr. Darcy. He recognized Mr. Hickey's look of urgency as soon as he opened the door.

"Mr. Darcy, sir, forgive me, but Mr. Wickham is driving his carriage up the gravel path directly and approaching the front entrance. As soon as I recognized him, I knew you would want to be alerted immediately."

"Wickham? George Wickham is here now?"

"Yes, sir, I saw him myself and came here as fast as I could."

"Dear God … George Wickham back at Pemberley again," said Mrs. Bergman.

"Thank you, Mr. Hickey," said Darcy. "You were correct in letting us know. I appreciate your quickness in letting me know of his presence. I will take it from here."

"Very well, sir. Is there anything else I can assist you with?"

"No, thank you. You may leave, but keep a sharp eye out for anyone else around here. We cannot be sure that Wickham did not bring anyone else with him."

"Yes, sir, I will." He bowed slightly, turned, and left the study.

"Mrs. Bergman, do you know if Miss Bennet is awake?"

"I do not, sir, but I will check on her immediately."

"Yes, please do, but do not alert her to what has happened. I do not want to alarm her any more than necessary," he said sternly.

"Yes, sir, right away." She turned quickly and immediately left the room, leaving the door ajar.

After Mrs. Bergman left, Darcy started to pace the floor while running his hand through his hair. His thoughts focused on his hatred for George Wickham again. His previous intentions regarding his mother and his recent mistreatment of Elizabeth all started to reappear in his growing anger for his boyhood friend. Darcy's thoughts were interrupted when he heard loud voices coming from the front entrance door. Shouting and cursing began, followed by loud footsteps. The door to the study flew open, and George Wickham entered, followed by Mr. Hickey.

"Well, Darcy, it is good to see you again. How long has it been—ten years or so since your father banished me from these hallowed halls? I can see not much has changed around here."

Wickham looked remarkably older and thinner than when Darcy had seen him last. His clothes were wrinkled, well worn, and covered with dust and dirt from traveling. His boots were military issue but were scuffed and appeared worn. He was in need of a haircut and shave, and a faint odor of alcohol wafted on his breath.

"Darcy, it has been brought to my attention that my wife is in your employ. She seems to have disappeared from her family home about one year ago and somehow turned up on your doorstep. I have been looking for her for quite some time. What a surprise for me to find out she was here—a very interesting situation. Do you agree?"

Darcy did not respond immediately to Wickham's statement but only stared at his adversary's unkempt appearance. He also did not want to unnecessarily provoke Wickham into an altercation that could turn ugly. While Darcy stared, Wickham walked slowly about the room before finally reaching the sideboard. He reached for the crystal decanter and poured a generous amount of whiskey into a matching thick-bottomed tumbler. He turned toward Darcy while raising his glass.

"Share a glass with me, Darcy? I have always appreciated your taste in Irish whiskey."

"What do you want here, Wickham?"

"Why, that should be obvious. I want my wife and the salary she has earned while employed here at your fine home." While speaking, George Wickham spread his arms across the room, exaggerating his words and indicating a grandeur he did not believe existed. "I also understand she has been spending an unusual amount of time with you personally. More time than what a servant would spend with her master. I certainly hope nothing out of your proper etiquette is occurring between the two of you. The scandal could ruin you and your fine name."

"How dare you speak of such things," said Darcy. His face was hot with anger and his fists clenched with rage. George Wickham was a terrible person and was speaking of Elizabeth, the woman he loved, with disrespect. He was furious with George Wickham. All the anger he felt toward this man was starting to come to the surface and boil over. He crossed the room and approached Wickham as if he might strike him, but he stopped short of his assault on him.

"Miss Bennet is a lady and an honest woman unworthy of your companionship."

"Watch it, Darcy; your comments are on the verge of guilt for infidelity," Wickham snickered.

Meanwhile, Elizabeth had awakened from her day's rest and dressed for the evening. Despite the cool evening, the room felt warm and close. She could not shake the feeling that something was wrong. She had heard the front door slam, and the sound of loud voices had drifted upstairs.

"Miss Bennet," said Mrs. Bergman, knocking loudly on her door. "The master has sent me to find you. There is some trouble downstairs. He has requested you stay upstairs for the time being."

"What is wrong? What is going on, and who is here?" Elizabeth asked with sudden concern.

"I am not sure, child, but I am sure the master will take care of the situation," said Mrs. Bergman.

"It is George Wickham; he is here; I just know it. He has found me and wants to take me from here. He could kill Fitzwilliam. That is who is talking downstairs. Please answer me truthfully, Mrs. Bergman."

"Yes dear, it is," Mrs. Bergman answered quietly but with apprehension.

"My God!" was all Elizabeth could say as she clasped her hands to her face. He was here to claim her as his wife and was probably going to take her with him this night. He had threatened to do this, and now the time had come. She had trembled at the thought of his return, fearing his ultimate touch and marital domination. Why did this have to happen? She had been hopeful that he would not find her and she would never have to see or speak to him again. But here he was, speaking with Fitzwilliam in the study regarding her and his intentions. What were they saying? Was he accusing her of infidelity? Surely he could not, but knowing George Wickham, he would make such accusations. It was true she had spent time with Mr. Darcy and they had flirted, but they had not consummated their relationship. Some would say that their behavior was scandalous and that their actions could ruin the reputation of Darcy, Elizabeth, his sister, and her family. Mrs. Jeffery could incriminate them as lovers if she wanted to, and maybe she did to those in London. That was probably how George Wickham had found her—by listening to lies told, and paid for, by those two who came to Pemberley, posing as delivery boys. *Oh, why did he have come here? How could this happen, and what is going to happen now that he has come here?*

Elizabeth left her room with Mrs. Bergman in tow and slowly and quietly walked down the hallway and down the staircase to the study. The door was now shut, but she could hear the loud voices. The conversation was inaudible, but the tone used was unmistakable. Her husband and Fitzwilliam were arguing about her. She wished she could hear their dialogue, but she could not. Her heart was pounding, and her anxiety made her breathing rapid, almost panting. While they were standing outside the door, it opened suddenly, causing Elizabeth to jump back to avoid being stuck. It slammed into the hallway, causing damage to the wall.

"Why there you are, my dear. I heard you were here. I came looking for you, and here you are; how convenient."

The smirk on George Wickham's face made her wince and feel small in his presence. The sound of his voice caused panic in her gut and a feeling of doom and failure. Darcy watched the reunion of his beloved Elizabeth and her estranged husband, George Wickham, with the reality of shock and surprise, which slowly changed to wrath and anger. He felt a lack of control with his emotion. He wanted to step between Elizabeth and her husband and demand he leave his home without her. He feared for their safety if he interfered now. Legally she was his wife, and in all reality, he had to recognize this—at least until he could decide what else he could do. Darcy was forced to turn away, unable to watch the look of hurt and pleading from Elizabeth as he mentally reviewed his immediate options. He had promised her safety from the abusive George Wickham, but at this moment he did not know if he could keep his promise. He feared for her immediate safety. A constable was presently too far away, and he had no immediate access to a weapon. He needed a plan to defuse the situation safely. Elizabeth wanted her beloved Fitzwilliam to stop the madness she was now part of. Unfortunately he could not without causing her physical injury.

"It is good to see you, Elizabeth," said Wickham. "You look well, but of course you would. My old friend here, Fitzwilliam Darcy, and his efficient staff have taken good care of you. But, unfortunately, it is time for you to leave. Please have the butler fetch your coat. You are leaving with me now."

"George," Elizabeth said as calmly as she could, "it is late. Surely we could wait until tomorrow's light."

"Wait? So you could spend more time with my old friend here, Mr. Fitzwilliam Darcy, the grand master of Pemberley? So he could make arrangements for you to sneak off? I think not. We will leave immediately. Now get your coat."

"Where are we going?" she asked.

"We are traveling to London. I have a business appointment there tonight," he answered impatiently.

"Tonight? Why tonight? Can it not wait? Traveling at night can be dangerous," cried Elizabeth in desperation.

"I said we are leaving now," shouted Wickham. He grabbed her arm and pulled her close enough to him for her to smell the whiskey on his breath and the unwashed odor on his skin and clothes. Still holding on to her, he dragged her down the hall to the steps of the front door. He forced her down the steps and into the waiting carriage. Darcy followed closely, knowing that his intervention would cause the situation to become out of control, resulting in harm to Elizabeth. She started to shiver from the cold and her worsening fear. Once inside the carriage, Wickham wrestled with Elizabeth's clothes, reaching under her skirts and grappling with her breasts. She was unable to stop his physical advances. The speed and rocking of the carriage as the horses followed the dark path made her nauseated and dizzy. At one point during the journey to London, she wished the carriage would spill over onto the side of the road. She felt that if she survived the accident, she might be able to forever run away from her husband, who was clearly in a dangerous mood. If she died in the accident, it still would be better than living her life with George Wickham.

Unable to let go of Elizabeth, Darcy rushed to the stables and ordered his horse saddled immediately. The forever loyal and efficient Mr. Hickey had anticipated a possible abduction of Elizabeth and had the fastest and

strongest horse saddled and ready to travel. Darcy was determined to
follow Wickham and Elizabeth into London, if that was indeed where they
were traveling. Darcy was sure George Wickham's business appointment
was a card game with high stakes and hopes of an easy profit. *Why did
he have to come back? Why did he have to take her away?* Darcy had to have
Elizabeth back. He loved her with all his heart and soul and was willing
to follow her anywhere as long as he could have her back. He did not care
about the gossip that would probably occur with their union. Their love
was real and strong, and able to withstand the confabulation of the evil
George Wickham.

It was well into the night when George Wickham and Elizabeth arrived
at the Northside Inn, located near the waterfront. Wickham's appointment
was indeed with three men, all with uncertain and disreputable pasts. A
card game was to start within an hour of their arrival. George stepped
down from the carriage and started toward the entrance of the inn.
He ignored Elizabeth and left her to step down from the carriage; she
nearly fell into the dark, muddy street. She could hardly see where she
was walking, but she followed Wickham into a dirty, smoke-filled room.
The tables were covered with empty glasses of liquor and partially filled
steins of beer. Men and women of questionable reputation filled the
room. The smell of unwashed bodies and urine immediately permeated
Elizabeth's nostrils. Several of the patrons stopped their conversations
and stared openly at Elizabeth. Many snickered, knowing of her marital
status with the unfaithful and adulterous George Wickham, thinking
of how stupid she must be to have actually married the disreputable
scoundrel. Elizabeth looked about the room for Wickham, finally seeing
him speaking with the three men he was to meet. Wickham saw her and
called out to her loudly to come over to join him.

"Elizabeth, get over here, and hurry up," he shouted. Elizabeth again
looked about the room, and she slowly crossed over to Wickham. Two
scantily dressed women approached Elizabeth and fingered her fine dress
and lace bodice. They had never seen such fine material. Their known
habits of servicing the male patrons left no doubt to Elizabeth that they
would steal her clothing if given the chance. Since she had sold all of her
jewelry months before, she did not have to worry about her personal
property. Unfortunately, she was wearing the pearl necklace given to her

from Fitzwilliam on Christmas day, but it was hidden underneath the collar of her dress. She hoped no one would notice she was wearing it.

She slowly approached Wickham, who was already drinking whiskey. He was laughing with the other men but stopped abruptly when she approached.

"This, gentlemen, is my dear estranged wife. We have been separated for a while but have found each other again. Apparently she has been staying with my old friend Mr. Fitzwilliam Darcy at his fine home, Pemberley. I found her there just this evening and persuaded her to accompany me here. Isn't that true, my dear?" He reached out, grabbed her face, and turned it toward him. He then noticed the gold chain around her neck and reached for it. "What is this, my dear? A present from the man you have been sleeping with while I was gone? I always knew you were a whore, and he a coward and cheat. I will take that from you. At least you are good for something." He pulled the neck chain from her, breaking it and causing her pain. A deep red welt formed around her neck.

"Very nice," he said, examining the large pearl. "At least he has good taste." She could not look at his eyes, but when she finally did, all she saw was hate and disgust for the man she had mistakenly married. When she did not answer him, he let go of her and pushed her aside, causing her to make a misstep and nearly fall.

"Come, gentlemen." Wickham called out. "Let us proceed with our business." He turned to Elizabeth. "Elizabeth, dear"—he reached out to grab her upper arm—"please come along; you just might pick up some useful information. It is about time you learned of my business and not that of your new lover, the honorable Mr. Darcy," he said with sarcasm as he dragged her into the room with him.

She followed reluctantly and without resistance into a smaller dark room holding only three tables. It took several minutes for her eyes to adjust to the dim, smoke-filled room. When they did, she saw several women kissing and caressing the few male patrons in the room. She had heard of women prostitutes but had never seen any before. She had never seen what they did for their customers. The sight frightened her, and she turned away.

"Come and sit down, my dear, and do keep your mouth shut. Like I said, maybe you will learn something of my business. And don't just stand there; pour me a drink!"

A bottle of whiskey was sitting on the table the other men were occupying. She found a used glass nearby and poured the liquor until the small glass was half full. She handed the glass to Wickham with an unsteady hand. He took it from her and drank its contents in one swallow, keeping the glass next to him. She then sat quietly in a chair several feet away from him, not wanting to know anything of the card game he was about to play. The cards were dealt, and the game started. A female prostitute walked up to Wickham and put her arms around his chest and shoulders, whispering in his ear. He laughed and kissed her bare shoulder. She released him and walked away slowly, looking back over her shoulder and smiling. Elizabeth watched but was too stunned to make any comment or reaction. While sitting there, her thoughts drifted to Fitzwilliam Darcy and the comfort and safety he would have given her if this had not happened. Where was he, and why had he not stopped this? She was sure he would not abandon her. Were all his words of love false like George Wickham's? Had she been a fool again? Why did this happen, and how could she possibly escape?

She listened to the conversations throughout the room without hearing the words. The laughter and movements exchanged between the men and women made her uncomfortable. Suddenly she was brought back to reality when George Wickham shouted, "Elizabeth, make yourself useful and pour me another drink. Hurry up, woman!" She did as she was told, hoping he would drink himself into a stupor; then she could possibly escape.

As the evening progressed, she observed George Wickham's temper becoming short and his movements becoming awkward. She knew the whiskey must have been affecting him, but she would say nothing to him about this. During the short time they lived together, she had learned when to keep her thoughts to herself and her mouth shut. His temper became violent when he drank, and she had suffered from its consequences in the past. She noticed that the bottle of whiskey was now gone, not sure who had consumed it. She rose quietly and slowly and walked to the sideboard. She found another half-full bottle and brought it to the table. She started to pour its amber liquid into his glass, but Wickham grabbed the bottle from her.

"Give me that," he ordered. With his unsteady hands, he spilled the bottle's contents onto the table, soaking the cards that had already been played. "You stupid fool!" Wickham shouted at Elizabeth. "Look what you have done now. You have never been good for anything." He turned quickly toward her and slapped her hard across her cheek. She staggered backward but maintained her balance by readily reaching out and grabbing a nearby table located behind her. Once steady, she stood upright and touched her face. It felt hot and wet. When she removed her hand, she saw blood from a cut on her lip. A reddened bruise on her cheek also arose immediately, causing pain and swelling. She did not speak but again sat quietly in the chair. The whiskey was soon forgotten, and the card game resumed. No one gave Elizabeth a second look.

The conversation between the card players grew louder. She had noticed there was no longer any laughter or kissing between the other couples sitting in the room. She turned back toward the card game and saw that visual exchanges had grown serious and intense. George Wickham was shifting his eyes between the cards he was holding and the other players at the table. Elizabeth had noticed a large sum of money lying in the middle of the table with more being added as the game progressed. She knew the game had taken a serious, and probably dangerous, turn. So this was how George Wickham made and lost his money. She could tell by his demeanor that he was losing money, though he continued to play. She grew more nervous and frightened, suspecting that trouble and violence could soon occur. The tension in the room began to grow, and the air became hot and close. George Wickham was now perspiring.

One of the card players called for a raise and tossed several more coins onto the table. Another player met the raise and contributed to the money pile. George Wickham was the next to call or fold. He looked intently at his cards but said nothing. A shift occurred under the table, which Elizabeth assumed were legs and feet becoming restless. She was wrong.

Taking Elizabeth by surprise, one of the card players stood up quickly and loudly kicked his chair away from the table. The other two players also stood, but slowly and quietly. All three players stared intently at George Wickham, waiting for him to make his move.

"Well, Wickham, what do you have to say for yourself?" said one of the players. The player's eyes were half closed, and his teeth tightly held a short, fat unsmoked cigar. His dirty clothes, unwashed body, and increasing impatience added to Elizabeth's growing fear.

Wickham continued to stare at his cards, making no eye contact with anyone in the room. The others, all experienced players, knew he did not hold a winning hand, but they continued to request he show his cards. He casually looked down at his money, picked up a few coins, and tossed them toward the large winners' pot. He placed his cards on the table. When they showed a straight flush, a winning hand, the other players knew Wickham had cheated. He looked up at the others players with a sneer on his face. The players stared back. Elizabeth did not know what had transpired, but she realized that George Wickham had cheated. She suddenly realized the movement she had heard under the table was not innocent but instead was the changing of the cards to produce a winning hand for her husband.

"Wickham, you are a cheat and a liar," stated one of the players.

"Yes, I saw him draw his last card from under the table," shouted another.

The third player agreed. "Yes, I saw it also. There is no possibility he could have been dealt this hand. He must have switched cards when the whiskey was spilled, and his whore probably helped him." Elizabeth looked up in sheer panic and did not know what to say or do. A look of terror was on her face, and she rapidly shook her head.

"No, sir, I promise you I did not do anything. I do not know what is happening here. Please, sir, I do not know what you are talking about," Elizabeth said in a frightened whisper. She started to stand but sat down again when Wickham turned to her with hate written on his face.

"Shut up, bitch!" yelled Wickham. The couple in the corner slowly stood and slipped out the door and into the main room, where they alerted others in the main room of what had happened. All conversation had stopped in the room, and a deadly calm had developed, as all in the room knew that the accusations of cheating would cause hostility. Patrons were starting to leave the tavern, afraid of being caught in possible crossfire among the players.

During the evening, no one had noticed that a tall, dark-haired, well-dressed man had entered the tavern. Darcy looked slowly about the main room, looking for Elizabeth, but he did not immediately see her.

"What is going on in there?" one of the tavern room guests asked the couple who had just left the smaller room.

The man answered, "That liar George Wickham is in there with three other card players who have just accused him of cheating. I suspect someone is going to get hurt."

"Maybe Wickham will finally learn his lesson and get what he deserves," said a woman with a laugh. She was the same woman who had whispered in George Wickham's ear earlier in the night.

"Excuse me, ma'am," called out Darcy. "Did you see a woman in there, possibly with Wickham? She has dark red hair and is wearing a fine green dress?" Darcy did not realize it, but Elizabeth's dress was similar to the one she had described to him when telling of how she first met George Wickham nearly one year before. So much had happened since then.

"There is a woman in there, all right; he says she's his wife. Ha! Probably just another one of George Wickham's whores," she answered. "She certainly don't look like no whore though." Laughter erupted throughout the tavern despite the tension that was growing. Darcy approached her as she continued to laugh.

"Tell me, the woman in there, is she all right? Do you know if she has been harmed at all?"

"How would I know? Besides, I don't care. Why would I care about one of George Wickham's whores? He's got plenty of them," she said causally. "He might have roughed her up a might, but otherwise she's good enough for another round."

Darcy looked nervously at the door leading into the small room where the card game had occurred. The door was closed, so he had no idea what was happening in there. His concern for Elizabeth was escalading rapidly, but he did not know how to pursue her recovery without injury occurring. He needed to do something to help her, but he also did not want to worsen her chances of being harmed by barging into an uncertain situation. What could he do? How could this situation have come this far?

The laughter in the main room of the tavern had died down, and the patrons of the main room had resumed their usual conversations and drinking. No one was concerned that an innocent woman was probably being threatened by her violent and dangerous husband in a situation worsened by liquor and a bad hand of cards. Darcy decided to walk slowly toward the door of the smaller room. As he grew closer, he could hear shouting coming from within the room. He heard the sound of heavy furniture being moved and possibly thrown. Darcy was unable to hear specific words spoken, but he certainly understood the situation was becoming worse. Suddenly, to everyone's surprise, shots from a handgun were heard. All conversation stopped in the main room. Despite guns being fired at establishments such as these at fairly regular intervals, everyone was anxious to know what had happened. The barkeeper immediately dropped his cleaning rag; grabbed his weapon, which was already loaded; moved from around the bar; and raced toward the closed door. He was followed closely by Mr. Darcy.

"Someone has summoned the constable," shouted the tavern owner. "Clean up the money on those tables, and you women get lost." The door was opened by the barkeeper, and both he and Darcy and stared at the horrid sight. The air was thick with cigar smoke mixed with the sulfurous scent of burned gunpowder from the pistol, making visibility difficult. A table was overturned, and the chairs had been thrown against the wall. The stench that emanated from the room was foul and strong. Money and cards, both soaked with whiskey, were scattered about the floor. George Wickham was lying on the dirty floor, blood spilling from underneath his body and spreading across the floor. A large-caliber bullet entrance was obvious in the center of his chest. His blank, half-closed, lifeless eyes stared upward toward the ceiling, confirming his obvious demise. One of the men Wickham had been playing cards with was still holding the smoking gun, pointing it directly at the now dead George Wickham. The other man was busy picking up the money, attempting to hide it from view. It had dropped to the floor from the overturned table. Neither card player showed any expression of remorse at the loss of their card-playing adversary, George Wickham.

The man holding the gun stated, "A man who cheats at cards deserves the consequences becoming him." He concealed the gun from the others, turned away from the body on the floor, and faced his partner, who was still picking up the money. "Make sure you get all of it; he owes me plenty this time."

"Hold on there, all of you," shouted the barkeeper. "The constable has been summoned. He'll want to talk with the likes of you two, so you had better get out of here while you can."

"Then I'll tell him exactly what happened," called out one of the bystanders. "That bastard, George Wickham is a liar and cheat. He pulled cards from under the table. This time he didn't get away with it. He got exactly what he deserved. We'll tell the constable that too!"

Elizabeth had been standing against the far wall during the altercation. She had wanted to be as far away from George Wickham and his card-playing associates as possible. She did not know how she had gotten to the wall, but the accusations and resulting event happened so quickly that she must have instinctively reacted to the shooting by bracing herself against the far wall. The last she remembered, she was sitting in a chair, not far from her husband's side. Now that he was dead, she could not speak or move. The shock of the evening's events were bottled and corked inside her. It wasn't until Darcy rushed to her side and held her close that she slumped to the floor, unconscious.

Darcy briefly and quickly examined her limp body for any obvious injuries. He found none but continued to hold her tightly. Her were skirts spread about the floor, her legs tucked close to her body. Her color was pale, and her eyes were closed.

He held her close and after several minutes whispered, "Elizabeth, are you injured? I am here now; everything will be all right. Do you hear me? I am here now. It is all over. I will take care of you." He kept whispering to her, hoping she would hear his words, while cradling her like a baby. "Elizabeth, please wake up. I am here now. You are safe." He was starting to panic, hoping she was not hurt during the shooting and scuffle. She batted her eyes for a moment, starting to awaken, until she was able to focus and see Darcy looking down at her.

She mumbled briefly, "Where am I? What happened? Fitzwilliam, is it really you?"

"Yes, my dear; I am here. You are safe with me now," he answered while holding her head close to his.

Again she did not respond immediately, but she finally had the strength to ask, "What has happened? I feel so shaky. I am cold and tired. Please tell me."

"There has been an accident, dear. George Wickham has been wounded but is being attended to by the tavern owner. How are you feeling? Are you hurt?"

"I do not know. My arm hurts, and it feels hot," she said.

With reluctance, Darcy allowed himself to look at her chest, breasts, abdomen, and lower body more closely. He saw no evidence of blood or injury. When he did inspect the arm closest to him, however, he noticed blood seeping from the sleeve of her dress.

Afraid of frightening her, he said with purpose, "Elizabeth, there is some blood on your sleeve. Let me look at your arm now. He loosened his grip on her, and slowly inspected the arm that was causing her pain. Her sleeve was torn, and indeed blood was oozing from a laceration on her upper arm. He could see it was not a severe wound, but a shard of glass from a broken whiskey glass was protruding from her arm.

"Elizabeth, dear," he said calmly, "it appears you have a piece of glass embedded in your arm. I am going to remove it, and it may be painful. Do you understand?"

"Yes, I do," she replied. "Please do what you must to remove it. I trust you."

Darcy searched their immediate surroundings and noticed a rag used to clean tables lying on the floor close by. It was within his reach, and he was able to grasp it with one hand while continuing to hold Elizabeth with the other. The rag did not appear wet or dirty. He slowly released his grasp on Elizabeth and laid her gently on the floor. Using the rag, he grasped the glass and gently but firmly pulled the remnant from her arm. She winced from the pain but did not call out from the discomfort. He wrapped the rag around her arm, maintaining pressure against the wound. The seepage of blood stopped almost immediately. Tears slowly ran down her cheek while she searched for his face. She watched him for a brief moment before turning her head away and closing her eyes. He dropped the glass shard and carefully tied the rag around her arm. He gently held her, whispering to her, "It's all over now; do you hear me? It's over. I love you."

The constable, barkeeper, and tavern owner entered the room, taking in the men and women, and finally focusing on the dead body lying in the middle of the floor. Darcy continued to hold Elizabeth, but she was sitting up, leaning against the back wall. The card players continued to stand, alternating stares between the constable and the lifeless body of George Wickham.

"What has happened here?" called out the constable. Patrons from the main room started to spill into the smaller room, where George Wickham lay dead on the floor. A few whispered accusations of cheating and infidelity, while most stared without emotion. Cheating at cards with a resulting shooting death was not an unusual event in some disreputable establishments located in the bowels of London. This was one of those places.

"I said," he called out again, "What happened here? Who fired the shot?"

"It's that bastard George Wickham again, sir," answered one of the women. "He came here to get rich, and instead he got dead!" She laughed. Others in the room also laughed.

"That's enough, all of you," he commanded. "Now I ask again, what happened here?"

One of the men looked nervously about the room and then said, "Well, sir, we was playing an innocent game of cards. George Wickham here got to drinking and started slapping around his wife." He pointed to Elizabeth, who was sitting against the wall, still wrapped in Darcy's arms. "I demanded a call of his cards, and he reached under the table and pulled up an ace and a king—cards that I know could not be in the deck. You know what I mean? The man was a cheat and a liar. Everyone here knows that."

"Anyone else have anything to say? You there"—he pointed to one of the suspected prostitute women—"what did you see?"

"Like he said, sir, George Wickham was cheating. I seen him do it," she answered.

The constable paused and looked around the room again until he focused on Elizabeth, pointing at her with his baton. He stared for a few moments, and then, stepping toward her, he asked, "Are you this man's wife?" now pointing to George Wickham's body.

Darcy called out to the constable, "Sir, can you see this woman has been injured. She needs to seek a physician's care and is unable to answer your questions. Let us leave here now. We will be able to answer your questions later, but not now." Darcy continued to hold Elizabeth tightly, watching for a possible worsening of her health.

"Who are you?" asked the constable.

"I am Mr. Fitzwilliam Darcy of Pemberley. Mrs. Wickham is in my employ. I am here to take her back to Pemberley so she may be looked after," he said.

The constable looked about the room and then focused on Elizabeth again. "Let me ask you this, woman," he said. "Are you indeed this man's wife?" He nodded to the body on the floor.

"Yes, I am," she whispered back, with her head buried in Darcy's shoulder.

"Did he cheat at cards like these folks said?"

"Yes, he did," she answered.

"How do you know that?" he asked back.

She paused momentarily. "I saw him do it," she answered in a whisper.

"I see," he said with hesitation, not sure how this well-dressed woman could be involved with a man like George Wickham. "Anybody else?" he called out. The room remained quiet, and no one else spoke. "All right, get this body out of here and clean this place up now. I don't want any more trouble in here tonight, you people hear me? I'll come back and arrest the whole lot of you." He did not wait for an answer but left without turning back. The tavern keeper followed the constable out.

"Officer," whispered the tavern keeper, "if you come back in the morning, I'm sure we can work something out pertaining to any wrongdoings that may have been going on here tonight."

"I would expect my usual pay. I will talk to you later. Like I said, clean up this mess tonight."

"Yes sir, and thank you sir. Good night," answered the tavern keeper.

"Elizabeth, please let me help you up. We need to leave here and get back to Pemberley. This is all over now; there is nothing left for us to do." She looked up at him and then turned toward the body, saying, "What about him?"

"I will take care of this; you do not need to worry. Please, dear, let us go home," he whispered, being careful no one else in the room could overhear.

"Yes, please take me home," she said, lifting her face to him.

He stood slowly, careful not to disturb the rag tied to her arm. Once he was sure the bleeding would not restart, he helped her up.

"Please, Elizabeth, just stand for a moment. You may be dizzy."

"No, I am fine, really," she said as she pushed her hair back out of her face. At some point during the evening, her hair had fallen down, and it was now cascading across her shoulders and back. She looked at Wickham's body and said, "My God, Fitzwilliam, how did all his happen?"

"It was an inevitable end for him. Please, Elizabeth, do not look at this. We should leave now."

"Yes, we need to get back to Pemberley." She carefully stepped around George Wickham's body, with Darcy holding her about the shoulders. She lowered her head as she passed into the main room. Little conversation was occurring while most of the patrons watched as the couple passed. Darcy stopped briefly to speak quietly to the tavern owner.

"Please make arrangements with the local undertaker. My solicitor will make contact with you in the morning to prepare for his disposal."

"Yes, sir, Mr. Darcy, sir; we can do that," he said as Elizabeth and Darcy left the tavern.

"Who was that man?" asked one of the patrons, who was watching Darcy and Elizabeth leave.

"That is Mr. Darcy of Pemberley. He is very rich—owns most of the farmland north of the city. George Wickham's wife works for him. She's one of the cooks there."

"I don't believe that for one minute," commented one of the women. "Not the way those two look at each other. I've seen that look before."

35

Elizabeth and Darcy stepped out in the near darkness of London as dawn was nearing. The air was cold, and a fine snow had fallen during the night. Darcy's horse was still tied to a post with several of his groomsmen standing watch. A carriage had been brought from Pemberley by Mr. Hickey to bring home the master and Miss Bennet. He had felt confident that Mr. Darcy would find Miss Bennet and bring her back to Pemberley and the family.

The couple walked as quickly to the carriage as their tired legs would allow. Elizabeth's legs were shaking—not from the cold but from energy expended. Darcy continued to hold tightly to Elizabeth's uninjured arm. Exposure to the cold air finally caused her to shiver. A brisk wind started, and Elizabeth tried to rub her arms against the cold but could not. The blood from her arm had dried, causing the rag to adhere to her skin. It was slightly uncomfortable, causing her to be aware of its existence.

"Elizabeth, are you in pain?" Darcy asked her.

"No, not really. The bandage is uncomfortable, and I am cold, but I am not in pain."

"Please, let me wrap my coat around you. We need to get you into the carriage and back home. I want to take you away from this wretched place and everything in it," he said more to himself than to Elizabeth.

"Yes," she answered while stepping up to the carriage, turning slightly to face him. "We need to get home." Neither showed any emotion as they stepped up into the carriage just before it pulled out into the near dawning light.

They rode silently back from London to Pemberley; the nearly two-hour trip was awkward for both of them. Neither Darcy nor Elizabeth knew what to say to each other. Elizabeth felt exhausted. Her eyes drifted downward with the gentle rocking of the carriage. Eventually she leaned against Darcy's shoulder and fell into a light sleep. Darcy, though, did not sleep. He could not stop the night's events from penetrating his thoughts. Seeing Elizabeth exposed to Wickham's darkest behavior made him seethe with anger. He had known George Wickham as a boy and now had seen for himself the monster George Wickham had become, but to expose Elizabeth to the sights in the tavern tonight was inexcusable. He wanted so much to protect her from the ugliness of sleazy taverns, but tonight he had not done so. He had failed Elizabeth after he had promised to protect her and provide her a safe and comfortable life. Tonight her life had been in peril and he had done nothing to defend her against her despicable husband. The only good event of tonight was Wickham's death, which had freed Elizabeth from his evil grip.

The carriage arrived back to Pemberley by midmorning, at which time the sun was passing above the tops of the trees. The horses had remained steady throughout the trip, but their fatigue was certainly evident. As they pulled up to the front portico, groomsmen immediately approached the carriage and opened the door.

"Elizabeth, dear," Darcy whispered when the coach stopped. "We are home now." She awoke immediately, clearly startled. "It is all right, Elizabeth; we are home now." Darcy exited the coach first, turned back toward Elizabeth, and helped her step down from their long ride. With his arms around her waist, he steadied her, anticipating her stumbling or falling. As the carriage and horses were led back to the stables, Darcy helped Elizabeth up the entrance stairs and into the mansion's vestibule. Both were tired, but Elizabeth's exhaustion was consuming her. Both her arm injury and the events of the night worsened her plight. As they stepped farther into the mansion, Mrs. Bergman rushed up to them, eager to assist in any way.

"Mr. Darcy, Miss Bennet, how glad I am to see you both," she said with fervor. "Is everything all right? Is it settled?" she asked. As soon as she finished her question, she could sense that everything was not all right and that something horrible had happened.

"No, Mrs. Bergman, we are not all right," Darcy said quietly to her. "Mr. Wickham has been killed—killed for cheating at cards. Unfortunately, Miss Bennet witnessed the whole affair. She has been hurt, and she is expended from tonight's events." Darcy then turned toward Elizabeth as if to speak to her but stopped when he saw how withdrawn she looked.

"My God, how awful," Mrs. Bergman said while eyeing Elizabeth. Elizabeth's head was bent downward, and her arms hung limply at her sides.

Elizabeth glanced up briefly at Mrs. Bergman and managed a slight smile. Her arm was starting to ache, and she reached for the wound with her uninjured hand.

"Elizabeth, dear," Darcy whispered. "I think you should retreat upstairs and rest. You are exhausted; you need to lie down." He then called out to several of the male servants, "Please help Miss Bennet upstairs, and Mrs. Bergman, assist her with a hot bath. I am sure it will help her feel better and help her rest. Her arm will need attention also."

"Mr. Darcy," said Mrs. Bergman while placing a calming hand on his arm, "I will take care of her. Now, please, you also need to rest."

"Thank you for your concern, Mrs. Bergman. I will rest, but first I must attend to Mr. Wickham's personal matters and funeral. I promised Miss Bennet I would make all the necessary arrangements."

"Yes, of course," she replied. She called out to several servant boys who were nearby. "You two boys; hurry and bring hot water upstairs to Miss Bennet's bath. Do it now." Both boys acknowledged Mrs. Bergman's orders and hurried off to the kitchen, where hot water was always ready. Mrs. Bergman put a comforting arm around Elizabeth's waist and gently steered her toward the stairway. Together they walked slowly up to Elizabeth's room.

Darcy watched Elizabeth ascend the stairway, but once she was behind closed doors, he returned to his study. Mr. Hickey had returned from the stables after personally seeing to it that his master's horses were watered, fed, and wiped down. Darcy was pacing impatiently when he entered the study.

"Mr. Hickey, thank you for following us to London last night. Your arrival with the carriage and retrieval of my horse were very welcome."

"Yes, sir, you are very welcome," he answered.

"Mr. Hickey," Darcy said while writing at his desk, "I need to send a message to my cousin Richard. He has connections with the military. I wish to have Mr. Wickham's body returned to His Majesty's Royal Army for interment. Actually, they can do whatever they wish with him, as long as he is out of London and away from here. I also have a note for my solicitor regarding tonight's circumstances."

"Amen to that, sir." Mr. Hickey nodded. "I'll see the message gets to him immediately, and good riddance to him." Darcy made no further comment but quickly finished his correspondence and handed it to Mr. Hickey.

"Please stay for a reply and return as soon as possible. I wish to give Miss Bennet some sense of closure after she has rested. I also wish to send word to Miss Bennet's family in Meryton. They need to be aware of her current situation. I am inviting them to come and stay at Pemberley for as long as they need. At a time like this, she should have her family nearby."

"Yes, sir, I'll be back rightly, and I'll send one of our fastest messengers to Meryton," Mr. Hickey answered. "You should have a reply by tomorrow nightfall." He took the sealed envelope from Mr. Darcy and secured it in his coat pocket. He left the study looking back at the tired and melancholy look on his master's face.

Elizabeth and Mrs. Bergman reached the dressing room adjacent to her bedchamber. The room did not have an outside light source, but the adjourning door was open, allowing light to enter the room. Elizabeth walked slowly into the bedchamber, which was light and cheerful. The windows had been opened slightly, permitting some fresh air to enter the room. She looked at herself in the full-length mirror and was shocked by what she saw. The woman in the reflection had suddenly turned ten years older and was wearing a dirty, torn, and bloodstained dress. Her hair had fallen and was knotted. She had dried beer, sweat, and the smell of whiskey and smoke upon her. She turned to Mrs. Bergman, who was watching her.

"Oh, Mrs. Bergman, it was just awful. Mr. Wickham took me to a London public house where he was meeting men who gamble at cards. There were women who knew him. It was apparent from their behavior that he knew them also—intimately. Do you understand what I am saying?"

"Yes, my dear, I do," she replied slowly. Mrs. Bergman could feel Elizabeth's deep sorrow and near defeat as she summarized the evening's events.

"He was drinking heavily, yelling, cursing, and being angry with the other gamblers. Then he cheated during the card game and was shot dead. One minute he was standing up, and the next, he was bleeding and dead on the floor. Oh, Mrs. Bergman, it was terrible. There was blood all over the floor and table we had been sitting at. Then the constable came. You know, I have never, ever seen a constable before, much less the inside of a public house. I have never seen women like that before either." Elizabeth seemed to be talking to herself more than to Mrs. Bergman. Her voice wavered, but no tears were spent.

"Please, dear, let me help you get undressed and ready for your bath. After that, you can rest. I need to clean and re-dress your arm wound also. In fact, the bathing tub should be ready by now."

"Thank you," was all Elizabeth could whisper. Elizabeth, with Mrs. Bergman's help, undressed slowly. She experienced difficulty due to fatigue and general myalgia. She stepped into the warm bath but immediately felt chilled. It seemed to take several minutes for her to feel warm again. Extreme exhaustion was starting to take over, and she could hardly lift her arms out of the water. The rag tied to her arm had loosened and fallen into the water. Elizabeth did not notice, but Mrs. Bergman did and retrieved the blood-soaked bandage from the water and placed it in a burning receptacle. The skin around the laceration was bruised, but otherwise the wound did not appear red or angry. Mrs. Bergman was relieved that no bleeding had reoccurred in the warm water. She turned back to Elizabeth only to find her nearly asleep in the water. She needed to wash Elizabeth's hair to remove the stale smell. She did this quickly and wrapped her hair in a towel. A fire had been started in Elizabeth's bedchamber, and her nightclothes had been laid out close to the warm fire. She hoped the warm clothes would help relieve some of Elizabeth's tension. Mrs. Bergman was anxious to dry Elizabeth's hair before she retired. She would not want her to sleep with wet hair and catch cold. She helped Elizabeth out of the tub, got her dressed, and wrapped a heavy, warm robe about her. While sitting by the fire, she combed out Elizabeth's hair to remove any tangles or possible remnants of glass. She was turned away from the door but heard a soft knock, calling attention to their visitor.

"Excuse me, ladies," Darcy whispered. "I wish to check on Elizabeth and make sure she is all right."

"She will be fine now that she is home; it may take a while, but she will be all right," Mrs. Bergman said with certainty. "I will leave you two alone." She handed the comb to Darcy and quietly left the room.

As soon as Mrs. Bergman left the room, Elizabeth reached out her hand to Fitzwilliam. He took it and kissed her fingers. He pulled close a nearby chair and sat next to her.

"How is your arm? I see Mrs. Bergman replaced the bar rag and put on a decent bandage."

"She did. She is such a wonderful person. I do not know what I would do without her. She has been so kind to me all these months I have been here. She has believed in me, and despite all that happened last night, she still cares for me."

Darcy could not look at Elizabeth's face, and with a sad tone he said with sincerity, "Elizabeth, I failed you. I had promised to protect you, and last night I did not. You were taken against your will by a monster, subjected to the evils of London's darkest circles, injured, and then forced to witness a murder—the murder of your own husband. I am so sorry. Can you ever forgive me?" After he finished, he looked up at her and saw the most beautiful woman he had ever seen, looking deep into his soul.

"Oh, Fitzwilliam, how can you say such things? My husband—excuse me, my late husband—was an evil man who thought of no one but himself. It was his actions, not the lack of yours that caused the events of last night and, ultimately, his death. There is nothing more we can say or do about this now."

Darcy buried his head in her hands and slightly wept. She did not speak and allowed him to display his grief—grief not for George Wickham but for his own thoughts of failure.

Finally she said, "Fitzwilliam, we are both safe now. We are both back home, and last night's events have passed. Sir, we are both tired. We need to rest; then we can both think clearly."

"Yes, of course you are right," he said quickly, still unable to look at her face.

"Fitzwilliam, please look at me. I love you, and I hope you still feel the same. Last night was so vile; you must think of me as one of those trollops forced to work in the back rooms of taverns. That is what George Wickham thought of me. My working to pay his debts and 'servicing' him whenever he required was all I was good for. I am ashamed of who I am, and I embarrassed you last night also. It is I who needs forgiveness."

"Elizabeth, you are wrong about that," Darcy suddenly said, now looking directly into her eyes. "You are beautiful, kind, sensitive, and considerate. I love you with all my heart, and I want you to be the mistress of Pemberley, now and forevermore—not as my trollop but as my wife."

Both were silent, and then Elizabeth said, "But we are from such different worlds."

"You possess the most charm and decency of any woman whom I wish to associate with. Marrying for money means nothing to me."

"That, sir, is because you have considerable wealth and I have nothing. In fact, I have less than nothing. Remember: I must pay back George Wickham's debts, or at the least pay back my father and uncle."

"That, ma'am, I would gladly pay for you. Or, if necessary, I would give away my wealth to have you as my wife."

Tears slowly flowed down her face, as she did not know what to say. "Sir, you speak words I cannot comprehend. You, the master of Pemberley, would give up everything—your wealth, pedigree, and station in society—for me?"

"Yes, I would, if it allowed you to be with me forever."

Elizabeth looked down for a brief moment until their eyes met again. She knew at that moment that their hearts and souls would be entwined forever.

"Speaking of your father, I have written to your family, telling them about Wickham. I have invited them, and your aunt and uncle, to come to Pemberley and stay with us. I would like to meet them and have them to know me and my family. I want them to realize that I truly love you and will honestly and gently take care of you."

"I have said before that we are from such different worlds, and you may be shocked to learn of mine," she said.

"Yes, but I will do whatever I can to have our two worlds come together."

"I do not deserve you," she said.

"Yes, you do. Now I want you to get some sleep. We can talk again this evening; now please let me help you up and get into bed."

"Thank you," she answered. He helped her up, careful not to disturb her bandage, and walked her to the bed.

"Before you lie down, let me braid your hair; it is still somewhat wet."

She looked at him with shock. "You know how to braid hair?"

"Of course. Remember: my sister was ten years old when our mother died. I learned to do many things for her after Mother passed. I am a man of many talents, and I still have a few secrets of my own."

"I believe you do." Elizabeth smiled. She turned her back to him while he competently braided her long red hair. He tied the end with a ribbon that had been left on her bedside stand.

"There, all done. Care to inspect my work?" he asked with a smile.

"No, I am sure it is fine. But please be careful, sir; I may have you braid my hair every night."

"Gladly accepted," he answered with a slight nod.

"Now, though, I must accept the offer of sleep; I can hardly keep my eyes open," she said.

"Rest well, dear; you need it. Sleep the day away if you must. There is nothing you need to be concerned about." She smiled and lay back on the bed while he covered her with a warm quilt. She was asleep before he left the room.

36

During the early evening, Elizabeth awoke. She was at first not sure where she was. Her sleep had been deep and, for the first time in many months, sound, but now she was frightened and shaken from the previous night's events. She sat at the edge of the bed, remembering the shooting and death of her husband. How dreadful it all was. She could still see his body lying on the floor, the blood seeping out from under him, and his half-open eyes looking up at the ceiling but seeing nothing. The fire had gone out, and the room had cooled down. She shivered, reached for the quilt, and wrapped herself tightly within its thick layers. She sat silently, thinking about her family and how much she missed them—especially her father. She wondered what he would think of her situation now and what advice he would offer when he arrived. As she sat on the bed's edge, a loud knock sounded at the door. She shifted her position in bed and looked toward the door. Mrs. Bergman entered, carrying a silver-colored gown. She could tell it was expensive and appeared to have a full skirt with a sequined bodice.

"Good morning, Mrs. Bergman, or is it evening? I do not know which." She smiled. "I must have slept the whole day. It looks like nightfall has approached."

"Yes, it has, dear. It is seven o'clock. Dinner will be served in about one hour. Mr. Darcy has been downstairs for about one-half hour, and he would like you to join him in the library when you are dressed and ready. I brought this dress for you to wear. Mr. Darcy instructed the maid to destroy your other dress. Now please, let me assist you with your toilet and dressing."

"Mrs. Bergman, why are you so good to me? After last night, I certainly do not deserve it."

"You, my dear, are the best thing that has ever happened to this family. The master of Pemberley, despite last evening's trouble, is the happiest I have ever seen him. Miss Darcy is playing the pianoforte with vigor again—something she had stopped doing after her mother died. This is all because you have come into our lives and awoken the spirit that has been sleeping in this family."

Elizabeth paused for a brief moment and said, "I am speechless, Mrs. Bergman."

"Just be who you are. That is all I need to say. Now let's get you ready for dinner and that handsome young man who is pacing the floor downstairs, waiting for you."

37

Elizabeth entered the library approximately forty-five minutes after she awoke. Her hair was clean and brushed but was not up off her collar. The braiding had left deep waves that cascaded over her shoulders. The light from the fireplace accented the red, causing a glow that was breathtaking. The dress brought by Mrs. Bergman fit almost perfectly. The length was slightly too much, causing Elizabeth to hold it up slightly as she walked. The bodice extended to the waist—something she was not used to—but she immediately liked the look when Georgiana wore the style at her ball. Her injured arm no longer needed a bandage and was already starting to heal nicely.

"Good evening, Elizabeth," said Darcy as she approached, entering the library. "Are you well rested? I certainly hope so."

"Yes." She smiled. "I actually slept very well. And you? Did you sleep well? After last night, we both needed some rest." She continued with a sad, unemotional expression. "Fitzwilliam, I must attend to funeral arrangements. I know George had no immediate relations, but there must be someone I should notify."

"No, Elizabeth, I know of no relations of Wickham," he said. "After he left here, he entered the military. After that, I was lost to him. I did not see him again until several weeks ago at the tavern in London. That was after my solicitor found him and told me about his whereabouts. I needed to see him for myself, to see if he was indeed alive."

"So what shall I do now? I cannot allow a pauper's grave in a potter's field."

"No, of course you could not. You are too kind and sensitive to others' needs for that to happen. I have taken the opportunity to contact his previous superior officer to give him a military burial despite his dismissal from service. Per their protocol, he could be cremated, and a new procedure called 'burial at sea' would be performed. It has been used for soldiers whose deaths occurred during wartime, but it is gaining popularity and acceptance for those who are no longer in active military duty. I hope you approve. I would never do anything that you do not approve of or that might upset you."

"No, of course not; thank you for your consideration. I accept the offer. Having to deal with a funeral and burial would be especially trying—especially after everything that happened last night."

"You are very welcome, dear; please have a seat." He motioned her toward the divan. "Would you like a glass of wine, or would you prefer a whiskey tonight?"

"Wine would be fine, thank you." As he poured the wine, he eyed her closely. He poured himself a short glass of whiskey.

"You look very nice tonight, my dear. I must tell you I have been very concerned about you. You experienced severe trauma last night, both physically and emotionally. I must admit it was difficult even for me. Are you sure you are all right?"

"Yes, I am. Even though last night was awful, it was also a final chapter for me. My abusive husband is dead, now leaving me an open door for me to start my life over."

Darcy slid over to her on the divan. "I hope that open door includes me, Elizabeth."

"It does," she replied with a smile.

"It is wonderful to see you smile again. I was worried that your beautiful face would have a permanent frown."

"I guess I was too, for a while." They were silent for a brief moment, both sipping their drinks. A rustle of skirts brought Mrs. Bergman into the room.

"A message for you, sir—just arrived by courier. I took the liberty of bringing it to you myself. I hope it is good news. God knows we could use some," she said anxiously.

Darcy opened the note quickly and read its contents completely, nodding his head in apparent approval.

Elizabeth spoke first. "Fitzwilliam, please tell me, what is it? What does it say?"

"Good news, dear. It is from your father. Your parents and sisters will be arriving in one week. Your father is very anxious to see you but has the estate and personal business to attend to before they can make the trip here. They are very upset about Mr. Wickham, of course, but very happy you are safe and comfortable here at Pemberley." He looked up at her and smiled. "Your uncle and aunt will be accompanying your family here also. Was it not your uncle who made provisions for you to come here?"

"Yes, it was," she answered, smiling at both Darcy and Mrs. Bergman.

"Well then, I must meet him and thank him for bringing you here to us—to me."

"Yes, we must thank him, dear," agreed Mrs. Bergman. "Now let me see to dinner. Miss Darcy should be coming downstairs momentarily." She smiled at them both, turned, and quietly left the room, shutting the door and leaving Elizabeth and Mr. Darcy alone.

"Elizabeth," Darcy said, sitting across from her, holding her hands. "You must still be tired."

"Yes, I am. It has been such a long twenty-four hours—such a long year. Fitzwilliam, my head is spinning from everything that has happened. In the past year, I was happy and unmarried, then married and happy for less than one day. During my short marriage, I was confused, sad, terrified, and then alone. Now I am widowed, but I am not unhappy about it. By rights I should be wearing black and grieving, but I am not; nor will I. Right now I feel confused—confused about George Wickham being dead, about my family coming to see me after being separated for such a long time, and about them meeting you and your sister." She smiled slightly as she looked up to see him. "I am so confused about all of this."

"Yes, I am sure you are," Darcy answered. "Elizabeth, we will go as slow as you need to with our new life. I will wait for you as long as it takes for you to understand and realize your feelings. Only then will you be able to move forward. When your confusion is gone, then we will be together for the rest of our lives. I promise."

"Yes, we will." She smiled broadly. "Now I will be the one to suggest we both have a short glass of whiskey before your sister joins us." They both stared at each other and then started to laugh.

38

Dinner was simple but complete: roasted chicken with baked potatoes and winter vegetables, fresh bread, and churned butter. Georgiana had been unaware of the events from the night before until dinner. Now she was talkative throughout the meal. She was overjoyed to see her brother smile and, at times, even laugh during the dinner. It had seemed so long since she had seen him so happy. It was as if he were born again. Elizabeth was the reason for his change in mood, and she hoped it would continue.

Georgiana broke the initial silence when dinner started. "Brother, Miss Bennet, Mrs. Enders and I have decided to have a very special dinner for when your family comes. I started planning this as soon as I heard they were coming. I hope that is acceptable with both of you."

"What do you think, Elizabeth? Would that be acceptable?" asked Darcy.

"Yes, that would be fine, but you really do not have to do that. Remember: my family are simple people. We do not have table service, linens, and china like this. We do have a cook, but we serve ourselves. Our food is grown in a garden we tend to ourselves, and our meat is raised, butchered, and cured by the local farmers."

"Elizabeth, dear," said Darcy with a chuckle, "Most of our food is grown and harvested and butchered right here on the estate also. We do order some foods that are unable to be grown here, but they are minimal amounts. So you see, Elizabeth, we are not much different in that respect."

Elizabeth smiled broadly and replied to him, "Fitzwilliam, you can be most persuasive when you need to be."

"I certainly try."

Dinner ended earlier than usual, and the trio retreated to the library for an after-dinner glass of wine. "Brother, may I join you and Miss Bennet in a celebratory glass also?" Georgiana asked.

"Georgiana, you are much too young to partake in drink. I think it best you do not," he answered. Darcy looked to Elizabeth for advice.

"Brother, please, just this once. We have so much to be thankful for now that Elizabeth is with us again, safe and sound, and you are finally betrothed." Darcy looked at Elizabeth, who gave a slight nod, and then permitted Georgiana a small glass of port. He poured the glass and handed it to her, being careful not to spill it on her dress. She took a small sip and made a dreadful face, finding the drink's taste bitter and unpalatable. "This is terrible tasting. Brother, why do you drink this?" she asked. Darcy and Elizabeth both chuckled at her disappointed expression.

"I am glad you dislike drink, sweetheart; I would not want you engaging in this too often."

The evening ended early, and all of them retired to their rooms. Darcy wished a good-night to his sister and then escorted Elizabeth to her room. Standing outside her door, he took her hand into his and lightly kissed her palm.

"Good night, dear. Please sleep well; you have more than earned a restful night. Do not worry about arising too early for breakfast. You may eat whenever you wish."

"Thank you, Fitzwilliam. You are too good to me."

"Elizabeth, you must know by now that nothing is too good for you. You deserve and will have everything I own. I promise you that."

"Oh, Fitzwilliam," Elizabeth said. A small tear escaped her left eye and trickled down her face. She started to brush it away, but Darcy reached for her hand and stopped her. He leaned close and gently kissed her tears away.

"Is that better?"

"Yes, it is," she whispered.

"Please get some sleep tonight; you are still spent from yesterday, and I will see you when you wake." She nodded in response, unable to say any more.

Still exhausted from her recent ordeal, she found sleep difficult. She undressed and put on her nightclothes. She brushed out her long, dark hair, not wishing for a maid to help her tonight. She preferred to be alone, hoping to sort out her scrambled thoughts. She slipped under the covers of her bed but found sleep difficult. She was anxious to see her family, yet she was reluctant for them to meet the Darcy family. She knew the Darcy family would also include Mrs. Bergman, Mrs. Enders, and Mr. Hickey. They had welcomed and supported her through her transition into the Pemberley estate, and she thought of them as her new family also. How could her mother and father understand that? She hoped they would. The disastrous marriage to Wickham continued to hold so much uncertainty for her.

Darcy himself was restless when he entered his bedchamber. His valet had laid out his clothes for evening retirement. He was not quite ready for sleep but removed his greatcoat, cravat, and boots, and he then put on his evening slippers. He had loosed his shirt collar and started to unbutton his shirt when he heard a loud scream come from down the hallway, near Elizabeth's room. He and several of the servants, including Mrs. Bergman, met him at Elizabeth's door. He entered without knocking and found Elizabeth in bed, thrashing about in fitful sleep. He quickly reached for her in bed and wrapped his arms around her, trying to pacify her obvious distress.

"Elizabeth, dear, wake up. You are having a bad dream. Do you hear me? Please wake up. You are safe here with us." Elizabeth slowly opened her eyes to see the staff members staring at her with concern. Darcy was sitting on her bed, holding her close.

"What happened? Why is everyone here?" she asked with a frightened tone.

"You were having a nightmare, Elizabeth, but you are all right now. May I get you a glass of wine or something else to calm your nerves?"

"No, thank you anyway. Just knowing you are all here is all I need." She sat up in bed and put her arms around Darcy's neck and buried her face into his shoulder.

Darcy turned and faced the staff who had responded to Elizabeth's screams. He said, "Thank you everyone. She is all right now. You may return to your rooms now." One by one, the staff left Elizabeth's room—except for Mrs. Bergman.

"If there is anything you need, dear, please call. Do you wish me to stay with you tonight?"

"No thank you, Mrs. Bergman," Darcy interjected. "I will stay with Miss Bennet tonight." Mrs. Bergman nodded and quietly left the room, but she left the bedroom door slightly ajar.

"How are you feeling now? Do you feel better?" he asked anxiously.

"Yes, I am better. I am sorry to have caused you such alarm. I do not know what came over me."

"Elizabeth, you are exhausted. You have had an emotional upheaval that none of us in this household could ever imagine. I am going to stay with you tonight. I will sit here next to you and hold on to your hand. You will not be alone tonight."

"Fitzwilliam, I am so sorry. I have been such an inconvenience. Ever since I stepped foot onto Pemberley, I have upset this entire house. I have never meant to cause you or anyone here any trouble."

"Elizabeth," he said, "you are the best and most exciting thing that has ever happened to this family. I love you, and you are going to stay with us—with me."

"Like I said before, you may not be so willing to have me once you meet my family," Elizabeth said.

"Your family is welcome here. I look forward to meeting them. Now, lie back, close your eyes, and get some rest."

Elizabeth did as she was told, falling asleep almost immediately. This time she stayed asleep until early the next morning.

Darcy stayed with Elizabeth until she awoke the next morning. He was relieved that she had no further night terrors and her sleep appeared restful. He was also relieved to be out of the chair he had stayed in all night next to her bed. When she first opened her eyes, she was unsure where she was and was startled, but she was immediately relieved to see Darcy's face and smile. She rolled onto her side in bed and reached out to touch his face. His whiskers were rough but comforting.

"Did you really sleep in that chair all night?" she asked.

"Yes, I did. I could not take my eyes off of you. Do you know you are beautiful even when you are sleeping?"

"I am so glad you stayed. I am sure that is why I did not have another night terror."

"Elizabeth, I would like you to get dressed. We will have breakfast, and then I would like to take you on a carriage ride into London today."

"Really, must we leave today? My family arrives soon," she answered.

"We will be back in plenty of time to prepare for your family. I would not want anything foreseeable to happen to interfere with your family coming. I do look forward to meeting them."

"You may change your mind once you meet my mother and younger sisters," she said with a smile. "They can be overwhelming at times. You will like my father; he is strong, smart, but gentle, like you."

"I will do whatever is necessary to ensure their visit is pleasant. Now, please, let us get dressed, have our breakfast, and be on our way. The maid will pack your bag for our overnight stay in London."

"Fitzwilliam, will I be meeting any of your family or friends? I really do not feel I am ready for that yet."

"No, you will not; nor will we be attending any social events. We do, though, have an important errand to attend to. My sister would like to come. We may need her help with some purchases I would like to make. Now, let us meet for breakfast. I would like to be on our way within the hour."

39

The leisurely trip to London took two days. A broken wheel axle and a lame horse prolonged their trip. Elizabeth again had difficulty sleeping during the trip, but thankfully she did not experience any further night terrors. Darcy noticed the lack of sleep in her eyes but did not question her about it. Mrs. Bergman, who also traveled with the group to London, noticed Elizabeth's weariness.

The town house in London was not nearly as grand as Pemberley, but Elizabeth immediately felt comfortable in the home, despite the closeness to the society she was reluctant to meet. The rooms were smaller, decorated with style and with an intimacy sometimes lacking at Pemberley. Georgiana introduced her to the house staff and gave her a tour of the house within an hour of their arrival. Elizabeth's fatigue had not wavered from her sleepless nights. She knew Georgiana wanted to start shopping and Fitzwilliam expected her to upgrade her wardrobe, but she did not feel up to going out immediately upon their arrival. The events of the past year were still haunting her. How could she expect to be mistress of Pemberley, a grand estate, when she felt so confused and fatigued? Was she asking too much of herself? Would she be unable to fulfill the task ahead of her? What about her family? What would they think of her now?

"Elizabeth, dear, why do you look so distressed? Let me show you your room so you can rest. We will have a quiet dinner tonight, and then I would like to take you out on a carriage ride tomorrow. I have a place I think you should see. It will help start to ease your mind and, I hope, help you understand what happened to you. Then we will be able to move forward with our lives."

"Fitzwilliam, what is it? Now I'm curious. What are you up to?" she asked.

"I will tell you all about it in the morning. For now, let us have a quiet dinner and evening, despite Georgiana's eagerness to start shopping." They both smiled, and then she took his arm and entered the dining room.

40

The next morning, Elizabeth entered the breakfast room to find Darcy and Georgiana already there. The coffee was poured, but neither had started breakfast. Darcy rose immediately when Elizabeth entered the room.

"Good morning, dear," he said as he eagerly kissed her hand. "How did you sleep?"

"Better, I believe. I do not recall awakening, and there were certainly no bad dreams," she answered.

"Thank God for that. I have taken the liberty to have your coffee poured. I hope it is still hot."

She took a sip and said, "Yes, it is, thank you."

"Good morning, Miss Bennet," said Georgiana.

"And the same to you," Elizabeth answered with a genuine smile. "Please, Georgiana, call me Elizabeth. I think we know each other well enough for that."

"Thank you, Miss Ben … I mean Elizabeth; I would like that very much."

Darcy helped her with her chair, and she acknowledged him with the same smile and nod. He could see from her eyes that she had not slept as well as she had told him. He hoped that after today her sleep would be more comforting.

"Fitzwilliam, where are we going today?" Elizabeth asked quietly. "You have been quite secretive about this trip you have planned."

Darcy cleared his throat, reached over, and put his hand over hers.

"Elizabeth, dear, we are going to the house you shared with George Wickham—the one down by the river's edge."

"What?" she gasped, nearly choking on her coffee. "Why on earth for? Why would you take me there, to that awful place?"

"Elizabeth, I believe the source of your nightmares and ill sleep is at that house. You are plagued with those demons you acquired there. The only way to rid you of them is to go back there and face them. I will be with you every step of the way. Together we will exorcise you of those horrible memories. Elizabeth, doing this will help the confusion you talk about. I believe driving out those haunting demons will help you sleep and allow you to move forward."

"Fitzwilliam, I do not know where the house is. I would not know how to find it again. I only know it was near the river's edge. There was no actual street or yard. I only remember that the house was dark and very dirty."

"I had my solicitor make some inquires, and he found the house. If you agree, we will travel there this morning and be back by evening." Elizabeth stared at Darcy and then at Georgiana, who only nodded in agreement, absorbing his words and then slowly agreeing with his suggestion.

"Should I go also? Maybe I may be of assistance," asked Georgiana.

Elizabeth spoke first. "No, Georgiana," she said sharply. "For your protection and safety, you may not go with us today. I am sure I speak for your brother also. This house is located in one of the most dangerous areas of London. I agree with Fitzwilliam; this is something he and I need to do alone. I do not know what we will find there. We will not risk your safety." She paused to collect her thoughts momentarily and then continued in a calmer voice, "Please forgive me, Georgiana; I did not mean to speak so harshly to you just now. I suspect this will be a difficult trip, and I would not want you exposed to the uncertainty that we may encounter today. Now that I know you, I understand and feel your brother's protective instincts toward you."

Georgiana was staring at her untouched breakfast and quietly replied, "I am not a child anymore, but I understand and appreciate your concerns."

"I agree you are not a child, so I am going to need your help—possibly tomorrow. I suspect your brother would like us to do some shopping so I may purchase some new dresses. I do not know what I should get or what styles are appropriate for various occasions. Would you be my guide and adviser? Will you take me shopping? I will need your help, for I am ignorant in such things. Could you show me the areas of London I have never seen?" Elizabeth reached over to touch Georgiana's hand as she spoke.

Georgiana suddenly brightened her expression and mood, agreeing happily to assist Elizabeth with what she would need when introduced as Mrs. Darcy, the mistress of Pemberley.

"Wonderful. It is settled. Let us plan on tomorrow for our shopping," said Elizabeth. Darcy did not contribute to the conversation but was very pleased that his two most favorite women were getting along so well.

41

Darcy decided to select a carriage that was old and in poor repair, though it was still finer than any seen in London's riverfront areas. He did not want to bring unusual attention to a fine carriage, its occupants, or their obvious station in London's society. He hired guards, casually dressed, to accompany them in case of an attempted robbery or hijacking. The journey to the house once occupied by Elizabeth and Wickham took several hours, and fortunately the trip was uneventful. At first Elizabeth enjoyed seeing the beautiful homes where Darcy's town house was located, but her apprehension grew as they left the well-kept comfortable houses and progressed to the river's edge and the city's more destitute population. The houses became smaller, less colorful, and obviously poorer in upkeep. She gripped Darcy's hand as the carriage moved through London's impoverished sections.

"Are you confident we will be safe here? This carriage is much too fine to be seen here. There are those who would think nothing of stopping our driver and robbing us."

"Elizabeth, I have ten men riding along with us as protectors. I promise you nothing is going to happen to us. I have hired armed guards to travel with us who have gone ahead of us to search the house for hostiles. We will be safe."

She looked at his confident eyes and reassuring expression to know that he had planned this trip with the assurance of their safety. Within minutes of their recent conversation, Elizabeth recognized the muddy street and broken-down house. The carriage pulled up to the now abandoned house. The same broken and dirty windows with an unwelcoming unlatched door brought Elizabeth to sit forward in her seat.

"There," she said. "That is the house. I recognize it."

"Driver!" Darcy called out. "Miss Bennet confirms this is the house." Both driver and Darcy noticed the presence of the armed guards employed for security who had been sent ahead for scouting.

"Are you ready, dear? We must face this." Elizabeth took a deep breath and nodded to Darcy while holding tightly to his arm.

"Yes, I am ready."

Darcy exited the carriage, and two of the guards were immediately at his side. "Have you entered the house?" he asked one of the guards.

"Yes, sir, the house is empty, and we have scouted the surrounding area. It appears secure, sir."

"Very good. As long as Miss Bennet is here, please stay alert for any potential trouble."

"Yes, sir," the guard answered.

Darcy helped Elizabeth out of the carriage. She did not immediately notice the armed escort and started walking directly toward the house. Holding on to Darcy's arm, she slowly approached the front door. She reached out to push open the door that had been repaired by the older neighbor man. The main room was dark and dirty, just as she remembered it. The furniture remained overturned from Wickham's last rampage of temper. A strong, offensive odor she did not recognize lingered in the air. Darcy held on to Elizabeth's waist with one hand and held her hand with the other. Anger started to swell within him as he entered the house. *How could any decent man allow his wife to live in such squalor?* Then he remembered that Wickham was not a decent man.

"The last morning that we fought, George was so angry he tossed these pieces of furniture as if they were children's toys. I see no one has touched any of it since. He certainly would not have righted anything once he discovered I was gone." She spoke as if in a daze.

They passed from the front room to the kitchen. The table was on its side, and the broken dishes still lay on the floor. Rat droppings were scattered about where the rodents had eaten whatever food had been discarded. Elizabeth's hairbrush lay among the filth left behind. She attempted to reach down and retrieve her personal article, but Darcy stopped her.

"Please leave it there. It is no use to you now." She turned to look at him, closed her eyes momentarily, and then turned her head away, pulling back her hand. She briefly told Darcy how she had used her hairbrush for cleaning. He let her vent, making no verbal comments regarding her ordeal, but he certainly would remember what he witnessed today.

She moved toward the bedroom but stopped at the door, finding it difficult to pass through the entryway. She started to tremble slightly. She felt on the verge of tears but was determined not to give into her fears.

Darcy whispered, "It will be all right, Elizabeth; I am right here with you. Remember: you are safe now." Together they passed through the doorway and into the small, dark room. Elizabeth's stained and torn underskirt that she had used to cover the filthy mattress was on the floor. The mattress was torn, and its contents had spilled out everywhere. The odor was horrendous, as a partially filled chamber pot and also Wickham's discarded cigar remained. She suddenly turned to Darcy, threw her arms around his neck, and buried her face into his shoulder.

"Oh, Fitzwilliam, it was so awful here. He yelled at me, he beat me, and he hurt me here. I was so afraid; I thought he would kill me. If I had not run away, I am sure he would have. He tore my dress that is lying on the floor. My father had bought it for me just before we were married. But he hurt me, and I decided I needed to escape from him and find my aunt and uncle's home. You found me the next day, wandering the streets while looking for their house."

Controlling his anger, he whispered, "I know, dear, I remember. That is why you had to come back here—to chase those demons away." He held Elizabeth tight against him, almost preventing her from breathing. They held each other for several minutes, and when they separated, she wiped her face with the back of her hand.

"I am ready to go outside now. I would like to show you the pump where I learned to fetch water. It was there that I met a very wise old woman who gave me the general direction to my aunt and uncle's house the day I escaped. She was the only friend I had here."

"Please show me then," he said calmly.

They left the bedroom and walked back through the kitchen, avoiding the broken dishes, and out the back door, which was now held up by only one hinge. They walked slowly down the path to the pump while holding hands tightly. Before walking very far, Darcy and Elizabeth met the old woman with the toothless grin—the one that Elizabeth had come to admire—walking back from the pump.

"Well there you are, sweetie. I was wondering what happened to you. I was hoping you was all right," the old woman said.

"Thank you, ma'am. I am well. This is my friend, Mr. Darcy. We just came back here to see how the house is."

"That shack don't need no look'n after. The rats own it anyways; they always did. Tell me, did you get rid of that worthless husband of yours?" Before Elizabeth could answer, the old woman continued. "I always knew you was a lady, and no lady belongs down here. Listen, I needs to get going—gotta make some supper for my old man. You take care of yourself now, honey." She walked past Elizabeth and Darcy and said loudly, "Make sure you leave that worthless husband. He was no good to anybody." With that she was out of sight and out of earshot.

Elizabeth looked at Darcy, and with a smile, she said, "You were correct in bringing me here. It was what I needed. I think those demons that have haunted me are gone now. Fitzwilliam let us go home now."

"Gladly, Elizabeth," he responded, smiling, as he continued to hold her hand tightly.

With that they walked quietly to the waiting carriage with guards standing by. Together they traveled back to the Darcy town house, still holding hands and lost in their own thoughts.

On arriving home, both Darcy and Elizabeth had relief from their anxiety of the day. After having a glass of wine and dinner, both slept well without incident.

42

The next day, Elizabeth, Darcy, and Georgiana traveled to one of the finest shopping districts in London. Elizabeth was somewhat apprehensive regarding the purchases she needed, but she knew Georgiana would guide her. It had been decided that Elizabeth would need material for several dresses and ball gowns. Darcy accompanied the ladies, acting as chaperone during the trip, but it was decided he would depart to the local bookstore while they were at the dressmaker's shop. He had made a few suggestions to his sister for Elizabeth's needs, but Georgiana already knew what her new sister would need. They agreed to meet by midday for lunch.

Elizabeth was measured, and several styles were selected for the dresses. Elizabeth rather liked the recently styled natural-waist dresses and decided to have two of them made. She was taken back to the fitting rooms, where she needed to remove her outer clothing. She had always made her own dresses and had never been physically exposed to such personal touch by a dressmaker. At first she was embarrassed during the more intimate measurements, but both Georgiana and her appointed dressmaker eventually made her feel more comfortable. The attention she was given was certainly something Elizabeth was not used to. Georgiana explained to her that as the mistress of Pemberley, she should expect such courtesy.

After reviewing several bolts of material, Elizabeth selected light colors of blue, green, and lavender. She also purchased a special light yellow silk for an eventual simple wedding dress. She knew she would never wear a white gown again. Matching shoes, coats, purses and other accessories completed her ensembles. Georgiana's contribution to the correct dress selection offered Elizabeth the solace and assurance she would need when she was introduced into London's society. It was decided that the dresses would be made and delivered to Pemberley within the week, just in time for the arrival of the Bennet family. Elizabeth was anxious to see her family again, but she was still concerned about her mother's inappropriate comments and her sisters' wild behavior. Knowing there was not much to be done about the impending meeting, she dismissed those thoughts and was determined to enjoy the rest of her day.

As planned, the three met for a late lunch. Seeing Elizabeth again after being away from her for the short hiatus of the morning's shopping made Darcy smile. Seeing the delight in her face and eyes from the morning's shopping heightened his feelings for her. She had been so melancholy during the past few months, and he was relieved to see her smile again. After the late luncheon, they traveled back to the town house. Georgiana chattered nonstop about the day's purchases, leaving Darcy and Elizabeth pleased with her decisions.

When they arrived back to the London town house, they were unexpectedly greeted by Mr. and Mrs. Gardnier, who arrived several days early. Unable to wait to see their favorite niece, they had made arrangements to complete any unfinished business and travel earlier than expected. They immediately found Elizabeth looking happy and healthy. She had gained some weight, and her face looked bright and animated. Her eyes were clear, and her smile contagious. This was the Elizabeth they knew and loved.

"Aunt, Uncle!" she cried out with surprise. She ran over to them and hugged them both. "I have missed you both so much. I am so happy to see you."

"Elizabeth, we have been so worried about you. Are you safe and well?" asked Mrs. Gardnier.

"Yes, yes I am. Please let me introduce to you to Mr. Darcy and his sister, Miss Georgiana Darcy." She turned to Darcy, who was taking off his coat and hat and was handing them to his butler. Elizabeth reached for his arm and led him to their unexpected guests. "Mr. Fitzwilliam Darcy, this is my aunt and uncle, Mr. and Mrs. Gardnier; these are the family members I have told you so much about. In fact, these are the same family

I was escaping to when I met you on the street those many months ago. They took care of me when I was hurt."

"My great pleasure to finally meet you both," Darcy said with a slight bow. "Welcome to my home. I have been so anxious to meet you; Elizabeth has told me so much about you. You have my sincere gratitude for helping Miss Bennet when she was such dire need." He turned toward his sister and said, "Please allow me to introduce my sister, Miss Georgiana Darcy."

"I am so pleased you are here," she said shyly to Elizabeth's relatives. "I hope our butler took your coats when you arrived."

"Yes, your staff was very accommodating upon our arrival. We are pleased to meet you also," said Mr. Gardnier to both of his hosts. "Please forgive our intrusion and early arrival. You cannot imagine how anxious we have been to see our niece again. Her father has written to us and told us of her most recent experience with that treacherous Mr. Wickham. We had to come and see for ourselves that she is safe and well."

"Of course, sir. Please come into the library, where we will be more comfortable," Darcy replied. Elizabeth took her aunt's arm and proceeded toward the library door, allowing Mrs. Gardnier to pass in front of her. Mr. Gardnier graciously followed the ladies, with Darcy close behind.

"Brother, let me see to some refreshments. I believe we have plenty of time before dinner," she whispered.

"Of course, and please let Cook know there will be two more for dinner."

"Yes, I will." Georgiana turned and nearly skipped toward Mrs. Bergman, who was already coming down the hallway with a serving tray of tea and cookies.

43

"Oh, Aunt, it was just awful. One minute I was at Pemberley and happy and the next I was in that dark, dirty tavern. The men were loud and drunk, and I will not tell you about the women," she whispered. "A fight started between George Wickham and two of the other men there. George was cheating during the card game and was noticed by several others for doing so. One of the men playing with him shot him dead. Fitzwilliam caught up with us and was able to rescue me and bring me home."

"Elizabeth, you use the word 'home.' Is this your home now?"

"Yes it is, Aunt. I am so happy here, and I feel safe, secure, and loved. Fitzwilliam is a wonderful man. I never understood what real love was before I met Mr. Darcy. I understand now." She looked over at Darcy, who was having his own conversation with Mr. Gardnier. Both had a snifter of brandy in hand and appeared to be having a pleasant talk. As if on cue, Elizabeth's and Darcy's eyes met, and it was obvious to both Mr. and Mrs. Gardnier that their secrets were no longer their own. Both couples smiled broadly, and it was then that the Gardnier's knew their niece's future was finally secure.

When Darcy's attention was again forced into conversation with Elizabeth's uncle, Mr. Gardnier asked, "So tell me, Mr. Darcy—what exactly are your intentions for our niece, and how are we to believe what you say? After all, our trust was broken with that cad Mr. Wickham."

"I understand your concern, sir, and I would be asking the same question if the tables were turned and it was Georgiana's future at stake."

"I assure you, sir, my brother—Elizabeth's father—and I have been in contact about this. He will be coming to your home in Derbyshire soon, and he will be asking these same questions. My brother will demand more direct answers than what we received from Mr. Wickham."

"Yes, sir, I understand that." Darcy's usual calm demeanor was starting to crack slightly, but knowing he would be asked these questions, he gathered his thoughts and proceeded to answer.

"Mr. Gardnier ..." he said. He was unable to proceed, however, as he heard a loud commotion just outside the library door. A knock at the door was followed by again shouts from several persons.

One voice was undoubtedly female. Darcy quickly stood, set his full snifter of brandy down, excused himself, and walked toward the door; but before he could open it, Mrs. Bennet burst into the room, shouting, "Where is my Lizzy?" Mr. Bennet followed immediately behind, appearing to be in distress but remaining quiet.

"Mama, Papa, you are here!" she exclaimed. "We did not expect you so soon. Oh, Papa, how I have missed you so much." Elizabeth jumped up from her seat, rushed to her father, and hugged him tightly. Mr. Bennet held her closely, tears starting to form at the corners of his eyes.

"I have missed you also, daughter. Are you well? Are you really safe?" he whispered to her.

"Yes, Papa, I am," she answered while hugging him again. "I am so glad you are here."

Mrs. Gardnier stood and walked slowly to Mrs. Bennet, took her hand, and smiled. "I think our Lizzy is finally safe and happy. I can see by the looks on the faces of these two young people that they are happily in love. I have seen that look before, and not with that awful Wickham," said Mrs. Gardnier to her sister-in-law, Mrs. Bennet.

"Love! What nonsense is that? There is no such thing, Elizabeth!" she shouted. "Come here and see me. I need to talk to you."

"Yes, Mama," she said quietly while still holding on to her father's hand. She walked slowly toward her mother, reached for her mother's hands, and gently kissed her cheek. Darcy heard Mrs. Bennet's command and slowly made his way across the room to Elizabeth's side. Pulling away from her mother, Elizabeth saw Darcy approaching and smiled broadly. He reached for her hand and took it eagerly, carefully watching the interaction between Elizabeth and her mother. Elizabeth firmly held Darcy's hand with both of hers.

"Mama, this is Mr. Fitzwilliam Darcy. This is the gentleman who rescued me after George Wickham took me from Pemberley and to that awful tavern here in London. Mr. Darcy came for me. After I was hurt, he bandaged my wounds and brought me back to Pemberley, and now here. He and his sister, along with the staff, have been so kind to me through this horrendous ordeal. They literally saved my life." Mrs. Bennet was quiet, listening intently to Elizabeth, and she then slowly turned toward Darcy. He reluctantly released Elizabeth's grip and bowed to Mrs. Bennet.

"Mrs. Bennet, I am honored to meet you. Elizabeth has spoken fondly of your family, and I am so glad to have you at my home. Thank you for coming."

"Mr. Darcy," Mrs. Bennet said quietly, "thank you for taking such good care of our Elizabeth. From your and Mrs. Gardnier's letters, we learned our daughter was in extreme distress and danger." Mr. Bennet overheard Elizabeth's introduction and came to his wife's side.

"Yes, Mr. Darcy, we are grateful for your assistance. Seeing my Elizabeth finally smiling again does more than you will ever know. We have been so worried about her. Thank you, sir, for taking care of our Elizabeth." Mr. Gardnier had also approached the group, and he nodded in agreement. Elizabeth's sisters, having been overlooked, stood quietly by at a distance, watching the exchange between the adults, overwhelmed by their surroundings; they displayed none of their usual silliness.

"Please, everyone, make yourselves comfortable. I invite you all to be my guests for tonight. I have already informed my cook to prepare for dinner, and my household staff is preparing rooms for you. I believe refreshments have been delivered already." Walking a short distance to where his sister was standing, Darcy introduced Georgiana to Elizabeth's family. Shyly, Georgiana curtseyed, and though uncomfortable, she proceeded to greet each guest. After final introductions, the young ladies retreated to the table of refreshments to further converse.

"Mama, Aunt Gardnier, would you like to refresh yourselves before dinner? I am sure rooms are ready for you."

"Yes, dear, we would be most grateful," Mrs. Bennet said curtly.

Elizabeth looked at Mr. Darcy and on cue said, "Yes, ladies, please allow my housekeeper to show you to your rooms. Dinner should be ready by 7:00 p.m., but please come to my library by 6:30 for a predinner cocktail. Gentlemen, shall we retreat to my study for a brandy?"

"Yes, that would be most appreciated, Mr. Darcy. I would like to speak with you," said Mr. Bennet.

"Mama, let me go with you now. I would like to tell both you and Aunt about today's shopping." With a slight smile, she nodded to Mr. Darcy. He, in return, bowed to the ladies. Elizabeth and Darcy's eyes met and lingered for more time than socially appropriate. The ladies, not missing this obvious show of affection, were led by Mrs. Bergman to the upper floors for rest, and the gentlemen retreated to Darcy's study.

Once in Darcy's study, and with the doors closed, Darcy poured a generous snifter of brandy for each of the men. He invited them to sit, hoping a pleasant and honest conversation could occur. Darcy knew he would be thoroughly interrogated regarding the events that had occurred since Elizabeth's arrival at Pemberley and his intentions regarding Elizabeth. Concerns regarding their current unconventional living arrangements would also be addressed. Once they were settled, an uncomfortable silence filled the room. It was Darcy himself who started the conversation that everyone knew needed to occur.

"Gentlemen, again, welcome to the Darcy town house. Finally I am afforded the opportunity to meet the family so important to Elizabeth."

"You use her name with too much familiarity, Mr. Darcy; I do not appreciate your liberty when referring to my daughter," said Mr. Bennet.

"I can understand your concern, sir, and as I said previously, I would feel the same if my sister were involved here, but I guarantee you I have the utmost honest intentions toward your daughter. Mr. Bennet, Mr. Gardnier, Elizabeth—I mean Miss Bennet—has stolen my heart. From the first day I met her, she captivated me. I have never met anyone as beautiful, honest, and wonderful as she. We have had long discussions regarding George Wickham and what she endured at his hand. In fact, yesterday we traveled together to the house they shared, and there we relived the anguish and torture she endured there." After a brief moment to gather his thoughts, Darcy continued. "Mr. Bennet, I love your daughter, and I intend to offer her a long and blissful life. You can see I have the financial means to do so, but if I had to, I would give up all of these worldly goods to be with her."

"You say many of the same words Mr. Wickham told me, yet he was deceitful and malicious to my daughter. Sir, you must understand my reservations in your argument."

"I do, sir," said Darcy now directly addressing Elizabeth's father. He stopped to gather his thoughts. "Please, sir, I cannot convey my intentions any more than I already have. I do not mean to offend you, sir, but obviously my motives for your daughter do not include her inheritance, wealth, or connections. My love for her is my only motive. What more can I do to win over your views of my intentions?"

"I need proof, sir, not just your word and fancy house. If my daughter should succumb to you, how will I know she will not be physically or emotionally harmed again? Your beautiful home and elegant possessions are impressive, but I need solid evidence that you are an honest gentleman."

Darcy nodded in understanding and asked, "What proof do you require to gain your acceptance regarding my intentions?"

Mr. Bennet's head was down in obvious thought. He glanced in his brother-in-law's direction, looking for his input to Mr. Darcy's question. "You must have a solicitor, sir."

"Yes, I do," Darcy answered.

"I too have connections, sir," said Mr. Gardnier. "May I contact your solicitor and inquire about your background, legal and illegal?"

Without hesitation, Darcy agreed. "You may, sir, I have nothing to hide. I have no criminal background, and I have had no illegal business dealings. I invite all of you to visit my permanent home in Derbyshire—an estate named Pemberley. I encourage you to traverse the property to see how I live and how your daughter will live. I invite you to speak, privately if you wish, with my staff, the tenants of Pemberley, and members of my church regarding my character. As I have said, I have nothing to hide."

"May I ask something else, sir?" asked Mr. Bennet.

"Yes, sir, you may," Darcy answered.

"If you are so honest, wealthy, and obviously well-mannered, how are you not already married? I can only imagine the opportunities you have had to marry. Why my Elizabeth?"

Darcy set his brandy down and put his hand to his mouth, trying to hold back a smile, before speaking. "I must admit, sir; I have had plenty of offers. The mothers of eligible daughters have pushed women onto me for years, but I have never found any one of those young ladies desirable. My family is prominent in London society, but I have never enjoyed attending any of the social events; nor have I gone out of my way to involve myself in the social aspects within my circle. That aspect of me is common knowledge about town. You may ask your connections about that. Until I met Elizabeth—forgive me again, Miss Bennet—I preferred to live my life alone. Now that I have met your daughter, I have no inclination to live alone."

"I see," said Mr. Bennet. "That is quite unusual for your lot."

"Yes, I suppose it is, but I promise you, sir, it is the truth," Darcy said with calm sincerity. "Mr. Bennet, I love your daughter, and I wish with all my heart, soul, and property for her to be my wife and mother of my children. She has enthralled me as no other has. Her laughter, honesty, intelligence, and gentle kindness are things not commonly found— especially in my lot. That, sir, is why I am not married."

"You are very open, Mr. Darcy. I like that. I appreciate your comments. You must understand I cannot immediately consent my daughter to you. She has just been widowed. An acceptable mourning period must be acknowledged. This will give my Elizabeth more time to know you better. I am concerned she may be experiencing what we may call 'rebounding.' Of course, she would need to agree to this, but I will be speaking to her about what we have discussed here this afternoon."

"Of course, Mr. Bennet. Thank you for listening to me."

"Now, if I may, Mr. Darcy, I would like to retreat to my room for a rest before dinner. Mr. Gardnier, are you staying?"

"No, brother, I think I will join my wife for a short respite." All three gentlemen finished their drinks, rose, bowed curtly, and left the study. Mrs. Bergman showed the guests to their rooms, leaving Darcy standing alone in the empty hallway.

45

The group gathered in the library shortly before seven o'clock, as planned. The adults enjoyed a glass of wine while the young ladies were served apple juice. A discreet smile was exchanged between Elizabeth and Darcy, as they would have preferred a jigger of whiskey instead of the wine. Elizabeth was wearing Darcy's mother's dress—the dress altered for her when she had newly arrived at Pemberley. The atmosphere was light and enjoyable until Mrs. Bennet noticed Elizabeth's fine dress.

"That is a very beautiful dress you are wearing, Elizabeth. I have never seen that one before. Where on earth did you get it from?"

"It belonged to Mr. Darcy's mother and was altered for me shortly after I came to Pemberley. I had so few clothes when I came here; he was good enough to have one of the maids modify it to fit me."

"That is very kind of him; I am sure he has given you several fine things since your arrival," she said sarcastically. Fortunately, dinner was announced, and everyone moved to the town house's dining room. It was smaller than the Pemberley dining room and not as elegant, but the table was set with fresh white linens and flowers, and the best china, crystal, and silver available were being used. Georgiana had overseen the table setting, remembering her own mother's preferences. Lady Anne Darcy would have wanted her son's future family properly entertained.

"Very nice, sister," Darcy whispered to her as they entered the dining room. "Thank you for doing this. This means a great deal to me."

"You are welcome, brother. You must know this means a great deal to me also." She was happy to see her brother smile and knew him well enough to know when he was displaying his best manners and behavior. He never enjoyed being a social host, but he never dismissed his responsibility when necessary. The outnumbered gentlemen helped the ladies with their chairs before seating themselves.

Darcy cleared his throat, raised his glass, and spoke. "Ladies, gentlemen—our welcome guests—thank you for being here at this table tonight so we may all enjoy each other's company and relish this wonderful food. Please let us say a silent prayer in gratitude." Everyone bowed in silent prayer for several moments before continuing with their wine and first course.

Cook had outdone herself in preparing a meal for so many on such short notice. The menu consisted of roasted duck with a cherry sauce, roasted potatoes, steamed fresh green vegetables, fruit, and bread with freshly made butter. The planned desserts included apple pie with chunks of cheese and a glass of port. Mrs. Bennet, now influenced by the abundant alcohol consumed during dinner, was the first to speak.

"Elizabeth, tell me, are you going to marry this man?" she asked pointing her fork directly at Darcy. "Your husband is barely cold in his grave, and you are contemplating marriage again? Do you even know where your husband is buried? You failed to tell your father about the location of your dead husband's remains."

"Mr. Darcy was very generous in taking care of that, Mama," she answered slowly and with a hint of hesitation. She had seen her mother intoxicated before and dreaded what might be in store for the dinner guests. "Mr. Wickham was buried at sea. This is something becoming more common with our military. His prior commander was notified, and the arrangements were made through him," answered Elizabeth.

"Were you present for this 'burial at sea'?" asked Mrs. Bennet.

"No, Mama, I was not," she answered meekly.

"Tell us, dear—what exactly is 'buried at sea'?" she now asked loudly.

The other members of the dinner party had stopped their own conversations and stared at Elizabeth.

"Mrs. Bennet," her husband said, "I am aware of this type of unusual but properly acceptable form of burial. His body was placed in a shroud and released overboard while the ship was out to sea. Many of our military are now being buried this way."

"It sounds rather cruel to me," she remarked.

"I assure you it is not, Mrs. Bennet; in fact, it is quite respectable," Mr. Bennet answered.

"Mama, burial at sea is no crueler than he was to me," Elizabeth said louder than she expected and with sudden anger. "The man you wanted me to marry was a monster. You must be aware of that by now."

Mrs. Bennet returned to her glass of wine before responding, now loud herself, "Elizabeth, your husband was a good man, God rest his soul. Your father and I selected him for you."

"Mother, good men do not yell, they do not hit, and they do not rape their wives," answered Elizabeth.

"Yes they do, if you do not obey them. What did you do to deserve the beatings you obviously deserved?" Mrs. Bennet asked.

"You forget, Mother. George Wickham was dishonest with us about who he was and what he was really after in our marriage, His intention was to acquire Longbourne after father's death and then abandon me and any children we may have had."

"You don't know that," insisted Mrs. Bennet.

"Yes I do! He told me so. Why are you being so stubborn and ignorant in this matter? Why don't you believe me? No man has the right to do what he did to me, not anyone, even to his wife. He came to me on our wedding night drunk and with another woman's perfume on his shirt collar."

"It is his right to do so. Maybe you did not fulfill your duties toward him," Mrs. Bennet answered.

"How dare you say such a thing, Mama," Elizabeth answered, now near tears.

The conversation lulled until she asked again, "Elizabeth, you did not answer my first question. Are you going to remain here and marry this man or are you going to come home to Longbourne?"

"I do not know yet, Mama. Mr. Darcy and I do not have any solid plans yet."

"It seems totally unacceptable to me that you would be contemplating marriage when your husband has recently passed and you are living in another man's home without the consent of your father and outside the accepted social rules and vows of marriage," said Mrs. Bennet.

"Mrs. Bennet," Mr. Bennet interrupted. "I think we have had enough discussion on this subject for tonight."

Darcy's demeanor turned cold as Mrs. Bennet continued to interrogate Elizabeth. Elizabeth's color paled, and she started to become anxious and restless. She put down her fork and gently dabbed at her mouth with her napkin. It was obvious to Darcy that she had finished eating despite her food being only half eaten.

"Please excuse me; I seem to have developed a sudden headache," Elizabeth stated. She stood, placed her napkin across her plate, and quietly left the room. The gentlemen stood while she excused herself. Darcy wanted to reach out to her but knew it was inappropriate. They were not yet officially engaged, but if he could again speak to Mr. Bennet, and if Elizabeth accepted him, they would be engaged before their guests left for Pemberley tomorrow.

"Since Elizabeth did not answer my question," Mrs. Bennet asked, after finishing her latest glass of wine, "tell me, Mr. Darcy, what are your intentions toward my daughter?"

"Mrs. Bennet," Mr. Bennet interjected, "Mr. Darcy and I have had this discussion already. We can discuss this at a later time. In the meantime, let us all finish this wonderful meal that our hosts have so graciously prepared for us." Darcy's demeanor did not change with Mr. Bennet's obvious intention to escape an uncomfortable conversation. He was anxious to leave the table but did not wish to be rude to his guests— especially since his guests were Elizabeth's family. If anyone else had been present, he would have left the room when Elizabeth did and ordered the guests to leave his home immediately and not return.

"I just don't understand Elizabeth," Mrs. Bennet said, now with a slur to her words. "I just do not know what that child is thinking."

"In what way, Mrs. Bennet?" asked her husband.

"She should be coming home to Longbourne, not staying here. Her husband was murdered; she should be observing a proper mourning period. She should be dressing in appropriate mourning clothes and not going out shopping. She is disgraceful to her family and her deceased husband, may he rest in peace."

"Mrs. Bennet," said Darcy with no hint of civility or manners. He pushed himself away from the table, stood, and threw his napkin onto his plate. "Your daughter Elizabeth has endured extreme cruelty at the hand of her husband, George Wickham. He slapped her, beat her, pulled her hair, verbally abused her, stripped her naked, and threw her into the street. In the presence of these young women, I will not speak of what else he did to her. I saw her myself wandering the streets of London, trying to find her aunt and uncle's home the day after she left that deplorable house her husband chose for her. She was exhausted, cut, bleeding, and in need of medical attention, all at the hand of George Wickham. Yesterday she and I traveled to the house that she lived in with him. It was filthy and rat infested. The clothing he tore from her in one of his fits of rage still lay on the floor. Her personal items were scattered about, no longer useable. Mr. and Mrs. Gardnier were witness to the injuries that were inflicted upon her by George Wickham. She cannot and does not want to mourn such a dishonorable man, even if he was her husband." With that, he removed himself from the table and left the room. The remaining guests and the servants standing at the sideboard were silent, unsure of what to do.

Finally it was Mr. Bennet who spoke. "Mrs. Bennet, girls," he said quietly, clearing his throat, "it has been a very long day. There will no more discussion tonight. I request we all retire for the night." He rose from the table, quietly placing his napkin on his plate, and waved his left arm, indicating for his family to follow him to their guest rooms. Reluctantly, Mrs. Bennet and their four daughters stood and left the dining room, leaving Georgiana and Mr. and Mrs. Gardnier remaining at the table. The three briefly eyed each other. It was Mr. Gardnier who spoke first.

"Georgiana, I must agree with my brother; it has been a long day. I feel Mrs. Gardnier and I must also retire. You are a most gracious hostess. We look forward to seeing you and Mr. Darcy in the morning, when tempers are less acute." Mr. Gardnier rose first, helping his wife with her chair. With a brief bow, they too left the dining room, leaving Georgiana alone. Feeling that she had failed as a hostess, she could not leave the room. When Mrs. Bergman appeared at the door, Georgiana looked up at her.

"This was a terrible evening. My brother and Elizabeth must be devastated."

"My dear, this will all work out for the best. You must trust yourself

and Mr. Darcy to make the correct decisions. He knows in his heart what
to do to make this right."

"You are correct as always, Mrs. Bergman; I will trust my brother,"
Georgiana answered.

"Now, Miss Darcy, you must get to bed. Mr. Darcy will need you
tomorrow to look and feel your best. It may be another difficult day. Do
not worry yourself about the dinner table; we will clean this all up."

"Yes, he will need me tomorrow, and thank you." She smiled meekly.
Georgiana left the dining room quickly, carrying great concern about
what the next day would bring.

46

Elizabeth had changed into her nightclothes and was sitting in front of the in fire in her bedchamber, her nightdress pulled over her knees, which were drawn up, her chin resting on them. Her bare toes were exposed under her nightdress. She was staring into the fire when she heard a soft knock at the door.

"Yes," she called out.

"May I come in?" asked Darcy.

"Yes, please do," she answered. He quietly opened the door and closed it gently, making little sound.

"Are you all right?" he asked.

"Yes, I am. Please sit with me." She gestured to him by placing her hand on the settee. He sat next to her, close enough that their legs touched. He placed his hand on the back of her neck. She turned her head toward him and said to him, "I am so sorry about my family tonight—especially my mother. She can be quite rude—especially if she drinks too much wine. I hope they did not upset you."

"Elizabeth, please do not worry about me. It is you I am concerned about. I love you, and nothing is going to stand in the way of our happiness. We will be married as soon as you are ready; then we will be united forever."

Elizabeth continued to look at him with her head still placed upon her drawn-up knees. "William, for the life of me, I cannot understand why you could possibly love me," she stated simply. "I warned you about my family."

"Elizabeth," he said as he moved closer to her. He placed his arms around her and kissed the top of her head. "I do not care about your past or your family. I fell in love with you the moment I found you injured and on the ground, next to the well. I knew then that I needed you with me for the rest of my life."

"Oh, William," she replied, now sitting up, unraveling her legs, and putting her bare feet on the floor. "I love you too, and I am ready to marry you as soon as we can. I do not need any mourning time. As far as I am concerned, my mourning took place when George Wickham was alive and torturing me." She paused to catch her breath. "When do you think we could marry?"

"How about the day after tomorrow? I will obtain a certificate of our intent to marry from my solicitor, and we could marry then. Our families are here now, so I see no reason why we could not have a ceremony here in our London town house. I will send a note to my aunt, uncle, and cousin, asking if they would be available to attend our ceremony also."

"Then it is set? Could it really be that soon?" Elizabeth asked.

"Yes, it can."

"Wait!" she called out. "Do we need some sort of affidavit declaring George Wickham's death?" she asked.

"My solicitor will take care of anything that is needed," he reassured her.

"Oh, William, please let us marry. There is nothing that I need or want. All I need is you, and you are with me here and now."

"Elizabeth, I love you."

They sat holding each other until the fire died down.

"Come let me help you to bed before you get cold," Darcy eventually said. "We have a big day tomorrow; after all, we are getting ready for our wedding day." He picked her up without any effort and laid her on her bed, gently pulling the covers up around her. "Good night, rest well, and we shall meet for breakfast and tell our families our good news."

"Good night, William," she said.

"Good night, my dear, and I like you calling me William."

Their lips touched briefly before he stood away from her bed and quietly stepped out of the room, gently closing the door.

47

The next morning, Elizabeth met her parents and Darcy at the breakfast table. She was well rested and smiling and had put on a clean, fresh dress for the day. Mr. Bennet had finished his meal and was already reading his favorite journal, *Farm Life*. Mrs. Bennet had just begun eating; Darcy was sitting with his coffee just poured but had not yet selected his breakfast. He was waiting for Elizabeth to join him. Darcy stood immediately when Elizabeth entered the room, while Mr. Bennet merely nodded while looking over the top of his reading. Mrs. Bennet did not acknowledge Elizabeth's arrival.

"Good morning, Elizabeth. You look very well this morning; I trust you slept well," Darcy said to her, purposely using her given name.

"I did indeed, William, thank you. Have the girls eaten yet?" she responded.

"Yes, I believe they did," Darcy answered. "They were up early, had a light meal, and left to discuss the latest London fashions. It is a beautiful day. I believe they would like to go shopping today. I can certainly arrange use of the carriage and proper escorts for them if they would like that."

"That would be nice for them. I am sure Georgiana would like to show my sisters some of the shopping stores we visited yesterday," Elizabeth commented.

"Elizabeth, would you like me to pour your coffee now?"

She smiled to him. "Yes, that would be nice. I will fix my own plate so we can eat together."

"Then I will join you," he answered. Together they approached the sideboard and selected their breakfast items.

As they sat down next to each other, Mrs. Bennet said, "I find it very disturbing that Mr. Darcy left my daughter's bedroom in the middle of the night. You are not married, and you have not yet completed a socially acceptable mourning period despite any complications of your marriage. Mr. Darcy is of a social standing and may do as he pleases. But you, Elizabeth—I expected more from you. What do you have to say for yourself?"

The silence that followed was unmistakably tense, and then Darcy started to speak. "Mrs. Bennet, I did—"

"Excuse me, Mr. Darcy, but I would like to hear from my daughter." Mrs. Bennet looked directly at Elizabeth, waiting for an answer. "Well, Elizabeth, what do you have to say?"

"I have nothing to say, Mama, except this: William came to my room after dinner, and we talked for several hours. There has been no inappropriate behavior between myself and Mr. Darcy. He has been nothing but a gentleman to me."

"So why was he in your bedroom last night?" Mrs. Bennet asked.

"We discussed our future plans together. In fact, we have decided to marry tomorrow, here at the town house, instead of in a few weeks from now at Pemberley. William's solicitor will be making all of the legal arrangements today."

"Does your father know about this?" Mrs. Bennet asked, now pointing her fork directly at Elizabeth.

"He does now, Mama." Elizabeth said in between bites of food.

"And does he approve?"

Elizabeth looked sternly at her father, who briefly looked up from his reading, and she answered for him. "Yes, he does." Mr. Bennet made no comment but continued his newspaper.

"I see," she said with obvious disapproval. "And you say this marriage will occur tomorrow?"

"Yes, Mama—that is if William's solicitor can correct any possible legal tangles."

"Legal tangles like the recent death of your husband?" she asked.

"Mama, we are not discussing George Wickham again. He is dead, buried at sea, and cannot hurt me or anyone else in this family again. Do you understand? If you do not understand or approve, maybe you would be more comfortable going back to Longbourne today."

An uncomfortable silence followed until Mrs. Bennet pointedly asked Elizabeth, "And will your family be invited to this wedding?"

"Of course, Mama; I want all of you here," Elizabeth said with a calm voice. "Please, you must understand I need to make my own decision about this. I love William," she said reaching for his hand. "And he loves me. We will make this work. For once you must believe me and trust my judgment."

"Your father and I will discuss this," Mrs. Bennet said, now staring at Elizabeth. Silence lingered before she pushed herself away from the table and left the room.

"Papa—"

"Daughter," Mr. Bennet said, "you and Mr. Darcy need to do what you think is best. Whatever you decide, your mother and I will support you."

"Thank you, Papa. You will not be disappointed."

Mr. Bennet smiled meekly and returned to his reading.

"Elizabeth," Darcy now interjected, "I will send word to my aunt, uncle and cousin asking if they can come here, to the town house, tomorrow morning. Of course Mr. Hickey should be here. We can have the ceremony tomorrow night, followed by a simple celebratory supper, if that is agreeable with you."

"That would be wonderful. I hope Mrs. Bergman and Mrs. Enders will not be too upset with us and with these hurried unexpected plans. I know how Mrs. Enders prefers a several-week notice for any parties."

"I am sure they will come through for us," he responded with a smile.

48

Shortly after breakfast, Elizabeth and Mr. Darcy traveled to Mr. Fellows's office. They were met eagerly by his staff and escorted into his inner office. They were offered tea but politely declined. Shortly after they were seated, Mr. Fellows entered the office.

"Mr. Darcy, what a pleasure to see you so soon," he said, reaching for Mr. Darcy's handshake.

"Good morning, Mr. Fellows. I apologize for not having an appointment. I hope this is not inconvenient for you."

"No, not at all, sir. I had no scheduled appointments for this morning." Suddenly turning, he realized that Darcy was not alone. "Excuse me, ma'am. You must be Mrs. Wickham," he said with a bow. "My deepest sympathies regarding the loss of your husband."

Shyly she answered, "Thank you, sir."

Turning back to Darcy, he proceeded to his desk and sat down. "Mr. Darcy, what may I do for you?"

"Again, sir, my apologies for coming without an appointment, but I am here with two urgent requests. First I would like you to look into having Mrs. Wickham's marriage to George Wickham annulled. They were married for such a short time before he was killed. As you know, the circumstances of him being shot in a disreputable tavern down by the waterfront led to his untimely death. Now, the consequences surrounding his death have been difficult for Mrs. Wickham, and she would like the marriage declared invalid. From my readings on marriage annulment, I believe she is eligible for this."

"I see. That may take some investigation, but I agree with you, and I am sure it can be accomplished. The church is recognizing some circumstances that can make a marriage annulment valid. One of these circumstances is when the contract between the man and woman is considered defective of willingness and/or defective of contract. This occurs when one of the parties enters the marriage under fraud or defect of intent. I feel we can make a case for both of these incidences. And from what Mr. Darcy has told me, George Wickham was guilty of fraudulently entering into the marriage contract. Am I correct, Mrs. Wickham?"

"Yes, sir, Mr. Fellows. That is true," she answered.

"The Pauline privilege is given to converts of Christianity to dissolve a marriage with an anabaptized spouse if either spouse interferes with the religious practices of another. In this case the marriage is not a sacrament, though this may not be considered an annulment. Would that be the case, Mrs. Wickham?"

"No, sir, I have been baptized, and I believe Mr. Wickham was also baptized, but I cannot be sure."

"Very well. We will further explore the defects of willingness and contract. It may take some time, but I think enough evidence exists for that decree."

"That is encouraging," Darcy replied. "Next, Mr. Fellows, Mrs. Wickham and I wish to marry as soon as tomorrow. My question to you, sir, is, Do we need a certificate of George Wickham's death to obtain a marriage license? We would prefer this prior to the banns being read."

"That should not be difficult to obtain. The church regularly keeps death records, and I believe a certificate of death was filed with the church after George Wickham's demise."

"Splendid. When we are able to obtain a marriage license?" asked Darcy.

"I can make those arrangements for you and have the necessary license by this afternoon. I will send a courier to your London town house this afternoon with the document. A church vicar should be available to perform your marriage ceremony tomorrow if you contact him today. The annulment may take longer, but I do not foresee any complications."

"Excellent, Mr. Fellows. We will go to the church promptly." Darcy and Elizabeth both stood and extended their thanks to their solicitor. After leaving the office, they traveled to the church and spoke to the vicar, making arrangements for the next day's wedding.

Arriving back at the town house by late afternoon, Darcy and Elizabeth were met by Darcy's aunt, uncle, and cousin, eager to see their nephew and anxious to understand his mysterious request. Georgiana, acting as hostess, was most grateful when her brother arrived home. She had not explained her brother's unplanned invitation to them, and Elizabeth's family were becoming restless, awaiting her arrival.

"There you are, Nephew," said Lord Matlock. "We have been wondering where you were. Georgiana has introduced Elizabeth's family to us. We have been enjoying their company immensely. Now, tell us, what is all this secrecy about?"

"Uncle, Aunt, Cousin Richard—thank you for coming, I did not expect you until tomorrow, but I am very glad you are here. Please, everyone, sit down and make yourselves comfortable." Wine and sherry were served to the adults by the butler, and punch was served to the young ladies. "I am glad you have met Elizabeth's family. Had I known you would be here this afternoon, we would have tried harder to be here to greet you. Please, let me introduce you to Miss Elizabeth Bennet, my fiancée."

"Fiancée! Well, well, when did all of this happen? Georgiana, you did not mention that these delightful people, whom we have been chatting with all afternoon, are to be our nephew's in-laws," said Lord Matlock.

"I did not feel it was my place to make such an announcement, brother," she replied, glancing anxiously about the room.

"Please, sweetheart, do not worry yourself about it. We are very excited that our families are here together with us." Darcy reached for

Elizabeth's hand and held it tightly in his own. He then announced to his guests, "Miss Bennet—excuse me, I mean Elizabeth—and I are getting married here tomorrow evening. We would like you to all remain here with us to be witness to the event and celebrate with us."

"Splendid, nephew. How glad we are to hear of your engagement and such a sudden marriage," stated Darcy's aunt, Lady Matlock.

"Aunt, Elizabeth and I have discussed marriage for quite some time now. It has been only recently that circumstances have allowed our marriage to take place."

"Lady Matlock," Mrs. Bennet said, "my daughter has just recently been widowed. A marriage so soon after her husband's death and without a proper period of mourning may cause a bit of a scandal among your society. We have discussed this at length, but these young people seem set on proceeding with their plans despite the proper mourning period."

"Is that correct, Nephew?" Lord Matlock asked, now suddenly alert.

"Yes, Uncle. Elizabeth's husband recently died, but we see no reason to postpone our plans because of it. My future mother-in-law is concerned about a proper mourning period, but Elizabeth and I have decided to proceed with our plans to marry tomorrow."

"Fitzwilliam," Lady Matlock said calmly, "Mrs. Bennet may be justified with her concerns. The gossip caused by this sudden marriage may impact you more than you realize. You may jeopardize future contacts for yourself and risk Georgiana's future."

Suddenly realizing that the younger sisters of Elizabeth and Georgiana were still in the room, Mr. Bennet cleared his throat and said to the young ladies, "Girls, if you would be so kind as to excuse the adults, it is becoming evident that we need to have to have a private discussion regarding this impending marriage." Georgiana was first to stand and invited Elizabeth's sisters to join her in the music room while she practiced her most recently purchased music.

After the children left the room, Darcy said, "Aunt, Elizabeth and I have discussed this. You know I couldn't care less about my social duties. If I did not have to, I would never leave Pemberley. Georgiana will not come out for another two years; any gossip that should occur regarding this marriage will be long passed by then."

"Do you really believe that?" Lady Matlock asked.

"Yes, I do," Darcy answered. "I would never do anything that could compromise my sister. You know that."

"Yes, I do, but I hear your heart talking and not your head. I can see you two love each other very much and want to marry as soon as possible. We all understand that, Fitzwilliam, but surely you must see the complications that this hasty marriage will cause. The gossip will be unrelenting. You could, and most likely will, compromise the futures of all your sisters. We certainly are not forbidding you to marry; we are just asking you to think about what problems this sudden marriage will cause," said Lady Matlock calmly.

"Fitzwilliam, we love you, and when we get to know Elizabeth better, we will love her too. What your aunt is telling you makes sense. Surely you must see our practical side of this proposal."

Darcy's face reddened, as it usually did when he was frustrated. He stood and nervously started to pace the room. Elizabeth remained seated and watched him with a tear-streaked face. She could feel the happy future she had anticipated rapidly disappearing and her life crumbling again. How could this happen after so much had happened to her in the past several months? The man she loved, and who truly loved her in return, was being pulled from her for no understandable reason. It seemed no one could empathize about how they felt toward each other.

Darcy stopped pacing, turned, and stared at his uncle and aunt. "Elizabeth and I will need to discuss this. We have heard your concerns and appreciate your comments, but the decision of our marriage occurring tomorrow needs to be made by only her and me. We cannot promise the answer that all of you are looking for, but we will give it our consideration," Darcy stated.

"That certainly is fair," Lord Matlock said. "Mr. Bennet, what do you think?"

"Mr. Gardnier, Elizabeth's uncle, and I have discussed many of the same concerns with Mr. Darcy and Elizabeth before you arrived today. I know my daughter can be quite headstrong when her mind is made up to do something, but I agree that we cannot let impulsiveness interfere with common sense and social acceptance. Mrs. Bennet and I would like our daughter and Mr. Darcy to wait for one year before they are married."

"Papa!" Elizabeth called out loudly. "You cannot be serious. That is unacceptable. William and I will not wait for one year to be married."

An uncomfortable silence lingered in the air before Mr. Darcy spoke. "As I said before, the decision of when to marry belongs to Elizabeth and me. We will be the ones to make the final decision. Now, if I am not mistaken, dinner is about to be served. Please let us all proceed to the dining room and attempt to enjoy the meal our talented and patient cook has prepared for us."

Epilogue

Later that same evening, Darcy and Elizabeth made the decision to compromise with their families. They would wait only three months to marry. During those three months, Darcy and Elizabeth were seen together at the occasional London party. Lady Matlock introduced Elizabeth to the elite circle of Darcy's family. This certainly satisfied any concerns the family had regarding Georgiana's future and the future of Elizabeth's sisters. Elizabeth agreed to live with Lord and Lady Matlock during the three-month hiatus of their engagement and while waiting for her marriage annulment to be completed. The gossip exchanged was minimal and faded quickly after the marriage ceremony took place. The ceremony, planned by Lady Matlock, took place at Pemberley, with approximately one hundred guests in attendance. Elizabeth wore the simple pale yellow dress she had bought while shopping with Darcy and Georgiana several months prior. The house was decorated with the colors of spring and its flowers. Mrs. Enders and her staff had developed and created many attractive and delicious foods for the occasion, which were much appreciated by both families. The newly married couple agreed to the lavish affair more for their sister's sake than their own. Many in London's society felt the wedding and celebration after was one of the finest seen in many years. There were no dry eyes in attendance when Darcy presented Elizabeth the same pearl necklace taken by George Wickham on the night of his death and retrieved by the tavern owner and given back to Mr. Darcy. During the ceremony, Darcy proclaimed his love for Elizabeth by repeating Shakespeare's Sonnet 116:

> Let me not to the marriage of true minds
> Admit impediments. Love is not love

Which alters when it alteration finds,
Or bends with the remover to remove:
O no! it is an ever-fixed mark
That looks on tempests and is never shaken;
It is the star to every wand'ring bark,
Whose worth's unknown, although his height be taken.
Love's not Time's fool, though rosy lips and cheeks
Within his bending sickle's compass come;
Love alters not with his brief hours and weeks,
But bears it out even to the edge of doom.
If this be error and upon me prov'd,
I never writ, nor no man ever lov'd.

Five years after their marriage, Mrs. Bennet took a sudden illness and died. Elizabeth was quite grieved but was glad her mother had been alive to see two of the nine children born to Elizabeth and Fitzwilliam Darcy. Mr. Bennet, along with Lord and Lady Matlock, lived many more years. The four remaining Bennet daughters eventually married and had families of their own. Georgiana attended an elite music school in Paris and eventually married a fellow music student. She remained in Paris and had several children of her own.

Mrs. Bergman and Mr. Hickey lived out their days at Pemberley, serving their master and mistress before eventually being cared for by the Darcy family in their later years.

"Elizabeth, could we ever be so happy?" Darcy asked after nearly forty years of marriage.

"No, I do not think so. I do not think so at all. Let us raise a glass of whiskey and celebrate," she said to him. His whiskey tasted good, and the kiss after tasted better.

Printed in the United States
By Bookmasters